ANNA

Graham Duncanson

Copyright © 2017 Graham Duncanson

All rights reserved, including the right to reproduce this book, or portions thereof in any form. No part of this text may be reproduced, transmitted, downloaded, decompiled, reverse engineered, or stored, in any form or introduced into any information storage and retrieval system, in any form or by any means, whether electronic or mechanical without the express written permission of the author.

This is a work of fiction. Names and characters are the product of the author's imagination and any resemblance to actual persons, living or dead, is entirely coincidental.

The views expressed in this work are solely those of the author and do not necessarily reflect the views of the publisher, and the publisher hereby disclaims any responsibility for them.

ISBN: 978-0-244-01733-0

Also by this author

Mating Lions
Fiona
Francesca

Chapter 1

When it all began in 1966

Anna was sad. It was the last day of their safari in Kenya. Tomorrow they would leave Samburu Game Park and drive to Nairobi to fly back to England in the evening. They had one more night at the beautiful lodge. Her parents and four older brothers who were in their twenties, were in the bar. As she was only fourteen, she was meant to be playing with her two younger cousins in the pool, supervised by her Aunt and Uncle. She had told them that she was going to read in her room, but decided to go for a walk beside the Uasin Nyiro River, to enjoy Africa one last time.

Suddenly there was a commotion in the river. A crocodile was trying to pull a very young zebra foal into the water. With no thought for her safety, Anna ran to the foal and tried to pull it away from the river. The croc was stronger than her. She and the foal were dragged into the river. She realised a man had grabbed her and was forcing a spear into the croc's mouth. The croc thrashed violently and then released the foal. The man pulled her and the foal out of the river on to the firm bank. He kept pulling until they were several yards away from the water.

The croc had bitten into the foal's jugular. There seemed to be blood everywhere. However it got to its feet and galloped after its mother into the riverine bush. The man was on his knees beside her and asked, "Where did it get you?"

Anna coughed up some river water and replied, "I'm fine." She looked up into a smiling face.

"I'm glad of that, as you look as if you have carried out a murder. The blood must belong to the foal and the croc. Come on we will clean you up and have a cup of tea. My camp is really near."

He picked up his spear and added, "I am glad I didn't lose that in the river I have only just bought it at the lodge shop. I'm Charlie." He held out his hand. Anna shook it and answered,

"I'm Anna."

"I heard there was a new girl, in her gap year, working in the lodge. Word will get back on the bush telegraph that you are seriously tough and wrestle with crocs!" Anna's heart missed a beat. She thought, *'He thinks I'm in my gap year.'* She said nothing. Charlie continued, "I'm a vet and I am up here, vaccinating some Government cattle. I should not camp so near the Park, but it is handy being near my plane on the Park airstrip."

Anna thought she ought to add something to the conversation.

"I am going to be a vet. Will that foal need any treatment?"

"Yes it needs Tetanus Antitoxin, antibiotics and possibly some stitches but we will never catch it now. Have you got your place at Vet College yet? If not, I would put today's drama in your diary. If I was interviewing you, I would be very impressed that you dived into a crocodile infested river to rescue a zebra foal. None of the other candidates will have done that, even if they have top 'A' level results." Anna said nothing, thinking, *'I'm totally out of my depth here in more ways than one.'*

They had reached Charlie's camp, which consisted of a small tent, a folding table, and a chair, next to a small fire with a metal bucket full of water.

Charlie laughed, "I did not expect to be entertaining very brave young ladies, but at least I have hot water and a shower. I will show you how it works. What I suggest is that you keep your clothes on and wash them on your body and then you can dry yourself and borrow some of my clothes. I even have shampoo for that beautiful blond hair!"

Having four older brothers, Anna was not shy and was used to men, but her courage nearly deserted her, as she realised she was not wearing a bra and was giving Charlie a very good view, and he was expecting her to wash herself out in the open. However she had proven herself in the Uasin Nyiro. Charlie thought she was in her gap year. She would keep up the illusion. He filled a canvass bag with hot water and then pulled it up with a rope over a branch. Underneath were a canvass camp bath and a plastic mat.

Anna said, "Why don't you join me and help me wash my hair?" She just could not believe what she had just said. She thought, *'Mother will kill me if she ever finds out.'*

So it was that they stood together in the camp bath, first wetting their hair and bodies with warm water when Charlie turned on the tap below the bag. Then he turned it off and, for a big man with big hands shampooed her hair very gently. Anna had a very strange feeling in her insides which when she thought about it later, was very sensual. He rinsed her hair twice and then they just stood under the water washing the soap off their clothes. When the water was finished, Charlie said, "You stay on the plastic sheet I will get you a towel and your shoes. There are thorns everywhere. You can get in the tent and take your clothes off. I will ring them out and you can look in my rucksack to find something to wear."

She just stood waiting and when he came back said with a smile, "You could always be a ladies hairdresser in your spare time."

Charlie laughed, "For God sake don't tell the rugby boys that!"

Anna passed out her wet clothes and dried herself. She found a bright white T shirt which was miles too big for her. She felt gloriously risqué when she came out of the tent. Charlie had wrung out all their clothes including her pants and hung them on the bushes to dry. He just had on a pair of shorts as he presented her with a mug of tea.

He said, "As the best ladies hairdresser in the NFD, I will find you a comb." Anna sat on the only chair, demurely keeping her knees together. He came out of the tent and said, "Hop up. I will make you into a real vet." He tied a brand new red calving rope around her waist. "You look like a beautiful Viking slave girl." He sat down and added, "Sit on my knee. I love combing girl's hair. I don't want to be accused of only doing half a job."

All Anna could think was, 'I think Dad would beat me with a hair brush if he knew about this, like he did, when I called my friend, Jane's father, a fucking pervert when he put his hand up my skirt. I am sitting on a guy's knee with no pants on, and I am sure he hasn't got any on either!'

However they chatted on, as if it was the most normal thing in the world. Anna asked him why he had not told her off for being such a fool, trying to rescue the foal. He replied he would have done the same, so how could he tell her off. He said he was really proud of her and he was sure she would make an excellent vet. He said more and more girls were becoming vets and he was certain that the trend would continue. Anna, without letting on that she wasn't working at the lodge, told him how she had to go to Nairobi the next day in the very back of a safari type Landrover. She said it always made her feel sick, as she had to sit looking across the vehicle.

Charlie asked, "Are you airsick?"

"I never have been, why?"

"Well I wondered if you wanted me to fly you down. I will have finished here by 9 o'clock and I am flying down to play rugby?"

Without any thought, Anna said, "That would be great. I would love that." Anna realised the African dusk was fast approaching. She knew she ought to get back, or she would be in real trouble.

"I had better get back. I will see you in the morning."

"I will walk back with you. There may be a Viking ship on the river; I don't want them to steal you back." He picked up his spear and it seemed natural to Anna to hold his other hand.

When they got near to the lodge she said, "Luckily there don't seem to be any Vikings. You have no need to come any further. Can I keep the calving rope and your shirt?"

He chuckled, "I think you had better as I don't think you have any pants on."

She reached up and kissed him quickly, "Thank you for saving my life."

She had got back just in time, the rest of the family were coming out of the bar. Her Dad said, "Hi, Anna did you have fun?"

She laughed and replied, "Yes I had a really good time." Her Mum said, "I am not sure I approve of your attire. Where ever did you get that T shirt, it is enormous."

Anna said with a little laugh, "Maybe I will grow into it."

Anna dreamed her way through supper, but she did pay attention to the travel arrangements for the next day. She was delighted that her brothers wanted to go to the big rugby game and so wanted them all to get away by 8 o'clock. On the other hand, her Aunt, Uncle and cousins were going to go a little later. After supper her mother said, "I think you ought to go to bed, Anna, as we have an early start."

"Yes, I had better. I will then be packed and ready for an early breakfast." She kissed both her Mum and Dad and walked to her room."

When she was out of earshot her Dad said, "I think this holiday has been the making of Anna. She is a real young adult now." Her Mum might have thought differently if she had not had a couple of G & Ts too many.

When Anna got to her room, she packed Charlie's T shirt and the red rope at the bottom of her bag. She was not sure, if he had actually meant her to keep them forever, but she thought he did really! The night before her mother had made her wear pyjamas which made her hot. She revelled in sleeping naked and she slept dreaming of Charlie. Charlie had been correct in his assessment of her. She was brave; most girls of her age would have had nightmares after being in a river with a crocodile.

She was the first to breakfast and left her bag by reception, smiling at the guard and saying, "She would not tell anyone that she had heard him snoring in the night provided he made sure her bag was put into that Landrover over there." He stroked her hair and replied, "*Ndio, Memsahib.*" She looked up at his wise old face and said, "*Asanti sana Mzee.*"

Then she went through to the wonderful Kenyan buffet breakfast. Pawpaw was her favourite fruit and mango her favourite juice. Soon she was joined by the rest of her family who were slightly the worse for wear. Anna could not wait for them to leave otherwise her plan would not work. At last they got into the big safari Landrover and drove off. Anna had no time to waste she gave the note she had prepared to the receptionist.

It read:

Dear Aunt Camilla

As I was up early and I am ready, I have gone with the folks. Many thanks for the offer of a lift but I will see you at the airport with them.

Love Anna

Then she was off out of the lodge along the river at a run. She only had her little travelling rucksack so she could go quickly, but she knew she was going to be late. She prayed Charlie would wait.

She arrived at his camp, which was totally cleared. She could see lorry tracks. Then she heard the plane start. She ran. It was slowly taxiing up the red '*murram*' airstrip. She sprinted and caught up with it. Charlie glanced to his right and saw her. He throttled back and braked. Then he opened the door and shouted, "Jump in, I had just given up on you, but I am so glad you made it."

Anna knew she looked a real mess. She had been sweating and now she was covered with red '*murram*'. She had so wanted to be the grown-up gap year girl, not the messy fourteen years old child. Charlie helped her with her seat belt and made sure the door was locked. He shouted, "You hold the stick and put your feet on the pedals and I will talk you through the take off. Here we go; we will taxi to the far end of the strip." As they were taxiing, Charlie said, "I will move your seat forward to make it easier for you." Anna felt his hairy arm between her bare thighs. Why hadn't she put on jeans? Actually it was rather a nice feeling. He half read her thoughts and said, "I am sorry getting you so dusty, but you will have a chance to have a shower at the aero-club. I have got your clothes from yesterday." Then with a cheeky grin he added, "It won't be as much fun as in the bush. I enjoyed combing your hair."

Anna replied, with a laugh, "I enjoyed it as well. Doesn't anyone wear pants on safari in the NFD?"

Once again, she could not believe what she had said. He really laughed then.

"Anna you are really one hell of a girl, wrestling with crocs is only one of your attributes. I have got good news for you. I saw the mare and foal this morning and he looked fine. I was worried that as a vet I had let him down after all your efforts."

They had reached the end of the runway. Charlie swung the plane around. Anna could feel the rudder pedals under her feet. Charlie shouted, "Have you ever been in a small plane before?"

"No, but it looks fun."

"You always take off into the wind, look behind to see there isn't another plane landing and shout on the radio. Then we give her full power and when we are happy, we let off the hand brake." Anna felt that arm against her thigh and they were off. They seemed to be accelerating alarmingly, but all she could think about was that arm and wonder what it would feel like if a rough hand was stroking her thigh. They soon were airborne and there was not quite so much noise, but the plane seemed to be lurching about. Charlie shouted, "Look out your side, there are your zebra." Anna was delighted, but she realised that she would never be able to tell anyone, particularly her family about the marvellous news that the zebra foal had survived and she had had this great experience, flying in a light aircraft. The lurching got less and the plane turned gently round on to a southern heading. It was odd feeling the stick and rudders moving, as if they had minds of their own. They were still climbing and Charlie said, "OK you have control."

Anna was terrified. She knew she had gone pale and her palms were sweating. Without thinking she wiped her left hand on Charlie's thigh. He laughed, "Well done you are flying her well. I take it you were drying your hand and not being friendly?" Anna was no longer pale but bright scarlet. A blush had spread all over her face and chest. She managed a, "I was just checking on your pant situation!"

Charlie laughed, "What a girl you are. The next thing, you will be wanting is to join the 'Mile High Club'.

Like a fool she asked, "What club is that?"

"It is when you make love while flying a plane at over a mile above the ground. That is Nanyuki ahead which is 6000ft already so we won't be able to get a mile higher than that, in this old Piper Colt. Sorry."

Anna nearly jumped out of her pants when she felt his hand on her thigh. She knew she ought to slap it, but it was rather good and she made an excuse that she needed both hands to fly the plane. Charlie gave her thigh a gentle squeeze and took his hand away. Then he said, "Look to your left there is Mount Kenya in all her glory. That is a sight worth a run to catch a plane."

Anna sighed, "This is magic. Kenya is such a spectacular country. Thanks for waiting for me. Can you fly now?" She could not stop herself from leaning over and kissing him on the cheek.

"Sorry you will have to make do with that. I think the 'Mile High Club' is out of my league, may be when I have finished at vet college."

Charlie chuckled, "I am a very patient man." Anna felt herself blushing again. The thought of making love to this lovely guy in a small plane gave her a very odd, but very exciting feeling.

Charlie started chatting then about college and how she would really enjoy it. Then he said, "In your last two years you have to spend six months in your vacations with a vet seeing practice. I would love it if you came out here and spent time with me." Anna wistfully replied, "That would be awesome!"

Then Anna did a bit more flying. She started to get the hang of it and was soon turning left and right, climbing and descending. When Charlie took over again he showed her various land marks before he said, "Can you see Nairobi?"

Anna could see the small farms and the more built up areas. He started talking on the radio and she only half understood what was happening. He pointed out two aircraft coming into land ahead of them. He said, "Hopefully, as we are inbound from a distance, they will let us come straight into land."

There was the airfield insight. They seemed to be coming in very fast over a road, and then they were down. As they were taxiing he said, "Well how was that for your first flight?" Anna could not stop herself. She kissed his cheek again and put her hand on his thigh. Then she added, "That was bloody marvellous!"

They parked up at the aero-club. Anna helped Charlie bring his kit into the room that he had reserved. He found her two towels and showed her to the showers. He said, "Pass out your dress. I will take it outside and give it a good shake. You can come back to the room wrapped in a towel."

With a wicked grin on her face she replied, "We are not in the NFD now so you put some pants on before I sit on your knee and let you comb my hair." He stuck out his tongue at her. She very carefully passed her dress out to him. He was not in the room when she came back from the shower. She locked the door and quickly got into her dress. She had unlocked the door and was brushing her hair when he came back.

"Look what I have found?" It was a hair dryer.

"Oh thank you Charlie. That's really kind." There was only one chair. The room was fairly Spartan. Anna continued, "You are an angel. Sit down and you can dry it, at the same time as brushing it. I have brought a brush in my small rucksack." Then with a cheeky smile she said, "I hope you have pants on."

Charlie with a guilty look replied, "I am sorry about yesterday. Yes I promise I have pants on."

Anna to try to tell him she was not actually upset said, "Do you wear a Jock-Strap when you play rugger. I think they are the most ridiculous piece of clothing."

Charlie smiled, "How do you know about Jock-Straps?"

"I have four elder brothers!"

Her hair was soon dry. She was slightly sad to get up off his knee. They were soon in Charlie's old Landrover driving to 'Parklands', which Anna gathered was a sports club, but the actual game was being played at a Rugger Club in the grounds called 'Nondescripts'. Charlie said, "Do you want to drive? Most girls love to drive my old Landrover, as it makes them feel as if they are real Kenyans." Anna thought, *'Bloody Hell. Why didn't I tell him? It is a bit late now.'* She said, "Don't worry I hope I will get another chance some other time. Now tell me about the game today."

Charlie then told her that they would see the 'Nondescripts' players training and then Charlie would go and change for the Kenyan game. It would be the national side against a touring side from England. The visitors were the Middlesex County Side which had won the county championship in the spring. Charlie said he understood they were really good and would actually destroy the Kenyan Side. Anna said, "Well I know you will do your best and I will be supporting you all the game."

Quite humbly Charlie replied, "Thank you Anna that will mean a lot to me. People say that as a player you should only be concentrating on the game, but a supporter's cheer can definitely make me play harder."

Anna could not stop herself. She put her hand on his thigh and said, "Good Luck. I won't say anything at the club, as I know that would only embarrass you, but I do hope you play well and don't get hurt. I can't wrestle crocs on my own you know." He covered her hand with his and said, "You are rather special Anna."

They both were a little shy then and both looked to the front.

Charlie was a mind of information and told Anna all about rugger training and various set moves. Anna paid attention and her young brain was like a piece of blotting paper. She adsorbed it all. Soon he had to go for the pre-match briefing. Anna was thrilled, as when no one could see, he squeezed her hand.

Then she saw her family walking across from Parklands. She waved and ran to meet them.

"I hope you had a good journey. At least you were spared my girly chatter." One of her brothers imitated her, "Mummy I feel sick!" Her mother was expecting a tantrum, instead Anna said,

"I am sorry. Am I that bad? I will try to grow up. Can I start by you telling me all about the game? I want to know why players are doing what they are doing. Why that foul gives a scrum away but another foul gives away a penalty. I want to know everything you would like a girl friend to know. I know how cross you get when girls get bored during games. Well I won't. I have had a wonderful time in Kenya so I am going to support them. Anyway we don't live in Middlesex."

Her Dad said, "OK Anna I will help you to understand the game. Well done finding out who is playing. That is a start."

"Thank you Dad, Middlesex will be in White, which I gather is the colour England plays in and Kenya will play in Green. Do I shout come on the 'Greens' or come on Kenya?"

"I think you shout come on Kenya", replied her Dad as her brothers looked at her with incredulity.

The game, sadly for Kenya, was as bad as Charlie had predicted. Kenya was down 24 points and it was only half way through the first half. There was a line out near to where Anna was standing in front of her father who had his hands on her shoulders. Anna had been shouting, "Come on Kenya." Then she suddenly shouted, "Come on forwards. Help number eight he can't do it on his own." Her father could not believe it. Somehow the Kenyan number eight shouldered his way forward to gain ten yards before turning and giving a short pass to another Kenyan player.

At half time, Kenya was down by 33 points and it was obvious to everyone that the game was really over. Anna asked her Dad all manner of questions during the break. Much to his surprise Kenya did not give up and nor did Anna who kept cheering which encouraged other spectators who were obviously locals to do the same.

It should never be forgotten that Nairobi is 5500 feet above sea level. The air is thinner. It takes three weeks to acclimatise to the alltitude. The visitors began to tire. The Kenyan team felt them weakening. They were granted a five yard scrum. The visitors were in trouble. The Kenyan team won the scrum. Charlie, at number 8, kept the ball at his feet as the Kenyan scrum inched towards the try line. The visitor's open head wing forward broke too early to cover the Kenyan scrum half. Charlie picked up the ball and he was over for a try. Anna's Dad felt her quivering like a greyhound in the slips. He held her shoulders. He was scared to death she was going to run on to the pitch in her excitement. However she calmed herself and with a great effort shouted, "Well done number 8!" Her father was certain the try scorer had heard her as he looked up and then walked back, as the Kenyan fullback converted the try. From then on the visitors had a difficult job holding the Kenyans, they gave away two penalties but they had much too big a lead and they were the definite winners when the final whistle went. Anna's Dad was pleased, as Anna did not run on the pitch like some of the younger children did, who obviously had fathers in the Kenyan side. However, just when the Kenyan number 8 walked in front of them she jumped forward and hugged him. Her Dad was glad her mother did not see, but he was sure that the man had squeezed her bottom and pulled her to him.

After the game Anna's family had time for one drink. Anna's Mum was surprised that Anna did not make a fuss about not being allowed into the bar.

Charlie had changed relatively quickly and looked for her. When he could not find her he came outside where there were several families drinking. She saw him, turned and walked to the side of the club house. He followed her. She looked to see no one could see them and pulled him right behind the building and kissed him passionately. Gasping as they split apart she said, "You were wonderful and certainly were the man of the match. I have to go now, as my lift wants to leave, but thank you for the best 24 hours of my life."

She turned and set off towards 'Parklands'. Charlie stood and scratched his head. He was exhausted by the game. All he could think of was. I wonder how I can find an excuse to go up to the Isiolo area again.

Anna raced across the grass to the Landrover which was parked up with other cars in the car park. As she swung herself into the back she shouted, "Sorry to delay you. Mum and Dad, this has been the most wonderful holiday thank you both so much." One of her brothers said, "Trust Anna to be late, we will probably miss our flight now!"

She retorted, "Well you four are true to form. I bet if there had been a Kenyan player in the Landrover he would have been a proper gentleman and given a young lady a seat in the front!"

Her mother said, "I was amazed at you Anna hugging that player at the end of the game. Most men would have been furious with you." One of her brother's added, "Particularly, as they lost so badly."

Anna was not going to back down.

"Well I thought he was the best player on the pitch and I think he played his heart out. He deserved a hug."

Her father agreed, "I think he was the best player. Since when have you been a rugger expert?"

"I do listen to you men you know. I think the number 8 is a vital player and he did score the only Kenyan try. The player wasn't cross. I felt him hug me back, even though he was too knackered to speak." Anna did not see, but her mother gave her a Dad a look which said, leave it. I don't think she is a child any longer.

Anna had changed. Her four brothers even noticed. She was helpful to everyone. She helped her Dad, as he got in a muddle with the tickets and the passports. She gave a dazzling smile to the chief air steward when he welcomed her on board, saying, "You must get heartily bored greeting us all. I do hope you get time for a little rest after you have given us supper."

He replied, "It is really great to be appreciated." Before they had even taken off a stewardess came to Anna with a glass of champagne saying, "The chief steward sent this to you Madam from first class." Anna's mother's mouth dropped open when Anna replied, "His name isn't Tony by any chance?" The stewardess said, "Yes it is. How did you know?"

"I saw him at the Kenyan Rugger game and I was told he would have been playing if he had not hurt his leg earlier in the season. Do thank him for me."

After the meal just before everyone was getting ready for the night the same stewardess came back and whispered to Anna, who then got up with her small bag, kissed her Mum goodnight and said she would see her in the morning.

Her Mum then whispered to her Dad, "Would you bloody believe it? Anna has been upgraded to first class, because she recognised the chief steward at the rugby game!"

Her father grunted, "I think her smile and those legs will get our Anna a long way in life."

Anna did not come back to tourist class but the stewardess brought a message that Anna would see her family by the carousel in baggage retrieval.

There was a massive queue at immigration. The whole family were very irritable when they got to the crush around the carousel. They were stopped by a shout and wave from Anna who had collected their entire luggage and loaded it up onto two trolleys. Anna said, "I thought I could be helpful. I came through with the crew. If one of you could take one trolley I can manage this one."

Anna's Mum gave her Dad a look which said I can't believe this. They got home in good time. Anna helped get the entire luggage indoors. She helped her mother sort out the washing and got a load on, as a start. Then she disappeared into her room saying she would be in her room getting ready for school, but if anyone needed any help just to give her a call. The rest of the family were sorting themselves out when she gave a shout at noon, "I have made some soup and toast, if anyone wants some sustenance?" Her mother could not believe that the kitchen table was laid. Not only was soup and toast ready but there was cheese, biscuits and fruit put out. There was a jug of water and glasses. Anna said, "I will be sad to go back to school tomorrow, but I will make the most of it. At least it is only six weeks to half term."

After lunch the boys all said they felt like some exercise and so they rang up some pals and agreed to meet at the rugby club. When they were gathering in the hall, Anna came down stairs in her tracksuit and said, "I would love some exercise. Can I come? I promise not to get in the way." Her brothers reluctantly acquiesced.

When they had all left and her father and mother were on their own, he said, "What has got into her? She is so mature. She could be eighteen. She obviously enjoyed the holiday. I did know it was something she has always wanted to do. It was great, as I don't think we will ever have all of us on holiday together again. He was wrong.

There were ten players at the club together with a thirteen year old boy called John who was the son of the Captain. The Captain greeted them, "Good to see you all. I expect you are all a bit unfit before the new season. Let's have a twenty minute workout first and then we will try some training moves." They set off jogging around the pitch to warm up. Anna whispered to John, "You come with me; we will run at the back." They talked together about school. The captain started calling for various stops e.g. 5 Press-ups, 5 star jumps etc. He noticed Anna had taken off her track suit and was encouraging John to do all the exercises. Then the Captain started getting them running faster. Anna and John kept up. After they had been going for quarter of an hour, he shouted, "OK, try and sprint a whole circuit of the pitch." He heard Anna say, "Stick with me John." The Captain was well in the lead of the other players at the half way mark, except he became aware that there was someone on his shoulder. It was Anna and John. Then he heard her say, "Let's go John." The two youngsters came by him, as if he was standing still. He tried to keep with them, but failed. When they reached the end Anna and John were jogging on the spot. He was doubled over breathing very heavily. When they all had finished, Anna shouted, as if she was a professional coach, "OK lads keep jogging on the spot so you don't stiffen up. All follow me. We will take it nice and steady, for five more minutes." She set off jogging. John followed with the Captain and the rest of the players. She then turned round and ran backwards, shouting, "Copy me, and punch the air." When they were all doing it, she kept going and turned. Then she shouted,

"Run with both arms up." Then she shouted, "Windmill your arms. Good. Get Ready. Down on your fronts." Down she went and John followed. She shouted, "Now up. Take five paces and go down again." She kept doing that until they had been around the pitch. Then she turned and shouted, "Face me. We will have only three more minutes. Let's give it our best. Star Jumps in your own time. One, Two, Three, Four, Five. Press-ups, in your own time. One, Two, Three, Four, Five. On your backs. Sit-ups, One, Two, Three, Four, Five, and up. Quicker now down again. Sit-ups, One, Two, Three, Four, Five, and up and jogging on the spot. Don't stop. OK Captain, do you want to take over now? Shall I put you all through a few moves?" The Captain was too knackered to say anything except, "Fine, fine."

Anna then said, "Keep jogging and all gather round. John, could you find a ball? OK, now I want three forwards on the left, with a scrum half behind. The rest of you line out as three quarters. She got the three forwards dribbling. Then she fell on the ball diving at their feet, shouting, "Now heel it." She was up and shouting, "Pass, pass," She kept shouting until it reached the wing. So it went on for half an hour until she shouted, "We will stop at that. Well done. I will try and get my brothers to bring me down when I get home at half term."

The players were knackered and her brothers were totally amazed. John said, "I hope I can come at half term that was marvellous." As Anna was putting on her tracksuit she said, "I don't think I will grow anymore, but I bet you will be an inch taller than me, when we next meet. Good Luck next term."

Back in the car, her eldest brother who was driving said, "When did you learn all that?"

Anna replied rather vaguely, "Oh I watched some training in Nairobi."

When they got in the house at home, Anna's youngest brother went into the sitting room, where their father was reading the paper and blurted out, "Anna was fantastic. She took the training session. She fell on the ball several times. I was worried she would get hurt."

Her father looked up and said, "I think it would be best if you don't tell your mother."

Chapter 2

Back to school September 1966

Anna's school, called Lancaster House, was at Broadstairs in Kent. It was for girls from eleven to eighteen. Anna was one of the youngest to go into the first year of her 'O' level years.

Next door was a boy's public school called 'Wingates' which took boys from thirteen to eighteen.

The Headmistress of Anna's school had noticed Anna and felt she was not performing either academically or athletically to her full potential. She wondered if she was repressed by having four much older brothers who all seemed physically big tough chaps. She actually felt sorry for her but obviously could not show her concern or any favouritism. She was surprised when Anna asked her secretary for a private interview. She was even more surprised by what Anna asked.

"I am sorry to bother you Mrs Woodhouse but three things have occurred to me this holiday. My parents very kindly took me and my four brothers on a marvellous safari in Kenya. It will probably be the last holiday we will have as a family, as they are all grown-up now. I have definitely decided that I want to be a vet. I know it is very difficult to get into Vet College particularly as a girl, but I am determined to try. For my best chance I need to get top grades in Biology, Chemistry and Physics at 'A' level, but before that I need the right 'O' levels. As you know languages are not my forte, however I can manage to get in if I have Latin 'O' level. I know all the other girls will be doing languages particularly if they are not doing sciences, but I wonder if I could study Latin. I know I would be on my own, but would you give me a chance until Christmas. I will try to prove to you I can do it. My parents do not know about this request, but they have a lot on their minds with my grandparents getting old and I don't want to bother them.

Mrs Woodhouse looked at her keenly and replied,

"You have obviously given this a lot of thought. I will give you a chance. I got a first in classics at Oxford. I was the only girl. I will help you, but if we both think it is not working we will review our plans. Now what else is troubling you?"

"On holiday I learnt to be a rugby coach." Mrs Woodhouse's eyebrows went up, but she said nothing. Anna continued,

"I have been coaching at my brothers' club and the Captain and team want me to train them more at half term and at Christmas. The Captain's son is a year younger than me and says he is very worried about playing rugby, as the under fourteen team is bullied by the older boys who coach them. I wondered if you would allow me to write to the Headmaster at 'Wingates' and let me offer my services to coach their under fourteen team?"

Mrs Woodhouse smiled and said,

"Does this young man go to 'Wingates'?" Anna replied,

"Oh no, Mrs Woodhouse he goes to a much better rugby school, 'Oundle'."

Mrs Woodhouse actually laughed,

"You know Anna, I have been a headmistress for over thirty years and I have never had such a strange request. Of course you may write and say you have had my permission to write. I think Mr Hancock will say that he has not got time to see you, but I am not going to stop you writing. Good luck. I will work out your Latin curriculum and put it in your pigeon hole tomorrow." Anna could hear her chuckling as she left.

Anna was lucky. Mr Hancock did not agree with older boys coaching younger boys at sport and he was struggling to find a coach for the under fourteens. The master, he had earmarked for the job, had been hurt in a climbing accident in the holidays. The master could only stand on the touch line, on crutches and shout which was not a good scenario. Mr Hancock could see that there was a danger that he would have to coach. He wrote back to Anna and said he would give her a trial on the following Wednesday at 2pm on pitch seven.

Obviously Mrs Woodhouse had spoken in the common room about Anna's strange request to coach rugby and so when Anna received the letter and gave it to Mrs Haywood who was in charge of

PE she was given permission to go. When Mrs Woodhouse saw Anna the following day, she asked kindly,

"Will you be OK going on your own?" Anna answered,

"I will be very nervous but I will face it on my own. I have had many more frightening things to cope with in my life. I won't betray your trust." Mrs Woodhouse was dying to ask what more frightening things Anna had had to face but she replied simply,

"I am sure you won't Anna. Good luck."

On Wednesday Anna was a bag of nerves. She had lied or at least had been very economical with the truth. Now she had to face the consequences. As she jogged over to 'Wingates', playing fields, which were next to those of her own school, she stiffened her resolve. *'Charlie thought I was eighteen. Now is the time to show him I can act like an eighteen year old.'*

She arrived at exactly 2pm. She was greeted by Mr Hancock, who introduced Mr Galbrieth who was on crutches. Mr Galbrieth was in his early twenties. He gave her an appraising stare. Anna thought, *'I will have to watch this one. At least I will be able to run faster than him for several months!'* He really annoyed her by saying,

"Well there you are young lady. There are thirty little urchins waiting for you to make them into rugby stars." She looked him in the eye and held his gaze and took off her tracksuit bottoms. His eyes looked down at her legs. She thought, *'Got you mate. You can look all you like but touch me and I will bite like that croc in the Uasin Nyiro.'*

She walked over to the boys who stared at her in surprise. Her opening line was,

"I helped to train the Kenyan squad. They are not the best internationals in the world, but they are hard and give it their all. That's all I am going to ask of you. Right let's do a couple of laps of the pitch. Then we will get two teams together for a practice before playing a proper game." The surface was quite muddy. Half way round the first circuit she shouted,

"Down on your fronts." Anna was down and up again before most of them had got down. She shouted,

"Quicker guys! We're not on holiday." They set off. Then, as soon as most of them had caught up, she shouted,

"Down on your fronts. Up, down again. Up down again on your backs. Quicker! Ten sit-ups." She knew she was plastered in mud. She also knew that most thirteen year olds would be fascinated.

So the training went on. She divided them in groups of five and had one group dribble towards her. Then she threw herself on the ball at their feet. Came up, turned and passed the ball to a little boy who had his mouth open. He was very surprised, but he managed to catch it. Anna, shouted,

"Well done. Now in groups of five dribble towards another group. Then go down on the ball get up pass it to one of your group, who chips it ahead. Then you are dribbling and the other group have to fall.

They all started enjoying themselves. One cocky boy tried to catch the ball and knocked it forward. Anna dived at the ball, was up in an instant and passed it to him. She never reprimanded him, just told him to carry on with a little chip.

After several different moves or actually they were good fun little games, Anna got them all around her. She didn't make the error of getting captains to choose teams but choose the teams herself. She got them to get the right colour shirt on and then they played a game. Anna did not have a whistle, but as she was right up with play she did not need one. She kept the game going by keeping shouting,

"Play the advantage."

She and the young players were so engrossed in the game that it took Anna time to register that all the other boys had finished and were standing watching the youngest boys in the school. A try was scored. Anna called,

"Very well done guys! We will call it a day now, after we have all just run to the far end. Let's go. She was there before them all. She slapped the two boys who were first to finish, on their backs, saying to them all.

"Great you gave it your all. I am proud of you."

She jogged to her tracksuit and put it on. She looked up to find Mr Hancock looking down with a kind smile on his face.

"That was excellent. I took the liberty of ringing Mrs Woodhouse during the game to ask her to release you regularly to come to help us. Thank you. Will you be OK getting back to Lancaster House?"

Anna replied,

"I will be fine Mr Hancock." Then with a cheeky smile she added,

"I am so smelly and muddy; no man is likely to come near me." He replied,

"I am not sure that is true, so if you ever feel threatened you only need ask. Take care." Anna turned and ran off.

She was met at Lancaster House by Mrs Woodhouse.

"Very well done Anna, Mr Hancock is very impressed. He just rang a second time to say how so sorry he was that you were so muddy, but that you had set such a marvellous example to all the boys. I therefore have arranged with matron to let you bath in her own flat, as all the other girls have long since showered and I suspect have used all the hot water.

Mr Hancock was very astute. He realised what Mr Galbrieth was like and so made sure he was taken off game supervision until next term, when they would be playing football.

Anna had great fun at half term. Her brothers were happy to take her to rugby training and all the team seemed pleased to see her. The Captain's son, John did not get home for half term, as it was not school policy to have half term at home, but he sent word through his father that he would look forward to seeing her in the Christmas holidays.

Anna's parents were very apprehensive when they were summoned to a meeting with Mrs Woodhouse, when they came to collect Anna for the Christmas Holiday. Mrs Woodhouse greeted them warmly but immediately worried them by saying,

"As I am sure you know, Anna, does not excel at languages. She came to me at the beginning of term to tell me she is passionate at becoming a vet. She had done her homework and has found that if she passes Latin 'O' level she has no requirement to pass a language 'O' level, so although the school does not teach Latin as a subject, I have allowed her to study on her own under my supervision. I am pleased to say she has been most diligent and I see no reason why she will not pass Latin 'O' Level at the appropriate time."

Anna's parents were surprised and quite relieved. However they were not prepared for Mrs Woodhouse's next statement.

"I think men and boys are very important in Anna's life." Her parent's hearts sank.

"Were you a keen rugger player Mr Anderton?"

Anna's father replied,

"I am afraid I was and I got a very poor degree at Oxford as a result of it."

"I rather guessed," answered Mrs Woodhouse,

"And your four sons?" She raised her eyebrows.

"I am afraid they are out of the same mould."

"Well we will have to guide Anna very carefully. At the moment she is very diligent with her academic studies but I do not want them to suffer on account of Rugby," said Mrs Woodhouse.

Anna's mother interrupted,

"I am very concerned. What has happened? Anna did watch a rugby game when we were on holiday and seemed to be excited by the game. She has been to rugby training with the boys, who surprisingly seem to welcome her which before now would have been unheard of."

"I see," said Mrs Woodhouse, she continued,

"Anna with my permission wrote to Mr Hancock, The Headmaster of 'Wingates', asking if she could train his under fourteen, team. I naturally thought he would totally dismiss the request but he didn't. He gave Anna a trial. Now he is most enthusiastic and he claims Anna has a natural gift for the task. She goes every Wednesday afternoon, returns covered in mud, exhausted but very cheerful."

Anna's mother butted in with almost a wail, "She is only a little girl, my little girl."

Anna's Dad did not know what to say and just put his arm around his wife's shoulder. Mrs Woodhouse continued,

"Obviously, I made arrangements that she could have a bath in the matron's flat as, being a games afternoon all the girls do sport here and tend to use all the hot water. However I was intrigued to know why Anna should want to take on such a task and also why she is so good at it. Make no mistake, she is good. I attended one session and Mr Hancock took me to the pitch. The boys, you must bear in mind are only a year younger than Anna, really respect her. They follow her every command and I noticed they all crowded around her at the end to thank her. Can either of you shed any light on this?"

Anna's mother just shook her head, but her father obviously thought he needed to say something. He said,

"It may be something which occurred on our family holiday in Kenya. Anna seems a changed person. She went out as a rather petulant fourteen year old and returned as a very helpful young lady. I would go further and say an adult. It was quite remarkable. However in answer to your question, my answer is, I don't know I'm afraid."

Mrs Woodhouse was a very wise woman. She replied,

"Thank you for that. I am sure Anna will tell us if she wants to, but we won't question her. We will leave it to her. Thank you for sparing me your time. I do hope you all have a good Christmas and we look forward to seeing Anna next term."

So nothing was said. Anna seemed pleased to see her parents. She was extremely helpful over Christmas and her brothers were happy to take her down to the Rugby Club. Anna did nothing to hide that she was pleased to see John, the captain's son, but her brothers did not notice anything other than that they were pals. Her parents were none the wiser at the end of the holiday.

The younger girls were not given a choice of what they did for PE. However the older girls were allowed to choose. So when Anna returned for the Easter term she elected to play lacrosse as a team sport and do athletics as individual sport. She excelled at the later and very soon became the fastest distance runner in the school. This was noticed by the staff, but Mrs Woodhouse was surprised by a letter from Mr Hancock saying that his games master was still on crutches and he wondered if Anna Anderton could possibly come on Wednesday afternoons and coach his cross country team.

Mrs Woodhouse called Anna into her office and showed her the letter. Anna read it and looked up. "Mr Hancock is a really lovely man and I enjoy his company and would like to help him. What do you advise Mrs Woodhouse?" Secretly Mrs Woodhouse was surprised by this very adult response. She replied,

"Well, when you asked him if you could train his rugby team he gave you a trial. Why don't you suggest you give his cross country team a trial? I think it is going to be very hard for you physically. I have watched you. You like to lead from the front. You may find this difficult."

Anna nodded and looked down giving the matter some thought. Then she said,

"I will do as you suggest. As the letter was written to you I guess you would need to reply." Mrs Woodhouse smiled and looked up at her.

"I think that is sensible. I will reply directly. Good luck next Wednesday."

Mr Hancock was in the reception hall to greet her, when Anna arrived at 2pm. He welcomed her and asked after her Christmas, as he led her through to a court yard. He casually said,

"There are eight in a team and we normally have two reserves, so you will have only a small squad." When Anna saw the squad she was appalled. There might be only ten but they were enormous. They were men. They were seniors and were turning eighteen if not actually eighteen. She paled and her legs turned to jelly. Then she thought about Charlie. She looked eighteen; she would just have to man up.

The team all looked at her with interest but not surprise. They had seen her training the under fourteens. Before Mr Hancock could say anything, Anna said,

"Hello I am Anna. I feel very privileged to be here. I will try to remember your names, but as I get tired I will forget. So if I make a mistake please shout your name. Let's start?" She held out her hand to the first boy, who rather weakly said,

"Mike," Anna gave him her best smile and shouted,

"Mike," The next boy shouted,

"John," Anna shouted,

"John." She went round the circle until a boy with red hair shouted,

"John." As quick as a flash, Anna shouted,

"Red John." She did not let go of his hand and shouted,

"Again!" He shouted,

"John." Anna smiled and shouted,

"Red John." He got the message and shouted,

"Red John," Anna shouted,

"Red John," and released his hand. They all were smiling now.

Mr Hancock said,

"I will leave you to it, but will come out at 3.30pm, to see you at the end."

Anna then took over.

"I have heard that stretching before warming up is not now thought to be ideal, so let's just have a little jog and you can tell me what you want out of me." They set off at a steady pace down the drive. Anna shouted,

"Let's stay in a bunch, with me in the middle and I can hear all of you. Ian can you lead? Mike, are you the Captain?" Mike shouted,

"Yes." Anna shouted,

"You are all faster and stronger than me by miles, so you will have to help me. We will warm up at the gate and take off our tracksuits. Then we will get going doing some exercises at intervals. Is that OK Mike?" He shouted,

"Fine." As they were warming up Anna said,

"I know a normal coach would have a vehicle and go ahead. We haven't got that luxury. So I don't slow you up, when I get tired you will have to carry me. It will be good for strengthening you up and will stop me dying. They were all laughing now.

So Anna and Mike set off at a pretty fast pace. Anna called the exercises. The boys were amazed that these often involved diving in the mud. After about an hour Anna felt herself tiring. She shouted, "Red John will be first to carry me. Jogging on the spot everyone." John went to pick her up in his arms, as she stood in front of him with her legs apart.

"No you great numpty. I am light but not that light. A fireman's lift would be better." Red John put his arm between her legs and she fell over his back. She instantly thought about Charlie adjusting the seat in the airplane. She shouted,

"Let's go, see if you can go a hundred yards then swop." The boys obviously enjoyed actually carrying her and often went further than a hundred yards. When they had all done their hundred yards, Anna shouted,

"That was great. Let's now go fairly steady and see how we get on. No more exercises." When they were getting near to their tracksuits, she shouted,

"Sprint now, last to the tracksuits gets a forfeit." Anna had to dig deep in her reserves to win the sprint. Jogging on the spot with her arms behind her head, she said,

"OK, bring your tracksuits and we will jog back to the school." Mr Hancock was outside waiting for them. They were only five minutes late. Anna said,

"Sorry we were late, Mr Hancock. The guys were too quick for me. I collapsed and they had to carry me most of the way."

Mr Hancock looked concerned,

"Are you sure you are OK now Anna?"

Mike butted in.

"She is only joking, Mr Hancock. Will you come back next week, Anna?" There seemed to be general agreement.

"I will be delighted to. I will think of your forfeit, Ian for next week. I had better go before it gets too dark, Goodbye." She was off running into the gloom, carrying her tracksuit. They could see her white shirt and pale bare legs.

Mr Hancock said,

"Well I'm glad she has accepted. You know it was actually you who were on trial. I did not dare tell her she would be training the senior squad. I thought that would terrify her." Mike said,

"I think the whole squad enjoyed this afternoon. If anyone can spur 'Wingates' to win races she can." So Anna came every Wednesday. They were always pleased to tell her, how well they had got on in the races that they had at the weekends.

Ian always seemed to be last when they did sprints. He therefore nearly always seemed to be getting forfeits. The last Wednesday of term was particularly muddy. It rained the whole afternoon. They were all very filthy and dirty. When they were on the last sprint over a ploughed field, unbeknown to Anna, Ian was behind her and managed to trip her up. She fell flat on her face and was really plastered. Anna never said anything about being tripped but said,

"I'm a lucky girl as this is the last training so I won't get a forfeit. Sorry about that Ian." Ian swept her in his arms and said,

"I think you had better have your forfeit now!" He ran carrying her into the changing room, in which was an enormous bath of hot water ready for them all to get in. He dropped her in. The others had all followed some were laughing but most of them were worried. Then they heard Mr Galbrieth shouting,

"What's happening in there?" Anna was by the side. She whispered,

"Quick all of you get in and hide me!" The boys stripped off and jumped in. Ian had his arm around Anna's shoulders. As Mr Galbrieth actually came in, Anna took a deep breath and Ian pushed her under. Anna was desperate for a breath, but she held on and as soon as Mr Galbrieth could no longer see her, Ian let her up for air. She sat in his lap gasping for breath. Sitting on Charlie's lap came straight into her mind. In between gasps, she murmured,

"Has he gone? I thought you were going to bloody drown me Ian." Ian said,

"I thought you would struggle if you had been really desperate. You were under for fifty seconds. I would have let you go if I thought you were in trouble. I promise." The ten boys were silent worrying what Anna was going to say. She stood up and said,

"I think that was three forfeits, one for being thrown in, and another for being half drowned and the third when I was too weak to resist, being impaled by something very hard and sharp in your lap." She leant down, kissed Ian, on the cheek and said,

"You owe me cheeky chops." She jumped out of the bath only to hear Mr Galbrieth coming back shouting,

"Will you boys stop cheering?"

Anna jumped back in the bath just in time. Ian's arm came over her shoulders, but he didn't have to duck her as the boys were silent except Mike shouted,

"Sorry Mr Galbrieth. It won't happen again." They all pretended to be washing. Anna whispered to Ian,

"How am I going to get out of here? It is not nearly dark enough yet. They won't be worried at my school, as they will just think the training has gone on longer." Ian with a cheeky grin said,

"Well you had better get your kit off and wash properly." To his amazement without showing herself above the water she got out of bra and shirt, shorts and pants and said,

"Who's got the soap? For God sake don't bloody cheer, we don't want Mr Galbrieth back here." So Anna sat naked with ten naked men and soaked. When Mike said they had better get out or Mr

Galbrieth would come back, Anna reached into Ian's groin and gave him a squeeze and whispered,

"I will make a deal, I won't make you stand up with your erection if you get me a big towel and hand it to me as I get out." Ian looked really embarrassed and whispered back,

"You have a deal. Don't touch me again or it will never go down. In fact just thinking about you will stop it going down."

"Well don't think about me," replied Anna, "think what Mr Galbrieth will say if you have to get out." All the rest got out before Ian who ran picked up a towel, wrapped around his waist and grabbed another towel for Anna. She managed to dry in a cubicle and he handed in her tracksuit. The others were all clothed and stood around her as she came out. They walked in a sort of formation around her outside until she said,

"I will be fine now guys." She ran off into the dark. She managed to get back and into her school clothes without any problems. She never let on to Mrs Woodhouse that she had been training the senior team and she certainly never let on about her bath.

Two days later just before the end of term she received an enormous parcel containing twenty fairly large Easter eggs. The note read; '*To Anna, Happy Easter. Thank you for training us this term. We hope these will help you to remember us. The Cross Country Squad.*'

Hidden underneath were her bra, pants, shorts and shirt beautifully washed and ironed and another note which read, 'These eggs are really meant to say, We think you are a bloody good sport and we wish we had half the balls that you have got!' Some of the other girls in her year had gathered round and to distract their attention, Anna said,

"How sweet of the little chaps. Come on girls help yourselves!" She pretended she had had her clothes under her arm and she managed to get rid of the note.

Her grandfather had managed to fall and break his hip, so two of her brothers came to pick her up from school at the end of the Easter term. Mrs Woodhouse was outside the school greeting and talking to parents. She made a conscious effort to come up to Anna and her brothers.

"I am sorry to hear about your Grandfather. Do give my regards to your parents. Needless to say Anna has an excellent report which will be in the post in the normal way. However I have just received this letter from Mr Hancock. I will reply as it is written to me, but I thought you might like to take it home to show your parents. I am surprised a thirteen year old would be brave enough to stand up in front of the whole school. You must have made a very great impression on the young man.

The letter read:

Dear Mrs Woodhouse

You will be pleased to hear how grateful I am for the help Anna has given coaching this term. Obviously the boys would not have wanted to embarrass her, if she had been present, but at the final assembly the Captain of the squad she has been coaching, stood up and said, "We would like to thank Anna Anderton for her outstanding courage and bravery. Three cheers for Anna. Then it was most moving as the WHOLE school stood up and cheered. It would have been inappropriate for me to cheer but I feel I must send her my heart-felt thanks. She has shown amazing fortitude, far in advance of her years. As her head mistress you must be very proud of her.

Yours sincerely
Bertie Hancock

Anna read it quickly and said,
"Thank you Mrs Woodhouse. I am sure I didn't deserve anything, but I am sure my parents will be very pleased.

Anna said nothing when her mother saw the letter and said,
"Very well done Anna. It seems as if you have a gift for coaching boys younger than you. It is most remarkable, as you are the youngest in the family and never had to help younger siblings."

Chapter 3

School continues December 1969

Anna was pleased that the letter was never brought up again and so she did not have to tell any lies. She probably would have largely forgotten that term if they had not gone for a two week holiday over the Christmas of her final year in the sixth form. Her parents were so delighted that all the family plus four girlfriends could go and so they took a chalet for ten in Wengen in Switzerland. The owners of the chalet said there was a little bedroom which was really a servant's bedsit which had a separate entrance which they could use, as in fact there were eleven of them. Anna said she was very happy to have that room, as she could then revise and not be a kill-joy with the rest of the party. Her mother was grateful because she felt guilty that Anna would be rather left out, as she was only seventeen. The other sleeping arrangements made Anna smile, as the girl friends had to share with each other. Her brothers were definitely not allowed to share with their girlfriends!

A pattern was established where Anna had breakfast with them all, and then went back to her room to work, while the others with a lot of messing about, eventually went off skiing. Part of the trouble was all her family including her mother were very good skiers, but of the four girls only one was a moderate skier and the other three were not much better than beginners. However they did not like skiing without their men, so there was inevitable tensions and delays. Anna actually was quite glad she was out of it. She just made arrangements with her Dad to meet him and her Mum and any other folk who wanted to join them at an agreed restaurant up the mountain at an agreed time for lunch. Some days if her work was going well, she just got the lift up and did only one run before lunch. On other days, if the weather was glorious and her work was not going well, she would quit work and go skiing a bit earlier, and hope she met up with them.

It was on one of these mornings when Anna met, not her family, but five of the Cross Country team of two years ago. They were all pleased to see her. They were, at University and were all good skiers, like Anna, so they were soon tearing down the mountain. They stopped for a Gluhwein and there was a lot of reminiscing about that term at school and of course the escapade in the changing rooms. Ian could not keep his eyes off Anna. When they were getting back onto their skis he made sure he was on his own with her. He said,

"Thank you so much for not getting me into trouble that afternoon. I was always being hauled up before the Headmaster, if you had made a fuss and reported me, I would have been expelled for sure." Anna just laughed and replied,

"I think, if I had told Mr Hancock about the water snake, you would have been sent to jail!" Before they all skied off they agreed to meet at a bar after supper.

After the family meal in the chalet, Anna's brothers and their girlfriends went off for a drink. Anna went as normal out of the chalet and up the wooden steps to her room. She worked for an hour and was tempted just to carry on working but she thought, she would go out and meet the Cross Country boys for just one drink, as they had arranged. She found them at the agreed bar, they were all in high spirits with their girlfriends, who to Anna's eyes were very glamorous. They obviously did not take the skiing very seriously, but revelled in the après ski. Anna had a couple of drinks and the boys really looked after her, but the girls rather ignored her. Against her better judgement they all went clubbing. Anna managed to ditch her free entrance cocktail, but they made her have a shot. The whole group were well away, but Anna kept her head, and did not drink. Ian had been near her most of the evening, so she whispered to him that she had to go, thanked him, kissed him on the cheek and left. She walked briskly back to her bedsit. She felt happy, as she knew she had drunk a little too much to do any worthwhile work, but that she would be fine to work after breakfast in the morning. Becoming a vet meant so much to her. She was desperate to get good 'A' level results in five months' time.

After three years, Charlie's T shirt was worn and in fact it had a tear which made it slightly revealing. Anna still loved wearing it. Charlie was still a real memory and now had become larger than life and the thought of him made her feel sexy. She was just dropping off to sleep when there was a knock at the door. Anna thought it was her Dad who might have seen her go out and was just checking she was home safe and sound. It was still before midnight.

It was Ian. He had followed her home. He was fairly drunk and pushed his way in saying,

"I tried not to knock and stood outside gazing at your window but you are so lovely I could not stop myself." Anna just laughed and said,

"You always do talk a lot of rubbish. Now off you go back to Charlotte your girlfriend who thinks the world of you. I bet she is lying in bed wearing a sexy nighty and you are here with a school girl wearing an old T shirt." Anna realised a little late that she had been foolish and what had meant to dampen his ardour was actually likely to enflame it. What neither of them knew was Charlotte had followed Ian and was at that moment standing in Anna's bathroom, having climbed through the window which she had left open, as the bedsit, being above the chalet's boiler, was always too hot.

Ian put his arms around Anna and tried to kiss her. She moved her mouth away and said really sharply,

"Ian, stop. You are making a fool of yourself. Remember I saved you two years ago. I will save you again, but we will have a deal, like before. You must go home now and I won't say a thing about this visit, or I will scream and my brothers, who are just through that pine wood wall, will come. They are seriously tough and will knock the living daylights out of you."

Ian still had his arm tightly round her. He opened his zip with his other hand. He felt Anna's hands, as his hand reached up between her thighs. He thought she was just going to try to push his hand away. He was wrong; she grabbed him with both hands. One hand squeezed his testicles like a vice and the other twisted his penis like a Chinese burn. He was in agony. Anna hissed.

"I am not going to scream for my brothers, you are!" They were both breathing in short harsh grasps. Ian said pitifully,

"I am sorry I thought you wanted me, I love you." He removed his hand from between her thighs and his arm from around her. Anna growled,

"You don't bloody love me, you fool, and it is just that you lust after a young school girl. You are never going to do anything like this to a girl again. Promise me." He whimpered,

"I promise." Anna released him and pushed him away saying,

"Don't you ever mess with me again either. I fought with a crocodile in the Uasin Nyiro. Just you remember that. Now I am still going to keep my side of the deal. Get out and this visit will be forgiven and not mentioned, but I will never forget. You are on oath. Now go!" She pushed him out the door, locking it behind him. He was still trying to do up his zip. She went to the little kitchen area and with shaking hands turned on the kettle and put some coffee in a mug. Then she remembered the open bathroom window. She thought Ian would be too humiliated, but she thought she would lock the window just to be on the safe side. She went into bathroom and found a weeping Charlotte. They stared at each other; Anna broke the spell and said,

"Would you like a coffee I have just put the kettle on. Can you lock the window?"

Charlotte came into room still crying. Anna said,

"Have a seat on the bed; the chair has a wonky leg. Do you take milk and sugar?" Charlotte answered,

"Yes please, I am not fussy. I don't wear a sexy nighty only thick pyjamas. Ian has never seen me in them."

Anna laughed,

"So you heard it all. Ian is a silly boy. You are so beautiful. I suppose he suddenly got the hots for me because I did not drop him in it, at school."

Charlotte asked,

"What happened at school? How did you save him? Had we better whisper or your brothers might come." Anna laughed again,

"No chance that is a stone wall. This bedsit is an add-on for a maid. I said that just to frighten him." As they drank their coffee Charlotte made her tell her what happened at school." At the end Charlotte said,

"I can't believe how brave you were lying naked in a big bath and you were only just fifteen. You must have been terrified, particularly feeling Ian all aroused."

Anna replied,

"Luckily I had felt a man before. I wasn't a bit terrified then, even though I was much younger, I was rather excited. Luckily that man was a real gent."

Charlotte had fully recovered now.

"I can't get over how bad Ian was tonight. Whatever should I do?

Anna replied,

"Ian is not all bad. He never hit me. He was just drunk enough to behave badly. I guess men at his age have too much testosterone. From what you said earlier, I realise you have never slept with him. He is just very frustrated, but I certainly don't think you should mention tonight. I don't feel I have broken my promise, as I have never told tales, but it will certainly look like that to Ian unless you tell him you followed him and heard it all."

Charlotte answered,

"I do like him, but not enough to sleep with him. If you will, I will just keep quiet. I am just so sorry he treated you so badly."

So Charlotte left and Anna went back to bed. Just before she drifted off, she thought of Charlie. She had known him for such a short time, but she was certain he would never have behaved like Ian. Equally she wondered if she would have stopped Charlie's hand if it was between her thighs. It was an erotic thought.

In the morning Anna got up as normal and had a good family breakfast. No one had even known that she had been out. She was not tired or in the least hung-over but by 10 o'clock she knew school work was not going to happen, so she got her skis and got on the cable car up the Mannlichen. The weather was perfect and she was soon in Grindelwald. She had heard the night before that the cross country boys were going to be skiing in this area. Sure enough they were waiting with their girlfriends for the train to Kleine Scheidegg. Ian was quiet, but the others were happy to see her. Charlotte gave her a hug. Obviously the skiing, with girlfriends, had not been a success, so they had decided to split and meet for lunch in Grindelwald. Anna asked the girls if she could ski with them. They were all fine with that and so they leisurely put on their skis waving the boys goodbye.

Anna said,

"I know these mountains rather well, would you like me to take you on a very secret way down?" Charlotte said,

"Please not Anna. I gather you are really good. I don't like anything which isn't a blue run." Anna replied,

"It is only blue run standard, and there is even a bit of flat to pole along which is why no one really goes that way."

"OK," said Hayley, who seemed to be bravest,

"I'm up for it. We will look after you Charlotte. We have got all the time in the world. Let the boys rush up and down we will enjoy the tranquillity and beauty of the mountains."

Anna led them on a long gentle traverse down from Kleine Scheidegg under the Grindelwald side of the Mannlichen. They reached a good viewing spot. Anna stopped so they could all enjoy it. Charlotte said,

"Thank you Anna for being so kind to us. This must be so boring for you." She looked and saw Anna was crying. She said,

"Anna why are you crying? Was it last night?" Anna replied,

"Goodness no! I haven't been along this path since I came with my Grandfather when I was twelve. He died a few days ago. I will keep my promise to him. Come on. He would not want me to be sad. Follow me it is not difficult. We need to keep our speed up, as we have a little bit of uphill at the end. Don't stop. Keep going. Follow me." She was off down a gentle slope between the trees in deep snow. The girls had never been in deep snow before, but they had faith in her. They never got going fast, but went at a steady pace. The snow was up to their knees in some places. It slowed them. Anna heard Charlotte shout,

"This is so exciting." Eventually Anna ground to a halt and started to pole herself along. There was no gradient so there was no need to herring-bone.

Suddenly they came out of the wood to a flat area. On their left about twenty feet up was a big rock. Anna stood with her arms up and shouted,

"Grandad." There was an echo back from the mountains. She gave a big spring using her arms and sticks to lift her so she could turn to face the others. She had tears in her eyes but was smiling.

"In 1924, a small intrepid group of British Skiers came on the train up from Wengen to Kleine Scheidegg. They climbed the Lauberhorn using skins on their skis and tried to find a new run down to Grindelwald. They ended up above that rock. The others stopped but one man was a little out of control and went straight over the rock, over that gulley behind me and managed to keep standing up. His nickname was Mac. They called it Mac's leap. No one has ever repeated it as far as I know. My Grandfather only showed it to me, not to my Father or elder brothers because he was frightened they might try to do the jump. He made me promise I wouldn't. Sorry I was crying. I rarely cry. I have never shown anyone else. My Grandfather was nicknamed Mac."

Then she said,

"Come on lets go for lunch. I am hungry." She led them down another blue run covered in deep snow until it joined the main route. Before Charlotte could be frightened Anna sang out,

"Follow me I will show you another secret way. She let them down an easy slope through cowsheds and goat huts so that they avoided the congested, icy, red route which everyone else took into the village. They arrived at the station.

They kicked off their skis. Charlotte flung her arms around Anna.

"That was marvellous. I burst into tears trying to get down that red run this morning, we avoided that. Thank you so much. The girls walked to the agreed restaurant. The boys had not arrived. As the girls came in, a very brown old man hugged Anna,

"Peter, these are my friends I have been bringing them down some of Granddad's secret ways." He laughed.

"You sit down we will have a drink together I heard he had died. Peter went behind the bar and came back with a shot glass for each of them and one for him. He and Anna raised their glasses, the girls followed. Peter and Anna said together,

"To Mac!" Anna kissed his weathered old cheek and said,

"Thank you Bravo." He chuckled,

"You are the only person who calls me that now. Remember what your Grandfather said, you must bring the man you are going to marry, for me to see, so I can give your offspring freedom of the mountains." It was Anna's turn to laugh.

"I may have found the man. I have temporarily mislaid him, but if I find him again and he passes my test. I will bring him here."

"Make sure you do," replied Bravo Peter.

The boys arrived and they all had a lively lunch. When they were waiting for the train, Ian came up to Anna and said,

"I am really sorry." She laughed and then whispered,
"Forget it. I have." Nothing more was said.

Anna really worked hard when she got back to school. She just concentrated on Chemistry, Biology and Physics as Charlie had suggested. Mrs Woodhouse gave her an excellent report and asked her parents to please give her as much support as they could. She was quite open in her report and said she was sure Anna would pass all three 'A' levels and would certainly get a place at University, but to be considered for Veterinary Science she needed three very good results. Anna worked really hard during the holidays. Her mother was marvellous and did not pester her. Her brothers had lives of their own and only one still lived at home.

Early on in the summer term, Mrs Woodhouse asked her to drop by her office after lunch one day. Anna was surprised to see Mr Hancock. She could not stop a smile coming on her face, as they were like two conspirators. Mrs Woodhouse welcomed her and Mr Hancock shook her hand, then Mrs Woodhouse said,

"As you know Anna, I was at Oxford and there is no Veterinary School there. However Mr Hancock was at St Catherine's at Cambridge. He has done some research. Bertie would you like to tell Anna your findings?"

Mr Hancock took over, "I did not want to do anything without your permission Anna, and so I have been very circumspect with my enquiries. It appears that the other five universities in the United Kingdom only take applicants for veterinary science on academic results with an interview to confirm a place. Cambridge on the other hand is different. You need to get, not only into the university, but also into a specific college. Obviously academic results are important, but sometimes if a college really wants a student they can overrule the university. An example would be if a boy is a very good rugby player or rower, a college would pull strings to get that boy. Now Mrs Woodhouse tells me that you are likely to get three 'A' levels but not very likely to get the very good 'A' levels needed to guarantee you a place. I am friendly with the admission secretary at St Catherine's college, as we were up at the same time. It is unfair as you are a superb athlete, but you are a girl and you are treated as a second class citizen." Mrs Woodhouse frowned.

"It will change I promise you Kathleen, but we must be realistic. Anna wants a place now, she can't wait for the world to make the sexes equal. Now I know Anna is an excellent coach, in fact she is not just excellent she is outstanding. Now apparently St Catherine's has already earmarked young male 'A' level candidates which they want to play rugger for the college. As soon as 'A' levels have finished they will call these chaps up to Cambridge and start putting them through their paces. I know the results of the 'A' levels do not come out until early August, but they are not really interested in these results, as they are going to take these young men anyway, unless they are totally hopeless academically. Now what I would like to ask Anna is would she like me to try to get her a chance to coach these chaps in front of the rugby selectors? If they think it is totally impossible for a girl to do the job, then Anna has lost nothing. But if they recognise her talent then it just might help."

Mrs Woodhouse was appalled,

"Really Bertie, Anna is only seventeen and you are asking her to coach eighteen year olds. She has only coached under-fourteens before." Mr Hancock replied,

"I agree but she started when she was only fifteen and she has been coaching eighteen year olds cross country, ever since."

"What," snapped Mrs Woodhouse, "I did not know that you had been training the senior squad? Is that true, Anna?"

Anna hung her head. Then she looked up into Mrs Woodhouse's cold stare.

"Yes, it is true, Mrs Woodhouse. I can't hide the fact. I knew it would worry you. I was nervous at first, but I conquered my nerves, and I really enjoyed it. I think having four much older brothers helped." A smile came on Mrs Woodhouse's face.

"Well I admire your honesty. I always wondered how a junior would have had the courage to get up in assembly." Mr Hancock added, "I have always wondered why ALL the school were so ecstatic with their cheering. Why was that?"

Anna smiled at them both and said,

"I suppose I can tell, as it is too late for anyone to get into trouble. I was only fifteen and they were eighteen and I just could not keep up with them for twelve miles, so I used to wear each one out, in turn, by making them carry me in a fireman's lift. I told the squad there was no way I could train them properly otherwise. They didn't seem to mind. At the end of the very last session, when it had rained all afternoon, one of them carried me into the changing room and dumped me in the big bath. There was a lot of laughter and Mr Galbrieth arrived so they all jumped in and I hid under water." Anna laughed,

"I nearly drowned trying to stay under long enough." Mr Hancock said,

"Surely Mr Galbrieth noticed they had their clothes on?"

Anna said simply,

"Oh they had taken those off."

Bertie and Kathleen looked at each other. They both shook their heads. Mrs Woodhouse said very gravely,

"You and I were entrusted with the welfare of a fifteen year old girl and allowed her to be in a bath with ten naked eighteen year old boys. I think we owe it to Anna to get her into Cambridge, even if we have to chain ourselves to the college railings."

So as soon as she had completed her exams Anna started training. She was not totally unfit, as she had run three or four times a week just to give herself a break from book work. Mr Hancock drove her to Cambridge after Mrs Woodhouse had shaken her hand and wished her the best of luck. Mr Hancock knew just where St Catherine's grounds were. They arrived early and walked companionably around the pitch until the sky darkened and it was obvious there was going to be a summer storm. They retired to the car.

Mr Hancock got out an umbrella and they walked towards three men, also with umbrellas who were standing by a pitch. They did not really noticed Anna and Mr Hancock purposely did not introduce her. One man said,

"This coach had better be bloody worth it. We are going to get soaked watching." A second much older man said,

"I will give him ten minutes." Mr Hancock said,

"Oh I thought you knew. It is a girl. Anna meet my old friends Jack Banham, Kit Burgess and I am sorry I don't know your name." The young man said,

"It is Christopher Long. I am the Blues coach." They all looked at Anna, as if she was a candidate for a Miss World Contest.

Kit Burgess said not unkindly,

"Well, I said I would give a man ten minutes, my wife would kill me if I gave you any less, Anna. What is your surname?"

Anna was already soaked but answered cheerfully,

"Anderton, Sir."

"No relation of Dennis Anderton who captained Kent in 1920?"

"He was my grandfather. Sadly he died just before Christmas. I never got a chance to say good bye as I was away at school."

Kit Burgess said,

"I am really sorry to hear that."

Anna said,

"Did you ever go skiing with Mac?"

"Yes, I did. Interesting you should call him Mac."

"I didn't," replied Anna,

"But I knew that was his nickname. I went to Mac's leap and shouted his name to say good bye just after Christmas. Bravo Peter said I was to bring any man I wanted to marry to see him, so he could introduce my offspring to the mountains." She then shed a tear and said,

"You will never give me the job now; you will think I am a right bloody softy." Kit Burgess said, as he put his arm round her shoulders,

"There will be no sex discrimination here. You just bloody well show us how good you are. Go on get out on the pitch and do your own private workup, so you can compose yourself. I can see the coach with the players just turning round the corner. Christopher will send the players out to you."

Anna was really grateful for his kindness. She took off her tracksuit which was already soaked and jogged out into the middle of the pitch. She had never felt so lonely. She thought, *'At least with this bloody rain they won't be able to see I have been crying. If it gets any wetter I will have to wrestle with a croc.'* By the time the players trotted out to her she was back to her usual cheerful self. Luckily there were only ten so she did her usual name shouting game. This time there was a 'Richard' and a 'Fair Richard'. She got a smile out of them. She got them dribbling and then threw herself on the ball and was up with it, even though it was so greasy. She suddenly felt she was invincible and got them really fired up. She realised that they too wanted to make an impression. One great big prop crashed into her and sent her flying into the mud. She was up before he realised what he had done and was shouting,

"Quicker, short passes keep it moving," There was a dropped pass which was knocked on. She dived on to the ball, shouting,

"Play the advantage, keep it moving."

After forty minutes she shouted,

"That's enough. Race to the coach. Last one gets a forfeit." She was purposely last and the big prop called Ed was second to last. One cheeky player said,

"What's your forfeit?" Anna shouted,

"Ed can throw me in the Cam off Queens Bridge if he meets me on a night out. They cheered her then, as they got back on the coach."

She jogged to the four men who were still sheltering under their umbrellas. Kit Burgess said,

"Mac would have been proud of you. You have got the job, but my colleagues and I would like you to have a gap year and start roughly in a year's time. Will you be able to do that?" Anna replied with a big smile,

"Thank you, I am sure I can. This bloody rain might make my face wet, but I am not crying now! I am sorry Mr Hancock I am going to make a real mess of your car." Mr Hancock laughed and said,

"You will make a mess of Kit's car when he gives you a lift home, when that prop throws you in the Cam." They were all laughing as they went their cars.

Chapter 4

Gap year September 1970

Anna was overjoyed when she got her 'A' Level results. She had done much better than expected and had got two good passes in Physics and Biology, and a distinction in Chemistry. She could relax. She was committed to her gap year, but had the marvellous bonus that she did not have to resit any exams. She knew where she wanted to go for the nine months. Her parents were not surprised that she wanted to go to Kenya. They were just worried that she did not have a job lined up. There was a distant cousin she could fall back on, but in reality she was on her own.

On the overnight flight she agonised on what she was going to do when she arrived. She knew, when she was being honest she was obsessed with finding Charlie. Should she find a job and somewhere to stay and then look for him, or should she just look for him. It had been four years. He might not even still be in the country. He might be married. He might even have children. She was sure he would welcome her because, although she knew they had been fairly intimate, it was only over a few hours. They had not slept together, so her arrival would not be embarrassing. Three things she was certain about were that he would still be a vet, flying and playing rugby. So she had plenty of leads. She decided she would get the airport bus into the centre of Nairobi and then get another bus to the Vet Labs at Kabete.

She found her rucksack on the carousel and in the safety of the arrivals hall she pushed her small bag into the big bag so she only had one to guard and look after. She had used her head and gone to the loo and cleaned her teeth on the plane, so she was ready to face the chaos of an African airport. With her pack on her back she walked boldly through customs. She was relieved she was not stopped. Once out of the exit doors she was looking up at the signs, when a big, tall man with his head down, not looking where he was going, came out of departures and bumped really quite hard into her.

She immediately thought about pickpockets, brought her hands to her sides in almost a defensive crouch and looked up into a very grumpy face.

To her utter amazement it was Charlie. As she had been thinking about him she recognised him instantly. His mind was on other things and was not so quick. The first he knew, her arms were round him. She could not stop herself from reaching up and kissing his surprised mouth. Then he held her away from him and said, "Anna, this is a miracle. Have you qualified already? Are you out here to see practice? Please come and stay with me."

Anna was so relieved; all she could do was laugh.

"Oh Charlie, it is so good to see you. Would you really like me to stay? I really came here to find you. I know I shouldn't have said that. I should act all casual but this indeed is a miracle."

"You are even more beautiful than I remembered. I am in a complete muddle. Come on let's get a coffee. I can't offer you some where to stay. I haven't anywhere to stay myself." Anna's heart sank but nothing could dampen her spirits. *'She had found him and he was as lovely and kind as ever.'*

They found a table. Anna sat with her rucksack while Charlie got them coffees. She was delighted that he had remembered and did not ask her how she took it. However when he sat down she could see he was worried. Instinctively she squeezed his hand and said,

"What has happened you look so worried? How can I help you? I am totally a free agent." With a smile on her face she said,

"I am at your service, that's provided you have pants on!" Charlie went very red and replied,

"I am so sorry about that." He lent forward and whispered in her ear,

"Actually I haven't got any on. I am heading up to the NFD. It is so much cooler without them."

"No change there then! Can I come?"

"I am so sorry you can't." He looked at Anna's devastated face and added,

"I am not coming back." Anna was totally confused. Charlie blundered on,

"I was due to drive to UK with my really good friend Len. He got Hepatitis. He just got out of hospital, but is much too sick to embark on the big trip we had organised. I have just put him on a daylight flight back to the UK. I think a night flight would have killed him, he looked so ill. Poor bugger he is not allowed a drink for six months. So I have decided, as I have got the trip all prepared, I am going to go alone. I am happy on my own in life, but this will be pretty scary. I will just have to be brave. I am sure I will enjoy it once I get started."

Then he said, "I was devastated when I managed to wangle a trip to Samburu two weeks after the rugger game only to find you had gone back to the UK. The lodge were confused, as they said your name was Rosemary Hatfield. Sadly I did not know your surname, but I called you Anna, which seemed to confuse them further. I am so glad I have found you now. I am not going to let you out of my sight until I have got all your contact details. Which Vet School did you get into? It is so sad me going off, as I would have loved you to have done some seeing practice with me. We could have had such fun. You must be in your last year unless you went to Cambridge and have two more years."

It all fell into place in Anna's mind. She was so pleased to see him, there was no way she was going to be all casual, but she did not really know what to say. There was an awkward silence. Then she managed to say, "I have got a place at Cambridge. I am just starting my gap year." Charlie looked at her in confusion and then his hand went to his mouth in horror. He said,

"You were not in your gap year four years ago? My God how old were you?" Anna answered,

"I am so sorry I misled you Charlie. I was not the girl working at the lodge. You just assumed I was. I am Anna Anderton and I was only fourteen." Charlie grasped both her hands and said,

"I am so sorry. I behaved abominably. I made you sit on my knee. Oh Anna you must think the very worst of me." Anna smiled at him,

"Charlie I don't think at all bad about you. I kept quiet about my age. I willingly got in the shower with you and then sat on your knee. Look at me." Charlie looked straight at her as she still held his hands.

"Never blame yourself, but I will always make sure you have pants on next time I sit on your knee. I am eighteen now. I think you are a lovely man." Charlie said,

"You were so brave with the crocodile. You even joked about feeling my excitement, when I was combing your hair. I am mortified. Well the least I can do is take you into Nairobi and we will have a really good lunch. Then you must tell me what your plans are." Anna replied,

"I won't wait until lunch. As I said earlier I have no plans. I have never been a girl to beat about the bush. Can I come with you back to the UK in Len's place? I have got a driving license. I do remember you asked me before if I wanted to drive." Charlie stood up and drew her across the table and kissed her gently on the lips and then said,

"I honestly can't think of anyone I would rather have as my co-driver." Anna laughed,

"You haven't seen my driving yet. I bet I will ruin your clutch. Will I need some visas? I have got only a little cash, but I have got five hundred pounds in traveller's cheques so I can pay my way. I even have got your T shirt to give back to you. It is very threadbare as I loved wearing it, as it reminded me of you." Then she burst into tears. Charlie hugged her. He stroked her hair.

"You have got me crying now. The number of nights I thought about you having fun with all the vet students, when actually you were at school." Anna's face was still wet but she did grin and say,

"Oh I did have some fun with the boys in the school next door." Charlie fondled her bottom. Anna went on,

"I never let any of them do that. In fact I don't remember giving you permission!" Charlie smiled,

"I was just brushing off a bit of dust."

"You are a complete rogue Charlie. You have not even told me your surname."

He held out his hand.

"Charlie Ferguson. Can I carry your rucksack, Miss Anderton and drive you to the Ethiopian Embassy to get your visa?"

Getting the visa was not straight forward. Anna had to leave; her passport, application form and forty Kenyan Shillings. Luckily she had several passport size photos as she needed two of these. Charlie signed the back of one saying he had known her for four years which amused them both. Anna whispered in his ear,

"I would like to add, 'NOT IN THE BIBLICAL SENSE.'" This seemed to amuse him. They could only return for the passport in two hours according to the clerk at the desk. When they were out on the street, Charlie said,

"I reckon working in an Embassy is a doddle. It is now past 10am and I am sure the chap who needs to sign your visa has not started work yet." Anna replied,

"Well I am going to put the time to good use and do some shopping. I am going to buy some girlie things. I said I was at your service, but I do remember before, that filthy piece of soap that I had to wash myself with, and the shampoo was little better than washing up liquid. Shall we meet back here in two hours?"

As soon as she was alone, Anna did some serious thinking. She remembered that actually Nairobi was quite sophisticated; she thought it might harbour the last decent chemist she would see for months. First she needed some money and she realised she could not cash a travellers cheque without her passport. She ran after Charlie. Luckily he had said he was going to the supermarket. She saw him and ran up to him grabbing a big packet of dates. With a cheeky grin said,

"Can we have these? I love dates!" He answered,

"We will certainly have lots and lots. I know you need some money as you haven't got a passport."

"How did you guess? I don't want to be the type of girl who always is borrowing money. I will pay you back!"

"I just think we are on the same wavelength. You have no idea how happy I am now and I was so apprehensive and worried earlier." He stuffed a bundle of notes into her hand, saying,

"Buy a brown T shirt and a brown bikini. It will be useful for you to travel in, as we are going through some seriously hot country and I know how dirty you get!" She stuck out her tongue at him and ran off.

When she got to the chemist she knew to buy extra 'Tampax' and extra antimalarial tablets. She wondered about contraception pills. She trusted Charlie. She did not trust herself. She knew she wanted to make sure of him before she slept with him, but somehow she knew he was going to be her first and there was no way she could coach the Cat's team if she was pregnant! Then she felt really guilty, *'she should be worried about her mother and father!'* She bought some pills. She was amazed how easy it was out here in Kenya. In England she would have had to go to her doctor.

She enjoyed some clothes shopping but only bought a T shirt and a bikini as Charlie had suggested. As she was walking back she saw a men's sports shop. She was surprised as the shop assistant was a young European guy who she guessed was in his gap year.

"How can I help Madam?"

Anna gave him a big smile and with a lot of courage said,

"I am really embarrassed to ask you but I need your advice. My boyfriend insists when he is travelling in the NFD it is too hot to wear Y fronts, but I think he should. What do you suggest?" The young man coloured and said,

"What about boxer shorts?" Anna said,

"You don't need to be embarrassed I have four elder brothers, but what are boxer shorts? I don't think he would like those silk things boxers wear?" The chap smiled,

"No they are made out of cotton, but are that sort of design." Then he went red and said,

"We have some very naughty pairs." Anna was a little intrigued and had lost her nerves. As he seemed a nice chap, she said,

"OK you had better show me. I hope you won't make me blush." The boxer shorts which were black, were produced. There was a make believe red tape measure down the fly and a caption down the back which read, '*Size does matter*'. Anna sniggered and said,

"They will be perfect." As she paid, she gave him a big smile and said,

"You have been most helpful, Thank you."

Charlie was already at the Landrover. He was obviously excited and said,

"Did you buy the T shirt and bikini?" Anna said,

"I am a good girl I do what I am told. Do you want to see?" She produced them and added,

"I got a dirty brown muddy colour, as you had instructed. You did not say, but I guessed you would have said that I was to get as small a bikini as possible." Charlie laughed,

"Wow, I am really looking forward to the NFD now."

"That is the maximum you are going to see. There is no way you are going to see any strap marks." Charlie pretended to look sad and said,

"I have brought you a present." Anna smiled,

"Can I see it? I love presents. I hope it wasn't expensive, as I have bought you a very cheap present." She tore open the small parcel to reveal a very skimpy pair of girl's lacy, black, knickers.

"Charlie you are a very naughty boy because I know, because they are so sexy that they will have been very expensive. Thank you." She gave him a quick kiss and said,

"I think you are right, we are on the same wavelength. I have got you a present." When Charlie saw the boxer shorts he really laughed.

"I think you are just as naughty as me."

They picked up Anna's passport and visa, stopped at a bank for her to get some money and then they were off on their adventure. First stop was to buy some pineapples at 'Delmonte', not far out of Nairobi. Charlie cheerfully bartered with Africans in Swahili.

They stopped for lunch at the 'Blue Post Hotel' at Thika and walked down to the bottom so they could look up at the waterfall.

After lunch Charlie suggested Anna drove. She was nervous and said so. Charlie put his hand on her thigh and said,

"There is no need to be nervous." Anna laughed,

"It is not really the driving; it is your hand which I am really nervous about!" Charlie drew it back immediately. She smiled,

"That was untrue. Thank you, your hand actually is rather reassuring."

She was pleased that she could remember some of the landmarks she had seen four years ago in the air. They headed for Nanyuki to stay with some of Charlie' farming pals. When she had driven up to Nanyuki she had not seen anything, as she had been crammed into the very back of the Landover facing inwards. She had felt very sick then. She felt on top of the world now.

Charlie's friends were Des and Kim. They had three children, George aged 14 and twins aged 11, Philip and Rufus. Kim was at home when they arrived, but Des was out on the ranch with the boys. She was surprised when Charlie introduced Anna. Kim said,

"How is Len getting up here? I am very pleased to see a girl. I am sick of being surrounded by boys!" Charlie told her about Len's illness. He did not mention meeting Anna four years earlier but implied they had met at the airport. Kim was incredulous,

"You are a brave girl setting off into the NFD with Charlie. It is pretty wild country. Now I am afraid we only have one spare room. Will you be OK?" Anna said,

"We will be fine. I think sharing a tent will be an experience. If he snores I will throttle him and so you can expect me back in a couple days. I will leave the vultures to sort out his body. I think that's what they do to their dead in Tibet."

Kim said, "Well Charlie, what do you say to that. Are you still glad you bumped into Anna at the airport?" She turned to Anna,

"You are so pretty I misread you. I should have realised what sort of girl you are, as I saw you were driving. I am going to really enjoy this evening. You are really welcome."

After having a cup of tea and a piece of cake, Kim asked Charlie if he would mind looking at her horse which was lame. She led them down to the ranch HQ. On the way she asked Anna if she rode. "I would have loved a pony but I had four elder brothers. It was rugby, rugby, rugby. So four years ago I decided if you can't beat it, join it. So now I am as keen on rugby as them." Kim did not notice Anna squeeze Charlie's hand, but replied,

"Actually I am a little the same. I always watch Des and the boys when they play. George, since he has been at school in England has been totally obsessed by rugby. According to him his school has the best under fourteen coach, not just in England but in the world!"

Anna was delighted that Charlie took a lot of time and trouble to explain to her about lame horses. Kim was pleased that he managed to find some pus in the horse's front foot, so the case was straight forward and Kim could treat it herself. It was a beautiful evening and they saw a herd of female impala on their way back to the house. It was dark when they got back. Kim was cross because Des and the boys were not home. She said to Anna,

"Des is hopeless. The twins will be dogged tired. They won't want to get ready for bed because Charlie's here. He is a god to the boys, as he has taken them flying. My plan was to get them all bathed while we had a drink, get them to eat supper and then pack them off to bed. We could then have a grown up dinner. It is not going to happen now."

Anna said, "Charlie and I will help."

Kim replied, "Well let's have a drink. I will try not to be cross with Des. He really is a great Dad. Charlie I'm sure you will have a 'Tusker'. Anna will join me with a G & T?"

Anna answered, "That would be great." She turned to Charlie,

"Could we buy some Gin and some tonics in Nanyuki tomorrow on our way through? I like beer, but it would be a nice change. If we were careful I think a lemon would last a few days." While Kim was getting the G & Ts, Anna whispered in Charlie's ear.

"You never know, when we are out in the wilds and I have had a couple of gins you might get a view of me wearing your present!" He gave her bottom a squeeze. She added,

"I don't remember giving permission for that. Don't forget we only met at the airport this morning." Charlie looked rather chastened. She whispered,

"I rather enjoyed it. You were very gentle." They moved apart before Kim came back.

They heard Des return as they had their first sips. Kim said,

"Better late than never! I will go out and give Des a hand."

George came bursting into the room.

"Charlie I am so glad you have come. Mum's cross, as the twins are tired and grumpy and won't come in for a bath." Then he saw Anna. Much to Charlie's surprise he said,

"Miss Anderton, this is marvellous. Will you do a rugby training session with my two brothers and me? Will you bath us all? That would be awesome." Anna laughed,

"Of course I will, but you better get your brothers, quick sharp." George was out of the room in a flash, shouting,

"Philip, Rufus, don't make a fuss. Miss Anderton is going to bath us. She is the best rugby coach in the world. She was thrown in the rugby bath by one of the seniors. She hid under the water for two minutes until the master had gone. So that the boys would not get into trouble she ran naked back to her school." George came in with the twins, grabbed Anna's hand, and dragged her through to the bathroom with the twins following.

Charlie, Des and Kim looked at each other totally perplexed. They could hear the water running with Anna calling,

"Get stripped off. You can be like the rugby seniors and all get in together. No splashing. I want you three to be the cleanest players in Kenya. We will have a training session at day break tomorrow so we don't hold Charlie up. That won't happen if there are any delays." Then the door swung closed and they could only hear muffled voices.

Des grabbed himself a beer and said,

"Come on you two, the best coach in the world seems to have everything under control. We can relax on the veranda."

They heard Kamau, their cook, bringing through the boys food. Then the boys were back. They heard Rufus moan,

"I hate green beans." Then Anna laughed,

"Bake beans make you fart. Green beans stop you farting. I don't want you farting at training tomorrow Rufus." Then she added,

"Well done Rufus. I will help you by eating two beans." There was general chatter about rugger. They heard Anna say,

"Keep eating I will just go back to the bath room and sort out your clothes and towels."

They heard Kamau bringing through the desert. Then Anna was back.

"Excellent three clean plates. Start on your desert it looks yummy." Philip said,

"Miss Anderton will you put us to bed? I normally only like Mummy to do it, but I think you would be OK." Then they heard Anna laugh,

"Only OK, am I? You wait until I give you a big kiss then I hope I will be more than OK."

Anna thanked Kamau and said to the boys, "Go on to the veranda and say goodnight to your Mum, Dad and Charlie. The first one back gets the biggest kiss."

Eventually Anna was back on to the veranda.

"Hello Des, we haven't really met. I'm Anna." Des held out his hand and said I remember you years ago supporting the Kenyan team at 'Nondes'. I remember thinking then, I would have played like a lion if I had been playing. You certainly stirred Charlie up. He got a lot of ribbing, because you hugged him when he was all sweaty before he had a shower. All his other girl friends have been a bit too precious." Anna laughed as she turned to Charlie.

"I hope you have brought a ten ton truck to bring all my hair products up into the NFD!"

Kim said, "So Charlie, I think you had better do some explaining. You might have bumped into Anna at the airport but obviously you had met before." Anna helped Charlie out saying,

"It was not Charlie's fault. I came out to find him." She told Des and Kim a rather edited version of event four years ago.

Then Charlie said,

"What about George's story about you at his school?"

Anna smiled sweetly at him and replied,

"Two minutes under water was a bit on an exaggeration!"

Kim said,

"Thank goodness you have left Lancaster House. I don't want you giving the twins any ideas when they get to 'Wingates'!"

It turned into a great evening. When they went to bed Kim said to Anna,

"I didn't really mean what I said about you leaving Lancaster House. You were amazing with the boys at bedtime. Since he has been to 'Wingates', George has had a thing about me seeing him in the nude. He did not seem to mind stripping off in front of you." Anna turned to Charlie and said,

"Don't you get any big ideas about stripping off in front of me. I will get out the present I gave you. Measure you and then have a good laugh." Charlie with a rather shamed face had to tell them about the new under pants.

Kim went on, "Also the twins let you put them to bed. They have been rather clingy to me since George has been in England. They are happy going to 'Pembroke' School at Gilgil, as there is a pretty young matron there. They only like girls."

"Don't we all," added Charlie. Anna pushed him into the bedroom.

"You certainly were not the first into bed and certainly don't get a big kiss. Anyway you stink of beer and so don't deserve a kiss at all."

When Des and Kim got to their room, Kim, who was just brushing her hair before bed, said,

"She is a wonderful girl, just what Charlie needs. She is amazing, considering she is only eighteen."

Des added, "She can share a bath with me anytime." He got a sharp whack with Kim's hairbrush.

In the morning at day break, George crept into Anna and Charlie's room. He was already in his rugby kit. Anna was instantly awake and jumped out of bed in her pyjamas, saying,

"I'm coming, get a ball and get the twins ready."

When they got back covered in red mud, Kim, Des and Charlie were having breakfast on the veranda. George said,

"That was awesome." Anna instructed,

"We are all starving. We will wash our hands before breakfast." When they were back and tucking into breakfast, Kim thanked Anna, for training the boys,

"I never thought you meant it. As far as we all are concerned you are the most welcome guest. Don't wait for Charlie to bring you. Then she added with a wink,

"Did he snore?" Anna replied,

"I guess he didn't, as I didn't have to throttle him" Then winking at Philip she added,

"I think he must have eaten his green beans last night!" The boys all sniggered.

After breakfast, Des made the boys have a bath. Charlie who had showered when he had got up, let Anna have a lovely long soak before they left. He knew that would be the last chance she would get to have a nice bath for weeks.

It did not take them long to get into Nanyuki. Charlie did some last minute food shopping. He remembered gin, tonic and a lemon; he was rewarded with a kiss on the cheek. Anna had filled up the Landrover and all the spare petrol jerry cans. She also filled up all the water jerry cans. They had one cold 'coke' for the road.

The tarmac ended in ten miles at Timau. Charlie told her they would not see any more tarmac until the outskirts of Addis Abba, the capital of Ethiopia. They chatted, as they came down the long descent off Mount Kenya to Isiolo. Charlie said,

"You were a real star. I am sure all my friends will like you. I could see Des was dying to kiss you goodbye but was too shy."

"Would you have been jealous?"

"No I am not the jealous kind."

Anna thought for a minute and said,

"I'm glad of that. I don't think I am either." They travelled on in companionable silence.

The fifty miles to Isiolo was soon over. They filled up with petrol in case there was none at Marsabit, went through the police barrier and then they were off into the NFD. They crossed the Uasin Nyiro River Bridge at Archers Post. As they came by the entrance to Samburu Game Park, Anna said, "They were happy days. I wonder if the zebra foal is still alive." She squeezed Charlie's leg.

"Thank you again for saving my life." It was now hot and she added,

"Can we stop and let me put on my bikini." With a smile Charlie said,

"I would like that a lot." Then she said,

"If you promise to keep your eyes on the road, I could change going along. I have it in my little travelling rucksack."

Charlie said, "I promise."

She managed to change with a few very sexy wriggles but she kept her eye on him and he didn't look round. Then she said.

"You are a very naughty boy."

"I'm not," He protested, "I never looked."

"I know you didn't, but I notice you are not wearing under pants."

"I am," He protested again, "I wearing my present." He looked down,

"It is just they don't hide me very well. Even if I don't see anything, just imagining you changing gets me excited." Anna laughed,

"I think we are both rather funny; you getting excited and me being glad that I can excite you so easily. When I get to Cambridge we will have to be scientific. I will measure you with the pants and see if you get more excited looking at me or just imaging me." Then she became sad and added,

"You will be out here 7000 miles away." Charlie to cheer her up said,

"I know we will take several months to do this trip, but it is only an overnight flight." She kissed him on the cheek and said, "Thank you Charlie. That was a sweet thing to say. You are a lovely boy."

They passed the big shear-faced rock called Lolokwe and covered another thirty miles before Charlie pulled off the road for lunch, under a big acacia tree. Anna opened the cold box which had some cold cokes, cheese sandwiches which Kamau had made and some tomatoes. For desert they had half a very juicy melon. Charlie took off his shirt, saying,

"I don't want to get juice all down my shirt." Before he said anymore, Anna said,

"No way Charlie! I will risk getting juice down my bikini top!"

They battled up the road for another three hours before they came to a massive sand river, or lugger at a village called Laisamis. Charlie had camped here before, so he knew of some lovely big trees a little distance away. He told Anna,

"We must not camp near to the lugger, as there are some dreadful, tiny, sand-flies which can get through mosquito netting. They cause serious itchy bites."

"I am grateful of local knowledge, also I never said thank you, to you yesterday for telling me all about lame horses. Can I book my place with you to see practice in three years' time?" He squeezed her hand.

"I would love that."

They set up their camp, initially Anna followed Charlie, but she soon got the hang of things. She was brewing up the tea when Charlie was setting up the camp shower. She shouted to him,

"I was so naïve four years ago. I will wait until dark and have a shower ON MY OWN but I will strip off and if you dare shine a light I will kill you!" He replied,

"Thank god, I was relatively well behaved four years ago or I would be mortified now."

He heard her chuckling,

"I did not have a bra on and I knew I was giving you a real eye full! I am much more demure now." It was Charlie's turn to chuckle,

"I suppose being naked with all those eighteen year old boys in the rugby bath has got exposing yourself, out of your system." He did not realise she was right behind him with the tea.

"Watch it Charlie Ferguson, unless you want to be scolded with hot tea!" Then she added,

"It was rather erotic and made me feel very sexy!"

It was a fun camp. Supper was good, as they still had fresh steaks to be cooked on the fire together with bake potatoes wrapped in tin foil and salad which all needed eating up before it went bad. Anna joined Charlie with a beer before she braved the shower. Charlie set the hot water up and then sat very obviously with his back to her. She had a good shower and hair wash. There was still enough hot water for him to have a good shower as well. They had two chairs, but Anna said,

"Will you brush my hair if I sit on your knee?" Charlie saw she had his old T shirt on which now gave him a tantalising view of her left breast. He replied,

"Of course but isn't that a bit risky?" She lifted up the T shirt to reveal the sexy knickers he had bought her.

"They are very skimpy but I think they are sufficient to keep that trouser snake out. Thank you for my present. Do you like them?"

"I like your lovely legs better. Come on I will love brushing your hair.

Soon they were ready for bed. Anna said as she climbed up the ladder,

"No peeping Charlie. I thought the new knickers, would be a bit hot to sleep in, so I have taken them off!" They lay on top of their sleeping bags in the tent on the roof rack in the dark. Charlie was just wrapped in a '*kikoi*' (an African equivalent of a sarong). He said,

"I take it I have to stay on my side of the mattress?" She replied,

"Sorry Charlie I think we will be too hot in more ways than one otherwise." Luckily Charlie had always slept, not only soundly, but also very still. They were in the same positions in the morning when they both woke at dawn. Anna reached over and squeezed his hand.

"Thank you Charlie you are a real gentleman." He replied,

"Now you are going to shoot our breakfast. I am going to enjoy putting my arms around you to help you with the gun." Anna laughed,

"That is certainly allowed."

Although it was easily warm enough for Anna to just wear her bikini, Charlie made her wear her brown T shirt and her lined waterproof jacket, as he said it would protect her shoulder from the kick of the gun. They walked down to the sand lugger. Charlie said,

"We have time for a practice. The sand grouse seem to have a clock. They fly in for about a quarter of an hour, for water which they store in their feathers for their chicks, and then they all disappear. They will come soon, so you must be ready. However we will practice. You put the gun tight to your shoulder, then there is much less kick. You look down the barrels keeping both eyes open and swing the barrel through the direction of the flying bird and pull the front trigger, then swing through another bird's flight and pull the second trigger. Well done that looks good. Now load the gun. Yes, that's right. Snap it shut and then when you are going to shoot push the safety catch forward and you are away. Here they come."

The first birds came flying in. Anna was not following through properly at first and then she got it and hit one. She had two misses then she hit another one.

"You have a go Charlie, so we have enough for breakfast." Charlie hit four and then stopped.

"That's enough. You did bloody well for your first time, as I get the impression you are like me, you do better at contact sports and athletics rather that hand/eye sports." Anna nodded her head.

"I am a little sorry for the sand grouse. I would not like shooting if it was just for sport, but I don't mind as we are eating them." Charlie agreed.

They did not pluck the birds but just skinned out their breasts and then fried them, and ate them with slices of bread. They were delicious. After they had washed up and were about to pack up, Anna took off her T shirt and stood in front of Charlie just in her tiny bikini.

"After last night I think I can trust you. Could you massage my shoulder it is bloody sore. Just my shoulder, my boobs are fine!" He sat on a camp chair and she sat on his knee facing him. Eventually she said,

"That was lovely, you were so gentle. Thank you."

They were travelling due north. The road was quite good, but they stayed at about forty miles an hour. They shared the driving swapping every hour. After about two and half hours they could see the green haze of Marsabit Mountain. Then they came to an airstrip. Charlie said,

"This is here, because often the Mountain is in cloud. Pilots can land here until the cloud lifts. I got seriously bored one day as I had to wait for three hours." Then he laughed,

"It was a lot better than crash landing in the forest. I think you will love it up here. It is five thousand feet and lovely, and cool. I think we both are a little hot."

He looked at Anna who had sweat running between her breasts. There was a lot of red dust and they both were filthy, as it stuck to their bodies. Anna looked at the front of his shorts and said, "Surely this sort of dirty look can't turn you on? Something has!" Charlie just said,

"Everything about you turns me on." Anna answered,

"I am not sure if I should be pleased or not. Obviously I am delighted that you find me attractive, but I don't want you to be besotted by me!" Charlie replied,

"I don't think I am, as I left you totally alone last night and slept like a log." Anna sighed,

"I think I am reassured. I also slept well. So let's hope we just find each other attractive mentally rather than physically." She thought, *'It is more than that for me. I really want him. I don't think I can resist making love to him.'*

As they started to climb, they also started to look out for a small, dirt road on their right. They planned to camp near one of the smaller lakes in the forest, where Charlie said they would be totally alone. He said that the water was not very inviting as there was a large amount of algae, but he thought they would find it very refreshing. Anna was driving and overshot the turning. She soon backed up and they set off into the forest.

The road was appalling. There had been no grading like there had been on the main road. Even going slowly the Landrover lurched about and Anna found it hard work. She stopped and asked Charlie to drive as she thought he, being stronger, he would find it easier. At last they came around a corner and there was a small green lake. Two elephants stood and watched them from the other side of the lake. Anna asked,

"Will they bother us?"

"I don't think so," replied Charlie. He drove the Landrover to a flat spot about twenty yards from the lake but several feet above it.

They stayed in the vehicle and watched the elephants. The elephants were in no hurry. They lazily sucked up water with their trunks and then squirted it, either into their mouths, or over their backs. They were big bull elephants and Charlie told Anna that their individual tusks might well weigh over one hundred pounds. He said they would be really sort after as trophies. He said it was lucky they were here on Marsabit Mountain and were safe in the National Park. Anna was appalled to think a wealthy hunter would want to pay thousands of pounds to shoot such beautiful animals which appeared so old and so majestic. She asked Charlie,

"Is it a male thing? Would you like to shoot an elephant?" Charlie replied,

"I can answer that really honestly. I would hate it. I have darted elephants for various reasons. The very first elephant, I darted, ran for over half a mile and then crashed down on to its brisket. I thought I had killed it, but it was still breathing and groaning when I reached it. I was so relieved, but then I had a hell of a job to roll it on to its side. Elephants are different from cows which are much better sitting on their briskets than lying stretched out in lateral recumbency. You have only got ten minutes with an elephant on its brisket. I was frantic and managed to get all the scientists and trackers mobilised to roll the poor elephant on to its side. We managed it. Then the elephant was fine and just lay there. I was then a complete fool. I was showing off. I gave the antidote with a flourish into one of the large veins on the back of the ear. I did not realise it acted so quickly. Within twenty seconds it was up and very angry! As I was running away I thought, *'thank goodness I was not a hunter'*. I could never have lived with myself if I had killed such a wonderful animal just for a trophy."

Anna lent towards him and kissed him on the lips and then said,

"I like that storey." When they looked back at the elephants there was a third even bigger elephant with such big tusks that they rested on the ground as he drank. Charlie gasped,

"That must be the famous elephant called 'Ahmed'. He lives on Marsabit Mountain and he has two younger elephants as companions. We are so lucky."

Anna kissed him again and then said,

"I think we are in more ways than one." They stayed in the Landrover kissing and cuddling until the elephants had disappeared into the forest. The cold hit Anna as she got out. She called,

"Look Charlie at my goose bumps?" He wrapped his arms around her and said,

"You must get some warm clothes on." She gave him a quick kiss,

"Unlike you to want me to put clothes on!"

They soon had a fire going and brewed some tea. Charlie got the metal bucket warming the shower water. Anna got the supper organised and he got the tent up on the roof. With the sleeping bags layed out. The tropical night came quickly as normal. Anna thought it felt so cold because she had been so hot in the Landrover and that the air was so damp and humid.

Charlie said,

"I have rigged up the shower. I am going to be brave and have a quick dip in the lake. Then I am going to run back and have a shower." With that he stripped off except for his gym-shoes and set off.

Anna thought, *'This could be very dangerous. I am not frightened of the elephants or indeed Charlie. I am frightened of myself.'* She stripped and ran after him. As she ran splashing though the shallow, freezing cold, water she tripped and fell headlong in to the green slime. Charlie turned to see her glowing white body. Anna called,

"Hug my Charlie I am freezing." Her nipples felt stone hard against his chest. Then she pushed him backwards into the water and he pulled her with him. He was up in a second. Grabbed her in his arms and then swung her up in a fireman's lift and ran back to the shower. They were both were laughing as they washed the green slimy algae off their bodies. Sadly the hot water was soon finished. Charlie gallantly rubbed, a soon shivering Anna, with a towel. Then they both ran to the fire and got their clothes on.

The corn-beef hash, with baked beans was very welcome. It was followed by fried bananas with brandy. Finally they had mugs of steaming coffee containing more brandy. As Anna sat gazing into the fire she thought, *'This is even more dangerous. I feel a bit pissed and so want him to cuddle me.'*

Charlie must have felt her apprehension, as he was very 'matter of fact', as he got her to help him pack everything safely into the Landrover. He knew there would be at least drizzle, if not rain during the night. When they had finished, they quickly had a pee on opposite sides of the camp and climbed fully clothed up the ladder into the tent. Charlie had bought up a towel so he dried Anna's feet before she wriggled into her sleeping bag with all her clothes on. She said sleepily,

"Thank you Charlie that was a lovely day." She thought she would go straight to sleep, but sleep eluded her. As the minutes ticked by she got colder and colder. She whispered,

"I am freezing, Charlie. Could we join are sleeping bags together?" He replied,

"I am bloody cold as well. We will have to be quick. I will shine the torch. You try and unzip them and then zip them together." It was not easy as her fingers were cold. Anna's teeth started to chatter before they eventually managed it.

Charlie ever the gentleman let her wriggle into the combined sleeping bag first which Anna felt was enormous. It did not seem so enormous, when a fully clothed Charlie got in with her. She was still cold but realised part of the problem was she had on too many clothes. She said,

"I have got too many clothes on. This is no good." He replied,

"I will help you take some off." She giggled and said,

"I didn't need to be a grade 'A' student to guess you would say that. OK but you must behave. I think it would be enough if I just got out of my jeans." This was not an easy operation. Eventually Anna just gave up and let him take off her pants at the same time. She giggled as she pulled off his trousers and felt his erection. She said,

"I don't think you are too cold. You had better take your sweater off as well."

Anna was so relieved that they both were laughing when eventually they got comfortable. Charlie cuddled her back. She did not mind that he his hand was on her chest. In fact she rather wished he had put it up under her top, but then as she felt him hard on her thighs she was well aware that things might get out of control very easily. She had not been taking the 'pill' for long enough to make her safe from pregnancy. At least she was now warm.

They both were still asleep when eventually the sky lightened enough for them to see. It was Anna's full bladder which woke her. She started to get out of their joint sleeping bag and woke Charlie. She murmured,

"I need a pee. You stay in the warm and keep your eyes shut!" The chuckle she heard was not very reassuring. The mist was down. It was a rotten morning and she could not even see the lake. She was back up into the tent as quickly as she could. As she was getting into the sleeping bag

Charlie said,

"I need a pee. Can I open my eyes or do you want me to break my neck falling down the ladder."

She giggled and replied,

"The ground is quite soft. Shall I bury you here?" She only just managed to bring her thighs tightly together to stop his hand.

"Tea would be nice as you are going to be down there. I will keep the sleeping bag warm."

Charlie laughed,

"Tea it is but I will need some serious warming up after I have made it."

As Anna wriggled into the nice warm bag she got a view of Charlie's bottom with his 'willy' hanging down. She called,

"Don't do the tent up. You might get something caught in it!" She snuggled down.

It was some minutes before she heard a clunk, as two mugs of tea were put on the top of the Landrover. The next thing was Charlie's head coming through the tent flap. He had a pair of bananas hanging over one ear and half a packet of biscuits held by the wrapper in his mouth. He dropped them in the tent and said,

"I have even brought breakfast. I know a modest girl like you would shut her eyes but you had better keep them open, as I don't want you burnt with hot tea. Can you grab the handle on the mug?" Anna could not help laughing. He went on,

"Your punishment for laughing at me and being so rude is you have to warm my feet between your hot thighs." Still laughing Anna said,

"No greater love has a women for a man than, to warm his feet, but normally she just brings him his slippers. Where are your socks?" She rummaged down the sleeping bag.

"I don't need a torch to find them. I can smell them."

When they had drunk their tea, and eaten the bananas and biscuits. Charlie said,

"When you were looking for my socks, did you find my pants? I will need them to hide my modesty." Anna laughed,

"I didn't find mine either."

"Oh good," replied Charlie, and before she could stop him he had rolled her on her back and was kissing her. She tried rather ineffectually to push him away particularly when she felt his hand between her legs. She kept her thighs together but it was difficult as he kissed her neck and her body cried out to her to open her thighs. She gasped,

"Oh Charlie please be careful. I mustn't get pregnant." Then she was lost as he gently rubbed her and she just let her thighs fall open and enjoyed the hot sensation in her tummy.

She climaxed and having kissed his neck, gasped,

"Thank you Charlie, for not entering me. I have not been taking the pill for long enough."

Charlie chuckled,

"So my advances were not unexpected?" She bit his ear lope sharply and said,

"Don't you get bloody conceited, but I bought them in Nairobi. I knew you would make a good breakfast!"

They both laughed, she gently fondled him and said,

"Sorry you will just have to be patient. However I will tell you. You will be my first and I am really looking forward to it!"

The weather may have been rubbish but they were a happy couple as they packed up the camp.

Charlie drove as the road was very rough. Soon he stopped, as the mud was getting worse. He showed Anna how to put on the chains. They were both wet and cold when they at last got them on all four wheels. He got her to drive as he thought fighting with the steering would help warm her up.

The Landrover was old and did not have power steering. Anna fought the road. Charlie said,

"My right hand is damn cold." Anna replied,

"Before you ask, the answer is, no. I think the only part of my jeans which is not caked in mud is in my crutch!" She battled on and suddenly the rain stopped and the mist started to clear.

They reached Lake Paradise and frightened some Greater Kudu, which Charlie said were very rare. The Lake was about four times the size of the lake they had camped beside. With a smirk Anna said, "Do you fancy a dip?" Charlie shivered.

"No way! At least we are getting near to Marsabit Town. Hopefully we will be able to get a cup of tea and a cake."

They churned their way down in the ruts down the main street and stopped at a shop. They were given a mug of African tea.

"This is different," said Anna,

"How do they make it?" Charlie replied,

"They add cold milk and water to sugar and tea and then boil it for a few minutes. It is good because there is a lot of Brucellosis in the cows out here and the boiling kills the bacteria which are excreted in the milk."

"What is Brucellosis?"

"It is a horrible zoonotic disease."

"Whoa, Charlie! Remember I am only in my gap year."

"Sorry I forgot."

Anna laughed,

"Charlie, you're hopeless!" Then she leaned over and kissed his cheek and added, "At least you didn't forget last night. I am still a virgin, but it was a bloody near thing."

Charlie coloured, "I am sorry."

He could not stop smiling when Anna answered, so matter of fact,

"I am just as much to blame. Somehow I knew I should keep my legs together but they just fell apart." She grinned,

"Of course it was your entire fault for getting me so excited! Now what is a zoonosis? I expect you are going to tell me it is a venereal disease."

Charlie laughed, "It is a disease which animals get which can infect humans. Actually Brucellosis is a venereal in cows i.e. it is spread by the bull but humans get it from drinking contaminated milk or vets can get it from examining aborting cows. It is a nasty disease in man called undulant fever or Bang's disease. It causes recurrent severe 'flu like symptoms and painful arthritis in joints. Do you still want to be a vet? "

It was Anna's turn to laugh,

"You expect me to share a sleeping bag with you, be banged, and have permanent 'flu. Becoming a vet will be the least of my worries." Charlie had a worried look on his face. Anna added,

"Don't look so concerned. I know I should not tell you and act hard to get, but I love the pants off you. That's if you choose to wear any!"

Charlie was saved further discomfiture by a Boran lady, who came out of the shop and offered them a square of cream coloured cake. Anna raised an eyebrow. Charlie said,

"Marsabit lemon cake?" Anna laughed and said,

"You don't half know how to impress a girl, Charlie. Are we at the Ritz or the Savoy?" He laughed in return and said,

"Not many girls see Greater Kudu." He was surprised when she kissed him and said,

"That's for last night, and the Greater Kudu."

They did a little shopping getting some fresh meat labelled 'Stack', which amused Anna. They bought some potatoes and tomatoes. She also found an aubergine and a melon and said,

"We will have a feast tonight." After filling up with petrol and water, they set off as the sun came out.

They were out of town, so while Charlie was taking off the wheel chains, Anna took off her jeans, shirt and sweater and put on her bikini. He did not notice. He was just putting the last chain into a hessian sack when she kissed him on the back of his neck saying,

"It is difficult to find a spot which is not covered in mud." He turned and said,

"You are gorgeous. I will take the windows off the Landrover so you will get a tan on your left side while I am driving then on your right side when you are driving." Anna replied,

"African sun is magic. Show me how to take the windows off?"

"Easy," said Charlie,

"Just loosen these two nuts. I keep the right size spanner by the steering wheel."

Anna said, "This is a vast improvement. It is like a racing Landrover."

Charlie added, "To encourage more airflow we can open these vents below the front windscreen.

The downside is we will get even more covered in dust, if we come up behind another vehicle. I will help you with hair washing at the end of the day!"

She stuck out her tongue and said,

"I bet you will!"

Once they had got going, Anna had a really good look at the map. She turned to look at Charlie. He was oblivious of her scrutiny. He was concentrating on the road. The road was dreadful, but he had a broad grin on his face. She asked,

"Am I right? We have got 150 miles to go to get to the border. Have you been up here before?"

Charlie answered,

"I have not actually been to Moyale town and the border but I have camped at a lovely spot below the escarpment, where we vaccinated several thousand Ethiopian cattle against Rinderpest, before they were bought by the Kenyan government for resale to Kenyan ranchers. I hope we will make it tonight. If we don't I have no worries we can camp anywhere in the desert. As you can see there is getting less and less bush." Anna said,

"I can see we are really in a desert now. There seems to be no people, no animals and no vehicles. I was watching you a second ago. You looked so happy. I guess you like it like this. I hope my presence does not spoil it for you."

He reached his left hand over and rubbed the inside of her thigh which gave her a lovely sensation.

"On the contrary it is because you are here that I am so happy. I know I would have enjoyed it with Len who is a good chum, but you are Anna, the girl of my dreams, who stole my heart four years ago."

Anna could see one tear running down his face. He brushed it away as if it had been caused by a bit of dust in his eye and pretended to be concentrating on his driving. Impulsively Anna said,

"Could you stop just a second, I think I have got some dust in my eye. Charlie brought the vehicle to a halt and they both got out and came behind it. Charlie, was not prepared, and nearly fell over, as Anna wrapped her arms around his neck and standing on tip toes gave him the most passionate kiss he had ever experienced. When they broke apart she said,

"I have never had anyone ever say anything so wonderful to me like that before. You are the man of my dreams. I love you because you are a bit of a softy. You never need to try to hide your emotions from me. Now I am bloody crying. I am hopeless!" They kissed again but very tenderly. Charlie smiled at her saying,

"It seems as if this dust causes a large amount of lacrimation." She replied,

"You wait Mr. 'I am a top veterinary scientist', I will teach you a thing or two when I qualify. Come on I can't wait for my promised hair wash and as I will be stiff from driving a gentle massage will also be expected."

They set off again with very dirty faces. They did not stop at lunch time but just changed drivers.

Charlie got a cold coke out of the cool box which they shared and a banana which he fed her. Anna ate it in a very lascivious way and then reached down to the front of his shorts, before remarking,

"Wow that really turns you on!" He gently rubbed the inside of her thigh. Anna said,

"OK, you have guessed that turns me on. You can do that all day, but you had better stop, as I am not driving properly."

It was lucky Anna was concentrating, as she topped a rise and saw in front of her a sea of sand with hundreds of different tracks cross a giant sand lugger. She had not been going very fast, so as she braked hard she remained on the hard road surface. She looked at Charlie,

"What do we do here?" He replied,

"I think we get out, have a walk and have a good look. Then we can decide on our best route." The whole lugger seemed to be just soft sand. There were no obvious holes or culverts. Charlie said,

"I think it is just a matter of grinding our way across."

When they got back to the Landrover, Anna went to get into the passenger seat. Charlie said,

"You drive, you will be fine. It is good practice." She replied,

"OK, I am sure you can help me if I get in a muddle." She thought, *'It is wonderful that he trusts me. I hope I don't cock it up. He does not seem to be the sort of guy who would shout at a girl. He certainly would not beat me. I wonder if I would enjoy it if he spanked me.'*

She must have had a smirk on her face as Charlie asked,

"What's amusing you?"

Anna blushed, not only her face but her chest as well. She laughed and said,

"When you were so kind to me earlier, I told you to always be honest with me, so I had better be the same with you. I was being very naughty. I was wondering if you would be cross with me if I got us stuck. Then I thought, I wonder if I would be excited if you spanked me." Charlie smiled and said,

"Come here". He held her close to him and fondled her bottom. Then he said,

"I certainly would not enjoy spanking you." Anna replied,

"Well that's settled then, no corporal punishment, but I enjoy those hands on my bottom and I enjoy it even more when you pull me close to you and I can feel you hard against me." She kissed him and said, "Now you had better start concentrating on giving me good advice and forget about my bottom. Your hands are filthy. I bet you can see where they have held me!"

Once they were back in the Landrover, Charlie fixed on the task in hand.

"Now apart from the gear lever there are these two other knobs. The red one gives you high range if it is pushed forward. That is what you have driving in all day. Only the back wheels are driving and you go at a good speed. If you put your foot on the clutch and pull the red lever back then you will automatically be in four wheel drive and in low range so you will go slowly but with a lot of power. Now if you are in high range with the red lever forward you can push the yellow knob down and you will be in four wheel drive but in high range."

"Bloody hell, Charlie, that's a serious lot of information!" Charlie laughed,

"But you are a bright girl. I am sure you have remembered it." Anna answered,

"However it begs the question what do I do?" Charlie said,

"I am teasing you. A carefully person puts the vehicle in first gear in low range and grinds their way along. If they get stuck, no one can blame them, as they have not made a mistake. A colourful person pushes the yellow knob down and hits the sand fast in high range, then, when they feel themselves slowing and sinking, pulls the red lever back and has more power and usually manages to keep going. However if there is a delay getting into low range, they get moaned at for making a cock up!" Anna gave him a quick kiss and said,

"There is a grave danger we are both going to be unhappy!"

"How come," said Charlie. Anna chuckled,

"Because if I make a cock up you are going to have to spank me and neither of us will enjoy it." She pushed the yellow knob down and accelerated down the slope into the sand changing up into second gear as she hit the sand. She roared along. As she started to slow she knocked it down into first gear and kept going. Eventually she began to slow. Then she pulled the red lever backwards and they kept going until they climbed up the far bank. She stopped and turned the engine off.

Charlie said in a very stern voice,

"Get out."

They met at the back of the vehicle. Anna protested,

"I made it, don't spank me." Charlie pulled her to him.

"You were a bloody star. I just need to give that petit bottom a really good fondle."

Anna laughed and pushed his hands inside her bikini bottoms before she put her arms around his neck, saying,

"I don't care how dirty and rough your hands are. I want to really feel them." Then she ground her pelvis forward and said,

"Christ, I want you. Sorry you will have to wait but not for long I promise." Then she kissed him really passionately.

They got back in the Landrover with Anna driving. Once she had got going, she pulled his right hand onto her tummy and pushed his palm into her bikini bottoms. Charlie rose to the occasion and soon she was moaning with pleasure. She sighed,

"Thank you Charlie. That was lovely. How soon do we get to your camping place?"

"About thirty miles I think."

However although it was only thirty miles the light was beginning to fade and they came to another wide lugger first. Anna stopped and they both looked at each other.

Then they both smiled as Anna said,

"So we are in agreement then."

"Are we?" replied Charlie.

"Yes," said Anna,

"Your look said, don't let's risk it tonight, but let's find somewhere to camp this side of the lugger. I totally agree." Charlie smiled and said,

"Great let's turn left as the escarpment is that side and we may be lucky and find some nice trees."

They found some trees. Charlie rigged up the shower while Anna made a fire and put up the tent on the roof of the Landrover. She left the two sleeping bags zipped together. Charlie put the windows back in, as he was worried they might have attracted thieves, but he thought it was very unlikely.

They braved the shower together. It was lovely under the warm water but a little chilly in the night air. They had good supper using the fresh provisions they had got in Marsabit. They had a cup of coffee, cleaned their teeth and soon were up in the tent.

Charlie came up behind her. When he saw the two sleeping bags joined together he said,

"So I might get lucky?" Anna giggled,

"You might but only to conserve body warmth."

"Off course," he replied,

"Can I help you get out of your jeans? I am always sad when you are cold and put them on after the shower."

"Go on you old rogue but don't fanny about as I want to be in the sack, Quick sharp." It was not in fact that cold and they both were naked when they got into the sack. Anna whispered,

"This is like using the yellow knob. There is a high risk of a cock up in more ways than one, but I love the feel of your body. We must be careful." She fondled him and then rubbed him, whispering "Come for me Charlie." They were passionately kissing as she felt him roll on top of her and climax onto her tummy. She hugged him, whispering,

"At least no cock ups tonight! Sleep well my Darling."

At dawn, Charlie woke on his back. He lay there thinking. He felt embarrassed about the previous night. It was as if he had taken advantage of her. Somehow he was worried about her feelings when she woke. He need not have worried, as she soon moved on top of him and nuzzled his chest before saying,

"You smell delightfully male. It is very erotic but we must stick to the red lever. I feel so bloody fertile the yellow knob would be disastrous. Soon she was moaning,

"Oh yes, please more of that."

When they eventually got up, getting going did not take long, as the embers of the fire were still hot and tea was soon made. Fried tomatoes on toast were like a feast. When they were all packed up, Anna pushed Charlie out of the way, gave him a quick kiss and said,

"I am not quite qualified yet; I need more practice with the yellow knob." They both were laughing when they set off.

Somehow the lugger did not seem as wide in the morning light. They sailed across with Anna shouting,

"I didn't even need the red lever, but that service you gave me earlier was magic!" Charlie smiled, *'Why had he worried? She was wonderful.'*

Soon they were climbing the steep road up the Ethiopian escarpment. There had been a few shacks at the bottom but the town of Moyale, if it could be called a town, was at the top. It was on the border. Charlie stroked the inside of Anna's thigh saying,

"This is new territory for me." With a smirk she replied,

"Really, I must have been dreaming in the tent." She loved it because it made him blush.

There was a garage, so they stopped for petrol and a final coke which was even cold, before they drove the half mile to the actual border. The barrier was down and no one seemed to be about. Eventually after Charlie had shouted,

"Hello, anyone about." A smiling Kenyan came out of a hut doing up his uniform.

"No border today. It is Sunday."

"Oh dear," replied Charlie,

"I had forgotten the days of the week. Couldn't you just stamp our passports and then we could try our luck with your friends in Ethiopia." The Kenyan laughed,

"Yes they work on Sundays but no one crosses because we don't work. The immigration officer has the stamp. He is having coffee with the police inspector. You could see if he will help, as you are obviously not commercial. Good luck. The inspector's house is the third, as you go back on the right." Anna was slightly confused, as he indicated to the left but she hoped Charlie had followed the directions. Charlie shouted his thanks, as she turned the Landrover around.

As they drove off Anna said,

"Which side are we looking?" Charlie responded,

"I am not sure." She smiled and said,

"You are a real numpty. Didn't you listen to him?" Charlie laughed,

"I have a theory that you never have an argument with a girl about directions or maps unless you have had sex with her."

"Well that's simple then. We only have seven thousand miles to go. You can stay celibate or we can have a dam good argument occasionally. Your choice!"

"That's easy," replied Charlie,

"I vote for a dam good argument several times a day."

"I disagree," replied Anna with a stern look on her face. Charlie lost his smile. She added,

"I say the odd argument in the day but lots of arguments at night and a gentle disagreement most mornings." Charlie stroked her thigh rather high up. Anna pushed his hand down nearer to her knee and said,

"No time for arguments now. You look your side and I will look mine. I guess we are looking for a blue Landrover."

They found a blue Landrover and parked behind it and walked with some trepidation up to the house. There was some laughter from the garden behind, so they skirted the house and walked into the garden. There were two Kenyans wearing shorts each with a bottle of Tusker. Anna was nervous as she thought they were intruding, but she was delighted when Charlie said,

"Samuel, what a surprise! Last time I saw you, you were sitting next to me with a loaded Tommy gun in your lap." The shorter of the two men leapt up and shook Charlie by the hand, exclaiming,

"Bwana Charles. It's good to see you. Meet Horatio Ngugi from Immigration." Turning to Anna he said,

"Madam you are also most welcome. I worked with Bwana Charles three years ago in North Eastern Province." Then he slapped Charlie on the back,

"However did you afford the bride price for such a beautiful lady?" Charlie laughed and replied,

"I have not met her father yet. I bought her a coffee at the airport and she has been with me ever since!" Anna blushed and managed to say,

"What's the going rate for brides in Moyale?" Horatio replied,

"They are very expensive this side of the border. Over seven camels and at least ten good cows in Kenya but the girls are much cheaper in Ethiopia!"

Anna rose to the occasion and responded, "Well I won't bother you Horatio. I will stay this side of the border and send Charlie alone!"

"We will certainly look after you," said Samuel,

"Now let me get you both a beer." Anna smiled when she saw the fridge on the veranda, in easy reach. She guessed the normal pastime in Moyale.

They ended up having a good goat curry and several beers. Their passports were stamped with a flourish and they both waved as Charlie drove off.

"Thanks for driving Charlie. Unless I sober up we had better unzip the sleeping bags tonight. I think it is the red lever first and then the yellow knob but either way I am legless, or should I say my legs will be way too far apart to be safe."

Charlie replied,

"You have no need to worry I will have Brewer's droop!"

"What's Brewer's droop?"

"It's when a guy has drunk too much and can't manage it." Anna sniggered,

"I bet you would bloody manage it, you old *'dume'* (Literally any male animal but in this context means a ram). Now think what you are doing. I know we have stamps in our passports but I think it would be bad form to crash into the barrier." The policemen were happy to see them and rapidly raised the barrier and cheerily waved them through.

Chapter 5

Ethiopia October 1970

Charlie only had to drive three hundred yards before they reached another barrier with a big bright flag, green, yellow and red with a five pointed star. Charlie said, "These guys were Christians in AD 300. I hope you are feeling holy?"

"No, only very pissed," was her reply.

The Ethiopia officials were very smart, both friendly and efficient. They were soon on their way out of the very small town on the North of the border. The road deteriorated rapidly. It became appalling. The Landrover crashed and thumped down unless Charlie went at little over 1 mph. At least it was dry. The bush was quite thick. There was no sign of people or any other transport. They stuck it for about an hour, before Charlie said,

"Let's look out for a camping spot. I am knackered." It took them another half an hour before they found two trees fifty yards off the road with a sandy area beneath them. As they drew up, Anna saw some Guinea Fowl and pointed them out to Charlie.

He quickly got out his shot gun from behind his seat and set off in hot pursuit with Anna close behind him. An athletic man can outrun a Guinea Fowl, so slowly Charlie got closer to them and then they took off. Heaving with exertion, Charlie stopped, raised his gun to his shoulder, pushed forward the safety catch and fired. The bird dropped like a stone. They ran forward and Charlie picked it up triumphantly saying,

"Supper! Sadly it has got long spurs so it will be old and tough but we can remedy that."

Anna put her arm around him.

"Well done Charlie. I am sure it will be feast. I think we both could have run faster if we had not had those 'Tuskers' at lunch."

They skinned the bird and Charlie showed her how to work the pressure cooker which was soon whistling on the fire. Potatoes were cooked in tin foil and they still had the Aubergine from Marsabit which they fried. Anna asked,

"Aren't they meant to be bitter if you don't soak them in salty water over night?" Charlie replied,

"So people say, but I have found them OK without the bother. We will have to ask, when we have Moussaka in Greece." Anna hugged him.

"We will need hot stews then, as it will be winter and dam cold. We must enjoy the sun and the warmth. I am sweating like a pig." Charlie grinned,

"I will enjoy the shower tonight." Anna laughed,

"I don't want you to get big headed but I will as well." They enjoyed their supper and their shower as the sun was setting. Anna had got used to being naked with him but she teased him, as whenever he looked at her he got an erection.

"Don't be shy Charlie. I am glad I excite you." It was quite hot so they lay cuddled on top of the sleeping bags. It cooled down around two in the morning and they wriggled into the sleeping sack.

The road was that bad that it was the middle of the afternoon when they reached Mega. They had a late lunch inside the walls of the Old Italian Fort. It was magic just getting out of the hot crashing Landrover. They played the fool in the fort. Pretending to be soldiers, Henry the 5th, Julius Caesar etc before heading north, out of the sleepy small town. The road had been graded and was much improved, so they got fifty miles under their belts.

Anna was driving when she saw a yellow-necked francolin. Charlie managed to shoot it out of the window. He was ashamed of being so unsporting, but it made an excellent supper. They were higher now and so it was cooler. It was dark by the time they showered. They climbed straight up into the tent. It was much warmer in the tent so Anna sat with her back to Charlie so that he could brush her hair. She felt him getting more and more excited so even though her hair was still wet they wriggled into the sleeping sack. She lay on top of him and whispered,

"Do you want me to really excite you?" He replied,

"You first," She answered,

"It is just too dangerous if you get me too excited I won't be able to stop." Then she sat up and having him directly under her gently moved her body up and down with her hands on his shoulders. She could feel him becoming frantic. She so wanted to let him inside her, but knew it would be disastrous. She got very worked up herself. She flopped onto his chest and kissed him passionately and felt him ejaculate between their two bodies. They continued to kiss gently until they both calmed down. Charlie whispered,

"You are so sexy. I love you to bits. Will you get excited for me?" She murmured,

"That would be magic." He managed to get her so aroused that she cried out,

"Yes, yes, Oh thank you." When she had relaxed, she said,

"Can you feel how wet you have made me. I am sure it won't be sore, when you enter me properly. You must not worry that you will hurt me. I so want to feel you deep inside me." They kissed again and they both were soon asleep.

The next day the road improved. They knew that they were slowly gaining altitude. First they noticed very small areas of cultivation and then later in the afternoon they came to bigger fields. Charlie thought the crop was millet. They found some lovely big eucalyptus trees which they were sure were not indigenous. There was no one about so they decided to camp. They soon had their table and chairs set up and were sitting down enjoying a cup of tea when there was a 'crack' and several leaves fell out of the tree above their table. They looked at each other in surprise. Anna asked,

"Are we being shot at?" Charlie replied,

"I'm not sure, but I think that was a catapult or a sling shot."

There was another 'crack' with more falling leaves. Anna jumped up.

"You stay put. It's some young boys. You were right. They do have sling-shots. I will see if I can make friends. They are less likely to be afraid of a girl." Soon Charlie could see five young boys surrounding Anna. He was worried, but then he relaxed as he could see her laughing. Soon they were teaching her to use the slingshot. Then they disappeared as a group and he could hear the odd 'crack'. He stoked up the fire and started to prepare supper. It was going to be corn beef hash with the remaining fresh tomatoes and aubergines. Eventually Anna returned, followed by the boys. They each solemnly shook his hand and Anna gave them a boiled sweet each. Charlie found a fruit cake and they all had a slice. They grinned and said what sounded to Anna as *ileskilin penicillin*. When they saw what Charlie was cooking they ran off. Anna said,

"I think it's their job to keep the birds off the crops. They have got platforms with coverings to keep the sun off them." Charlie added,

"There is no doubt you have a way with little boys." She kissed him and replied,

"Maybe I have a way with a certain big boy?"

Much to their delight the boys returned with an aubergine and three tomatoes.

Anna said, "*Ileskilin penicillin.*" This made them laugh. Then they shook hands and went off back into the millet. Charlie said,

"I think we have made some friends. I don't think we need worry that they will pinch anything." Anna laughed and said,

"I think I will wait until dark before I shower."

They had a good meal as they decided the fresh vegetables were best eaten. After it was dark they had a shower together and were quickly into the tent as it was distinctly cold. Charlie cuddled her back with his top hand fondling her breast and whispered,

"You have certainly got a way with this big boy!"

The following day the road improved and they began to see many more people. They laughed together as they passed group after group of Ethiopians wearing the same, very bright coloured, sweaters. A few miles further on it would be a different bright colour. Obviously a very good salesman had come on the road a few days earlier. They passed through Debre Zeit. Sadly Charlie did not have any contacts at the veterinary school, as they both would have been interested in having a look around.

They arrived in Addis Abba as it was getting dark. Charlie was driving. Anna asked,

"Where are we going to stay?"

"It's a surprise." Anna put her hand on his thigh and said,

"I love surprises." Charlie kept climbing up into the city towards the only tall building. He swung into the car park of the Addis Hilton. Anna stroked his thigh and said,

"You really know how to spoil a girl. Can we share a really long bath? You were so kind to me at Des and Kim's." Charlie squeezed her hand saying,

"That sounds good fun."

They felt very scruffy when they checked in. Charlie amused the Ethiopian girl at reception by saying,

"She should not bother to get a porter, as Kenyan men were very strong and he would carry their bags."

They were given a room on the top floor which gave them a wonderful view of the city. There was a fridge in their room so they both got a beer which they took to the bathroom. Anna washed her hair in the shower while Charlie ran a bath. He then had a shower before he joined her in a deep bath, splashing water all over the floor. With great fun they managed to arrange it, so that Anna was sitting in his lap. She said,

"This is a real treat. Thank you so much, Charlie. Can we be really decadent and have supper in the room? Then I don't have to put any clothes on."

"I would like that a lot," replied Charlie, "The longer you're naked the more I like it."Anna smiled,

"I'm glad nothing has changed then."

She brought his hands up onto her breasts.

"I love your big rough hands there. I feel protected and loved."

He very gently squeezed her nipples.

Anna said,

"That is a real bonus. Can you feel my nipples harden?" Charlie kissed her neck and then whispered, "You are so lovely. You are good enough to eat."

After their bath they had a combined clothes washing session in the bath and basin. Charlie rinsed after Anna had washed. Then they both wrung out together. The room had a small balcony with two chairs and a small table. Wrapped in towels they festooned their clothes on the balcony. There was no wind so they thought they would be safe and not end up in the car park.

The room service menu was not brilliant, but when the food arrived it was presented nicely. They got some more beers as there were only four in the fridge. They made themselves coffee in the room and after putting their tray outside, crashed into bed. It was a real luxury with pristine clean sheets. By mutual consent there was no lovemaking as they did not want to mess up the sheets.

In the morning they went down for a late breakfast which was a magnificent buffet. While Charlie checked out, Anna took their bags and the almost dry clothes out to the Landrover. When Charlie came out he found her changing a flat tyre. He was really proud of her, as she had started on her own and not come moaning into him. He said so, and was given a reward of a passionate kiss, even though there were several people in the car park.

While the tyre was being fixed at a garage they walked to a bank to get out some more money. They then walked further down into town and checked in another hotel. It was an old and much more modest hostelry, called the Teque Taitu. Apparently it had been built in 1898.

On the way back to the garage they were hustled by two youths. Anna looked down and saw one trying to pick Charlie's pocket. Without a thought she whirled around and hit him hard on his chin with a right upper cut. The pickpocket landed on his bottom and fell onto his back. Charlie was rather slow off the mark and thought the lad had collapsed. He lent down and said,

"Are you OK?"

The other youth ran off. Exasperated, Anna with her hands on hips retorted,

"Of course he is OK. He was trying to pick your pocket so I punched him. You great numpty! Leave him alone. We will scarper in case the other one has gone for reinforcements!" She dragged Charlie off down the street. There was no pursuit and they soon arrived at the garage.

Later over a beer, Charlie asked if her hand was sore. Anna answered that she must have caught the youth just right as she had only slightly bruised her knuckles. She dismissed Charlie's enquiry with a shrug of her shoulders and a comment about having four elder brothers. Then she laughed,

"No more cuddling in bed, for you, Charlie. I will be sitting in a chair with the shot gun as your minder!" Charlie grimaced. Anna was not sure whether the grimace was because he felt such a fool or because he didn't relish sleeping on his own.

They had a lazy afternoon and after an early shower, decided to have a night out on the town. The first bar was not very inviting, as it was filled with rather loud men. However the second was much better and had various groups of young people. Charlie was sure they were students. He asked the barman what was the local drink. He was told it was Tej which by the description and sign language was brewed from honey. It was very pleasant. Obviously he had been overheard, as a girl from one of the groups, came over to them.

"My name is Zenobia."

"I am Anna and this is Charlie." They shook hands and Charlie went to get three more Tej. Zenobia explained to Anna that she and her four friends were all at university in Addis Ababa. Soon the seven of them were all chatting. Zenobia insisted that Charlie and Anna came back to her house for a traditional Ethiopian meal. It was really good fun. There was a large bronze dish covered in a type of rubbery bread which was very different from what Anna was used to. Around the dish were several small dishes, each containing different ingredients. Anna recognised aubergine, okra, tomatoes but there were several meat dishes which were a mystery. The food was all on a large, low table. They sat around on big cushions. They ate by breaking off some bread and scooping up some of the food in the small bowls. It was quite in order to scoop up a delicacy and give it to someone. Anna smiled, as Zenobia was often finding delicacies for Charlie who often dropped food when he was scooping. The boys were too shy to scoop up anything for Anna.

Zenobia spoke the best English, but the other Ethiopians all tried. Needless to say Anna and Charlie were hopeless at speaking or understanding Aramaic. There was quite a large amount of Tej drunk.

Anna felt fairly pickled when she and Charlie got up to leave and to walk back to their hotel which mercifully was not far away.

Their problems then started as the front door was locked and very solid. No one came, even when Charlie knocked really loudly. Charlie said,

"Blast this. We are in a ground floor room. Let's go round the back." At the back of the hotel was a twelve foot wall with sharp spikes on top. Charlie leant against the wall and cupped his hands so that Anna could climb up him and eventually hold the sharp spikes standing on his shoulders. Then as she pulled herself up, he could put the palms of his hands under the bottom of her feet to help her. It was only when she was crouching on the top of the wall holding on to the spikes that she looked down into the garden at the back of the hotel.

She looked into the eyes of an angry lion which immediately sprang up at her. It was stopped by a second row of spikes pointing downwards on the inside. Anna was terrified and let go of the spikes, falling on top of a surprised Charlie. It was lucky he caught her as she was quite high up. She did not scream, so he had no idea what was happening. He just held her to him as she was obviously scared.

After a couple of minutes she stammered,

"I am sorry to be so pathetic. There's a lion in there and he eyeballed me and then sprang. My limbs went to jelly." She buried her face in his neck as he continued to hug her. Then he stroked her hair saying,

"Don't worry we will have another go at waking someone up."

When they got back to the door, Charlie was much more forceful and beat the door with a fist sized stone which he had picked up in the garden. Eventually an old man let them in. The hallway was dark but they managed to find their room. Charlie locked the door and then checked the French windows which had bars and were bolted. Still in their clothes they cuddled together on the bed. Anna said,

"I am sorry. I behaved like a pathetic young girl. Shall I fly back to the UK and you can find someone else?"

"No way, you are a great co-driver. Everyone goes to pieces the first time a lion charges at them. I am sure you will be fine sitting in that chair being my minder!"

"You are the bloody limit, Charlie Ferguson. A girl is terrified out of her wits and all you do is take the piss out of her. If you think I am going to sleep anywhere in this room with that bloody lion just outside the door, you have got another think coming." Charlie said nothing but kissed her on her neck which he knew she loved. As he felt her relax he whispered,

"Who said anything about sleep? I will never forget how brave you were with the crocodile." She hissed,

"What did you do? Get me to take my knickers off and then get me to sit on your bloody trouser snake."

Somehow Charlie had managed to undo the top button of her jeans and slid his hand inside her knickers. Anna stammered,

"I hope you realise whenever we have an argument in future, I will remind you how you took my virginity. Not gently and sensually but by terrifying me so badly that I didn't realise what you were about to do." Charlie stopped moving his hand.

He could hear a hint of laughter in her voice,

"Don't bloody stop now." He realised that she was actually lying on her back and her legs were wide apart. She started to kiss him passionately and gently push her pubis up to his hand. In fact she was so open for him that two of his fingers entered her and she groaned with pleasure.

"Now do you still want me to sleep in the chair and be your minder?" There was no answer from Charlie who was frantically trying to unbutton her shirt.

"I think if you asked very nicely you might be given a very 'Happy Ending' if you gently take all my clothes off and gave me a sensual cuddle and we can forget about you needing a minder." He kissed her neck. She shivered with delight and he said,

"You are so lovely. I will be very gentle." Anna felt his hand gently on her back under her shirt undoing her bra. He gently stroked her back. Then he kissed her again and Anna felt him fumbling with the buttons on her shirt. She was dying to help him. The lion had frightened her so much she was becoming desperate for him to take her and so all she could think about was for him to be deep inside her. It seemed forever before she felt his big hands on her breasts and then unexpectedly she felt his lips on her hard nipples. Yes that was magic. His hand was still in her knickers. The terror of the lion was forgotten and she thrust up to his hand.

Everything was a blur now. She felt wide open and longed for him to enter her but he was kissing her passionately and rubbing her so beautifully that she wanted the sensation to last forever. Her arms were tight around his neck. She thrust up to feel him. She broke off from their kiss and whispered,

"Oh Charlie I love you so much." She heard his reply,

"My darling, Anna. I love you. You are so beautiful I can't resist you." She pushed up to him.

"Take me Charlie. I want you deep inside me."

She felt him pushing into her. She opened her thighs as wide as she could. She felt his big hands on her bottom. She moaned with the intensity of the feeling. Charlie hesitated.

She groaned, "Don't stop Charlie!"

Charlie gently guided himself into her, pulled her bottom to him and with one thrust ejaculated deep inside her, crying,

"I am sorry, I just could not hold back any longer."

Anna felt herself gripping him and whispering,

"I did not want you to. That was lovely."

In a few minutes she felt his breathing coming back to normal and he rolled off her. Anna asked,

"Will you help me to have an orgasm?" Charlie replied,

"I would love to. Is this right?"

"Yes, you can rub a little harder. That's magic. Don't stop. Yes I am coming." She gave a little sigh.

Later she asked,

"Was I as good as other girls?" Charlie kissed her and said,

"You were my first and you were bloody marvellous." Anna was incredulous,

"Were you really a virgin?" Charlie said,

"I am sorry I came so quickly. You were just so exciting."

Anna laughed and said,

"I hope you always find me as exciting. Cuddle my back." They were soon asleep.

In the morning Charlie slipped out of bed to have a wee. He was standing in front of the loo when he felt two arms around him.

"Hurry up, slow coach. You are quick when you should be slow and slow when you should be quick but I love you to bits. Keep the bed warm!" Charlie thought, *'What a girl she is!'* Anna came running, naked, back into the room and burrowed into the bed and wrapped herself around him. Before he knew really what was happening, he was on his back and Anna was on top of him. Then she gently pushed him inside of her and sat up. She undulated her pelvis so provocatively that even though he was trying to hold his breath he could not stop himself, when she ground on to him and flopped forward whispering,

"Don't stop I am so ready for you." He would have cried out if she hadn't covered his mouth with kisses. As he wrapped his arms around her, Anna said,

"I am so sorry I was so wet with that lion last night. I hope I won't let you down like that again." Charlie replied as he fondled her bottom,

"You do talk a lot of nonsense. I'm very proud of you. Most girls would have screamed the place down and certainly would not have gone to sleep with him just outside the window. I feel guilty that I took advantage of you." Anna felt the return of his desire and replied,

"How about taking advantage of me again?"

Breakfast was very late and so they hardly left the outskirts of Addis before noon after they had bought some fresh food.

On the road they saw hundreds of donkeys laden with cut grass coming into the city.

The road deteriorated. Charlie explained that they would have been more comfortable in a modern four wheel drive vehicle. Not only was the Landrover old, but also he had put on extra hard springs. Driving was hard work but Anna manfully did her share. She was delighted that although the Landrover was bucking like a mule Charlie went to sleep and only woke up when she had found a good place to camp. She kissed him, saying,

"Did I wear you out last night?" He laughed,

"You could say that. This looks a good camping spot.

"I noticed you bought some bottles of Tej. I imagine you hope to have your wicked way with me tonight. I hope you have not organised a lion to terrify me!"

Charlie blustered, "I promise I didn't know anything about the lion."

"I know you didn't but I did notice Zenobia fancied you. I expect all the best bits of supper to be put on my plate." She kissed him again.

"Come on you old rogue, let's get this camp set up and have a lovely shower before supper."

When they eventually were snuggled up in the two sleeping bags zipped together, Anna was enjoying the warmth of his body as it was quite cold, but she sensed something was wrong. She pushed him on to his back and lay on top of him.

"Out with it Charlie Ferguson, what is bothering you?"

Very hesitantly Charlie replied,

"Is there something wrong with me? Why do I ejaculate so quickly? Surely we should both have an orgasm together." Anna had the sense not to giggle and make fun of him. He might be an experienced vet, but obviously she knew more about her body than he did. He had been sensible not hiding the fact that he had never made love to a girl before. She gently stroked his cheek.

"I think it is that boys and girls are so different and we somehow want to make love facing each other. In reality that is very stimulating for boys but actually it is not that exciting for girls. I think your penis is not actually rubbing me in the right place. Obviously I love you kissing and fondling me and it was wonderful to feel you deep inside me last night. However I think male apes mount the female from behind." Charlie said,

"I guess we are like all the other animal species." Anna continued,

"You don't need to worry, Charlie. I love the way you stimulate me. It fact you do it so well. I am not faking when I have an orgasm. It is the most wonderful feeling, but it takes time to get there and I guess, but I don't know, that virile men like you, just ejaculate really quickly. I think if you were really pissed you would not be so quick. Also you would need more time the second time." She stroked him gently and added,

"I will enjoy shagging you in lots of different positions. Sometimes I will tease you and not let you in until I am on the brink and then we can both come together. I know we are in a big sleeping bag but I think it would be easier if we were on top of it. I think it is too bloody cold to get out. Come on Charlie; let's see how you get on."

With that she rolled off him and on to her tummy. She loved the feel of him on top of her and the feel of his hand between her legs. Eventually when they both calmed down, Anna said,

"I hope you are not worried now Charlie. That was a bloody good shag." Charlie kissed her gently, "That was heavenly, I love you so much Anna. Sleep well my darling." He felt a squeeze on his wrist and she was asleep.

In the morning it was drizzling but nothing could really dampen their spirits. They were young, on a marvellous adventure and very much in love.

However after the third time Charlie lost control of the Landrover on the slimy mud road he decided to put on the wheel chains. It was a mission, as they had not packed the Landrover very well and the hessian bag with the heavy chains was right at the bottom. Anna helped as best she could, but she knew she was not as strong as a big man. When they got back into the Landrover she asked Charlie what Len was like. Charlie said he was a good bloke and was helpful like Anna was. Then he smiled and said she might not be so very big and strong but she had style. Look how she had knocked out the pickpocket. Look how she drove so well in soft sand. Anna was pleased. In fact she was delighted he was so positive.

They ground on through the mud. At least the chains were giving them some traction, but they were very noisy. Anna tried to look at the map. She thought they should soon reach the Blue Nile, before a place called Dejen. They came round a corner and suddenly they were on to a smart paved road. Charlie stopped to take the chains off, as the hard road would, not only ruin their tyres, but also would make the noise even worse. As they were struggling with the chains the rain stopped and the sun came out. Charlie said,

"Well this is a turn up for the better."Anna replied,

"Let's hope so. I think we are near to a bridge crossing the Blue Nile." As the road was so good Charlie speeded up. Soon they seemed to be airborne on a high viaduct. There was an enormous green sign with large white letters which read; **'Caution Viaduct ahead has started moving and may be hazardous to traffic. All motorists are advised to drive carefully and very slowly.'**

"Bloody Hell! I am glad you are driving, Charlie. I don't mind which knob you use, but the sooner we are across this bridge the better. Down below us is the Blue Nile which according to the guide book is totally inaccessible and is full of enormous crocodiles. This makes falling in the Uasin Nyiro a doddle." Then she laughed,

"If I could choose my life again, I would still opt to sit on your lap with neither of us wearing pants. What an adventure!"

When they eventually reached the other side they both exhaled, as Charlie drove off the road into a large quarry. Anna got out and started climbing up the ladder to get on to the tent which was strapped down on the roof rack for travelling. Charlie looked up. She was taking her clothes off. Suddenly the danger they had been in was forgotten. As she lay on top of him she giggled,

"There is nothing like a little danger to make me want an argument."

When eventually she rolled off him, she said,

"I am not sure if a little danger makes you slower or if you are trying harder, but that was magic. Thank you." Charlie gently kissed her neck and then said,

"I could never imagine a safari like this." He looked up. There was a row of little boys looking down at them. They all had very serious faces. Charlie was mortified, but Anna just laughed as she got dressed.

"In future if we are going to have an audience of little boys, whose ancestors have been Christians since AD 300, we better make love in the missionary position or we will confuse them."

"All I can say Anna is, I am so embarrassed. I already know you have a way with little boys, but I think you should stick to rugby or sling shot." Then he grinned and added, "Please never stop teasing this big boy."

They drove off to find another campsite.

Later as they were eating their supper, Charlie asked,

"Did the Ethiopian engineering really worry you?"

"Not really. I think I am a lucky girl. I seem to have an inbuilt positive mental attitude. You making love to me in full view of little Ethiopian boys was much more memorable than an Ethiopian viaduct which was about to collapse and plunge us three hundred feet into a crocodile infested river. Either way why do you ask?"

"Well I have a desire to go to a place called Lalibela. It is really famous for having a large number of monolithic churches. They were cut out of single rocks by the early Christians. The road to get there is virtually impassable except on mules. However there is an airstrip relatively near which was built by the Italians in 1940. I wonder if you would mind flying there."

"Not at all. I loved our flight back from Samburu four years ago."

"Sadly I would not be flying we would have to go in an Ethiopians Airways plane." Anna laughed.

"I won't mind. I imagine you won't want to join the mile high club in full view of the other passengers. We will have to wait to join when we are back in Kenya." Then she was suddenly sad.

"Oh Charlie. I am so going to miss you when I am at Cambridge."

Charlie got up and came around the small camp table and kissed the back of her neck and said,

"I love you. We will work something out. Don't be sad."

"You're right. It is time for me to get back my positive mental attitude and do the washing up, while you make the coffee."

Charlie did not forget her sadness. He just could not see a way around Anna being at Cambridge and him at work out in Africa. He would have to scheme something.

The following day on their way to Gondar they took a detour to try to fine the Tisseat Falls. They went on various tracks; you could not call them roads. They never found the falls, as they arrived at a very dilapidated old wooden bridge. They looked at the bridge and then they both burst out laughing. She had tears in her eyes.

"What a pity we are both agreed. We won't have an argument now but I promise you, Charlie, we will have a bloody good disagreement tonight inside the tent, so you are not so embarrassed."

After they had booked their flights to Lalibela, for the following day, they enjoyed looking around Gondar with its old castle. For some reason which they could not discover, they were not allow into Fasciolides Keep. It was in the centre of the much older castle and was in good repair. Charlie thought that perhaps it was used by the army.

They took a look at two cheap hotels, but Anna turned her nose up at both of them, so they went out of town past the airstrip and found a beautiful forested area to camp in. They had bought some fresh provisions so the meal was a feast. They washed it down with a couple of pints of Tej. Anna's only comment, as she wriggled into the sleeping sack was,

"Hurry up Charlie, that Tej makes me feel really randy."

They were in high spirits when they arrived at the airstrip in the morning. Apart from six black robed priests they were the only passengers. They all waited in a corrugated iron hut for the flight which was coming from Addis Abba. When the very old DC3 came to a stop by the hut, Anna shouted in Charlie's ear,

"I don't think they dare cut the engines in case they can't get them started again. This is going to be an experience. There is no way this plane can get a mile high! Anyhow I asked those priests to come along to keep you in order."

They had to climb a ladder, behind the wing, to get into the fuselage. Anna found it very strange as they had to walk up a slope to get into their seats. She raised her eye brows at Charlie. He shouted,

"These Dakotas have a tail wheel." She shouted back,

"I thought you said it was a DC3?"

"It is just another name. I wonder what the cabin staff has got us for lunch?"

It was sometime before they were presented with a very hard bread roll and a luke-warm bottle of 'Fanta Orange'. The take off had been extremely noisy. Most girls would have been terrified. Not Anna. "I will never forget when you flew me down from Samburu. I must have had a surge of female hormone as I had a wonderful feeling low down in my tummy, when your hairy arm rubbed the inside of my thighs, when you adjusted the seat. Will I learn all about hormones at Vet College? My biology teacher at school was only in her twenties and was rather shy and so did not explain very much." Charlie chuckled,

"Well, you certainly were a very helpful and explicit teacher to those little boys in the quarry!"

Anna stuck out her tongue at him.

The landing was very bumpy and noisy. The aircraft got very hot as they were taxiing. Anna was pleased when they eventually ground to a halt and the cabin crew opened the door. She was not very pleased, as there was a high wind, and gritty dust was funnelled in. This stuck to her T shirt and she knew she looked a mess. They climbed down the ladder. They were thankful they only had small rucksacks. Charlie helped a priest with his bag. They then had a hot walk to the tin shack which masqueraded as a terminal. At the back of the shack was a dilapidated old bus out in the hot sun. Charlie said,

"I don't like the look of that!" Anna laughed. She had seen two mules resting in the shade of an old tree.

"What about hiring those mules? I pity yours. In fact in the interest of animal welfare, I think you should walk!"

"No, way. I will try some of my fluent Aramaic and do some negotiations."

The mules were hired from a cheerful Ethiope. A blanket was thrown on their backs. Anna stood beside her mule on its left hand side. Charlie went to post her up. The mule danced away from her and she fell laughing in the dust. The Ethiope was very concerned. He helped her up and indicated that she should mount from the other side. This time it stood like a rock. Charlie laughed,

"You learn something every day. Obviously they mount from the right. That's something to remember in your animal management exam in your first year at Cambridge." This made Anna a little sad, but she kept her feelings to herself. She dreaded the thought of leaving Charlie and going to Cambridge.

It was a long dusty ride up to Lalibela. Charlie shouted,

"Without a saddle this is very hard on the bollocks." Anna replied,

"So no argument tonight. You won't be up to the job! In fact without a saddle this is really quite stimulating. You might hear me give a satisfied sigh in a moment."

To take his mind off his sore bollocks, Charlie tried to learn some Aramaic. To make the mule go faster you had to shout, "Mudge, mudge." To make it slow down and stop you had shout, "Uum." Anna's mule seemed to Uum automatically as soon as she stopped shouting, "Mudge, mudge!"

They were the only guests in the little hotel which had 6 tiny rooms. The shower was outside overlooked by a large stone building which was the seminary. Anna laughed,

"I am either going to wait until dark, or have a shower in my bikini. I don't mind a few little boys seeing me naked, but I am damned if I am going to give a whole load of priests an eyeful!"

In fact the monolithic churches which had been hewn out of the rock in 300 AD were amazing and well worth the visit. They enjoyed winding their way amongst them. There was no problem going into their incense filled interiors.

The goat stew with rubbery bread was different! Luckily Charlie managed to get a bottle of very rough local wine. As it was a litre bottle they were both slightly pissed when they got into the extremely small bed. Anna said,

"I think I should be on top as your balls have been crushed. You might damage them further bouncing about on top of me, as you will be hours coming after all that wine!"

Anna was not sure but she thought she heard him growl,

"You cheeky madam. I'll bloody show you. I don't care how many sex-starved priests can hear us!"

With that Anna was rolled on to her tummy and felt a very stimulating tongue as her thighs were pushed apart by a bristly chin. She clutched her pillow and buried her face, so, neither the priests, nor Charlie heard her moaning,

"Bloody hell that was good. Take me, Charlie. Christ I want you deep inside me." Charlie did not need to hear her, as that was just what he had in mind!

They woke together with Anna cuddling Charlie's back. She had to or she would have fallen out of the tiny bed. She kissed the back of his neck and very gently fondled him.

"How are the balls this morning? I was slightly pissed last night but I seem to remember they were working rather well!"

"It is very kind of you to ask. Could we just make sure they are OK?" Anna rubbed herself against his back and kept fondling him.

"Yes everything feels in order. Now this next manoeuvre will have to be accomplished with care or I will fall out of bed. How we managed last night, I can't imagine. I remember you would not let me come on top last night but I am going to insist this morning. Mind you I did enjoy the rampant stallion."

Eventually they got up and tried the shower. It was only tepid and made Anna shiver but breakfast was good. There was a large amount of tea, scrambled egg and fresh tomatoes. To save Charlie's balls they went to the airstrip in the bus with two other large Ethiopian families. The younger children were fascinated by Anna's long blond hair.

The Ethiopian DC3 was only half an hour late which everyone seemed to think was good! They all got in, but it was quite a squeeze. Anna was certain several of the smaller children had not got seats but no one seemed bothered. There was the normal crashing as they were speeding up to reach take off speed and then mercifully they were airborne. They were given their bun and orange drink. Then Anna smelt curry. They were cooking up a curry on a Primus stove at the back of the plane. It was only when they were near to Gondar that disaster happened. There was a bump of turbulence the stove fell on its side and a curtain caught alight. Charlie jumped up, ran the ten feet to the rear of the plane and grabbed a fire extinguisher. Anna pulled three of the younger children into their seats.

Then the screaming started. Anna started pushing the children forward away from the fire. She then got them to lie down where there was less smoke. The air stewardess had run forward and told the pilot. She came back with a second extinguisher, but could not work it. The fire was gaining on Charlie. Anna ran to him with the extinguisher she had taken off the panicking stewardess and the two of them were facing the fire together.

The pilot must have lost his cool as his landing was very bouncy. Charlie fell awkwardly and felt his ankle give alarmingly. It hurt like hell but he regained his feet and continued spraying the fire. The smoke was really dense now. At last Anna felt the plane stop. Charlie managed to get the door open. Anna joined him literally throwing the passengers off the plane. It was about an eight foot drop. The air made the fire worse. He continued to fight the fire, as Anna continued pushing the children off.

Luckily unbeknown to them the pilots had got the front door open. The drop there, was twelve feet but they had managed to get several passengers out before they and the stewardesses jumped themselves. Anna found a very small child hiding under a seat. She grabbed him and Charlie bundled them both out, before he jumped. He managed to take most of the fall on his good leg. Anna dropped the child and shouted,

"Run, run." Before hoisting Charlie in a fireman's lift and carrying him, as quickly as she could, away from the plane. She had only managed about fifteen yards before the plane exploded. The blast knocked her over on to the grass. Charlie landed on her shoulder and grunted. Anna said, "Sorry that must have been worse than riding a mule. Your poor balls!"

Charlie was doubled up in the foetal position and could not speak. She started to drag him further from the plane in the thick smoke which added to their problems. However soon Charlie could crawl and they both got to safety. It was a miracle that no one was seriously hurt or burnt. In fact Charlie was one of the worst. Anna found an old broom behind a corrugated iron shed. He used it as a crutch to limp to the Landrover. Anna drove them to where they had camped before. Charlie's ankle was very sore but he didn't think he had broken it. He remembered his sister, who was a physiotherapist saying, "Use an ankle, and rest a knee." So he tried not to make a fuss, but he was very grateful that Anna did everything for him. That night in bed, Anna said,

"I suppose you want to make sure your balls are OK?" Charlie replied,

"I think that would be wise." He lay on his back and Anna came down on him. Her golden hair lay on his tummy. When he was spent he heard her laugh,

"All seems in order Mr Ferguson. Could one of those big rough old hands return the compliment or is your ankle too sore?"

"The pain will be excruciating, but anything for such a brave girl. You were a star in the plane." She kissed him gently and said with a laugh,

"Thanks for the compliment but don't hang about."

Charlie was certain she actually sighed in her sleep.

In the morning, Anna was really worried that Charlie had fractured his ankle, as he could not walk without the broom. However he insisted he was OK, so she had to let him go on without seeing a doctor. The only thing he would agree to was another night in Gondar, so they had a lazy day reading in their beautiful camp. Anna had a good look at the ankle in the evening. There was a lot of bruising but less swelling and he did not seem in as much pain. She kept him sitting in a camp chair and brought jobs to him, like peeling potatoes. She helped him to shower which he loved. It would have been impossible for him to climb the ladder to the tent on the roof so they slept on the mattress on the ground like they had done the previous night. Luckily there was no rain.

In the morning Anna did most of the packing up and obviously she did the driving. Initially the going was good, but as they lost height the road deteriorated and Anna could see he was in a lot of pain. She stopped in a good shady area and rearranged the Landrover. She had to be careful what she put in the passenger seat-well, as that got very hot, as it was only just above the exhaust. However she knew the thick plastic water containers which were full of water would not come to any harm. Charlie then could sit with his legs up on her lap leaning against the door which she locked so he would not fall out. He was then much more comfortable. She just had to put up with his smelly feet!

They found a lovely camping spot by a stream and some big trees. These provided some welcome shade. There did not seem to be anyone about, so they both had a refreshing sit in the stream. Anna had to help Charlie as his ankle was still very sore, but he kept saying it was getting better as she helped him to get out of the water and then to dry him. He kissed her and said,

"You are a much better nurse than Len would ever have been." She smiled,

"May be I have other attributes?" Charlie replied,

"You are bloody good at setting up camp." She kissed him,

"It's lucky I love you, or a remark like that might have got you a kick on your good ankle! As it is, it has meant that I will be sleeping on top of the Landrover, well out of any danger of you bouncing about on top of me!" Charlie made a hang-dog face. As it was she relented and they both slept cuddled up on the ground.

The next day the road deteriorated further as they lost height off the uplands of Ethiopia and descended to the hot dry country of the Sudan. They did not reach the border as they had hoped and made a camp in a drier area, but still in Ethiopia. They had to go back to their old camping routine which they had used in the NFD. Charlie enjoyed Anna washing him in the safari shower. He tried to climb the ladder to get on the top of the Landrover, but he just could not make it, so they slept on the ground. They did not need a tent as there was no danger of rain. It was too dry for mosquitoes, so they did not need a net.

They just slept on their mattress in their joined sleeping bags. They were both too tired for any high-jinks. They were woken by the heat of the dawning day. Now they were at a much lower altitude, it promised to be a really hot one. Anna packed up with Charlie hoping about and helping as best he could. They were soon off. Anna fought with the appalling road. They were delighted when they drew to a halt at the barrier which was the Ethiopian border at a small village called Metema.

Initially the Ethiopian Askaris were very friendly, but then an officer arrived and started to throw his weight about. He insisted that Anna drove the Landrover into the police compound and everything was got out of it. He insisted that each jerry can containing, either water, or petrol, was opened up so one of the Askaris could smell the contents. Charlie then made a big mistake. He gave the officer half a bottle of whiskey. A man in an immaculate grey suit came out of a building and walked up to Charlie. He said in excellent English,

"The border is closed. You will make your camp under that tree in this police compound until I have permission from Addis Abba for you to proceed." Much to Anna and Charlie's annoyance they were detained for two more days. Each morning they were told by the officer in uniform who was obviously less senior than the officer in a suit that he had no news from the capital.

On the third morning after they had finished breakfast, Anna said,

"I think we must try something different?"

Charlie was slightly alarmed when he saw her behind the door of the Landrover take off her bra and only do up the bottom four buttons of her shirt, when she replaced it. She then took their last full bottle of whiskey, Charlie's prized bottle of 'Glen Fiddich', and wrapped it in a brown paper bag and walked purposefully to the border post. Once she was on the veranda before the officer in uniform could say anything, she said very loudly,

"I have come to see the gentleman in charge of the border alone!"

The man in the suit shouted through the open door,

"You may allow the lady to come in Captain and then please shut the door."

Anna walked into the office and up to the desk behind which sat the man in the suit. She leant forward so her shirt fell open and she presented him with the whisky.

"My man made a mistake and gave the captain his gift of half a bottle of ordinary whiskey before I could give you this whole bottle of special whiskey." He could not drag his eyes away from her pert white breasts, highlighted by the tan line from her bikini. He managed to say,

"Thank you madam. I am pleased to accept your gift. Mistakes are easily made."

At last he lifted his eyes, "I heard from Addis Abba this morning that you may proceed into the Sudan. Your passports please." His eyes fell again, as Anna reached into her shirt pocket for the passports. He dragged them away, reached for his stamp and with a flourish stamped them. He just looked at Anna when she said,

"Thank you. Goodbye." She turned, opened the door and buttoned up her shirt as she passed the Captain. She thought, *'No harm in him thinking his boss managed to grope me. It will appeal to his boss and increase his boss's standing.'*

When she got back to the camp, she said to Charlie,

"Permission seems to have been granted by Addis. Let's get going before they change their minds."

Charlie asked,

"How did you manage that?"

"Sorry I had to give the man in a suit your bottle of 'Glen Fiddich' and show him my tits. Are you cross?"

"Bloody hell yes, about the whiskey."

"Wrong thing to say Charlie. You are definitely spending our first night in the Sudan on your own on the ground." Charlie stuttered,

"I meant I was cross that you had to expose yourself and give him the whiskey."

"Better, at least you agree with the man in a suit. He said that mistakes are easily made!" Without further mishaps they were allowed to drive through the border.

Chapter 6

The Sudan November 1970

The road could not be described as anything more that an extremely bumpy rough track winding its way through the acacia scrub. After 20 gruelling miles Anna started to worry that they had missed the Sudanese border post. However they both were reluctant to turn back. Anna just kept following the track. They were in fact in no mans land as they had left Ethiopia, but had not entered the Sudan.

Eventually they came to a concrete sign saying 'Gedaref'. They knew then that they were definitely in the Sudan, as it was marked on the map. They came to the Main Street and there was a blue sign saying 'Police Station'. Anna parked in front of the building. She went into the police station with Charlie limping behind her. A smart policeman saluted behind a high reception desk. He asked her what she wanted. When she told him that they had just driven in from Ethiopia, he asked them to follow him and led them into a clean room with a table and three chairs. He indicated that they should sit down. He then left, closing the door behind him.

Charlie whispered in her ear,

"These guys are all Moslems. You had better keep your shirt buttons done up!"

"You cheeky bugger. I don't normally expose myself to officials. I was just worried we would be camping in that compound for weeks. You have got me worried now. I wish these shorts were not quite so short."

"Well I love them. They show off your great legs."

She tossed her head, "Flattery will help you to redeem yourself. Remember to keep trying. You still might be on your own on the ground." Charlie hoped she didn't mean it.

The door opened, a tall African, wearing a galabier entered and in immaculate Oxford English apologised for delaying them. Anna apologised for bothering him and explained how they were worried that they had entered the Sudan illegally, but that they had failed to find the Sudanese border post. The man smiled,

"Sadly we do not have one. I am the Chief of Police, so I act as Immigration Officer. Can I see your passports, please?"

They handed them over. He looked through them carefully.

"We have never had travellers from Kenya before. I see you do not have visas to enter the Sudan. Where do you wish to go in my country?" Anna replied,

"I'm so sorry we did not realise we needed visas. We hoped to drive down the Nile into Egypt."

"I don't think there will be a problem if you sign a form for me here and then report to the Ministry of the Interior when you arrive in Khartoum. I will get two forms in English for you to sign." He left them again closing the door quietly. Anna whispered,

"He is very polite. Isn't it strange that the high up chaps don't have uniforms on. It is so confusing." Then with a smirk she added.

"A girl does not know when to undo the buttons of her shirt." Charlie growled,

"Or give away my good whiskey." Luckily the door opened before she could remind him that he still could be sleeping on his own.

The form they each had to sign was hilarious, as they had to promise while in the Sudan that they would never drive on any railway lines. They had learnt their lesson in Ethiopia so neither of them laughed. He stamped their passports and then very carefully wrote a long paragraph in Arabic underneath. Anna was slightly nervous as she was worried he was somehow defacing them, but there was little she could do about it. He wished them a very enjoyable stay in the Sudan and showed them out of the building.

They decided to leave the Landrover where it was and go to do some food shopping. Anna was pleased that Charlie seemed to be moving less painfully, although he still used the old broom. They managed to buy the hind leg of a sheep. At least, Charlie thought it was a sheep, as it had quite a large amount of fat which he said a goat would not have laid down. At the butchery they also bought four sheep's kidneys. Anna was delighted they also found a fruit and vegetable shop. They bought, onions, tomatoes and grapefruit. Lastly they bought two flat round unleavened bread loaves and a dozen eggs. She was going to make them a good brunch as it was now 11 o'clock and then a really good meal that night.

As they came out of the final shop they were stopped by two men wearing galabiers, in fact they only had seen men and they had all been wearing white galabiers. They looked fairly scruffy and Charlie who had learnt his lesson from the pickpocket in Ethiopia was about to tell them in no uncertain terms to go away. Anna luckily stopped him and asked the men what they wanted. The two men produced their police warrants and asked for their papers. They carefully looked at the passports and read the Arabic writing. They bowed deferentially and handed them back.

On the way back when they were nearing the Landrover they were stopped by two more men and the same procedure occurred. Anna whispered to Charlie, as she was helping him to get into the Landrover.

"The place must be full of secret police. Whatever that writing says, I am glad we have got it!" He replied, "Oh, I don't know I would enjoy you not wearing a bra and undoing the top button's of your shirt!

"You are impossible Charlie Ferguson. Oh well, you lusting over my tits is better than you moaning about the loss of your precious whiskey." Anna was actually pleased to see him smiling, as he eased himself into the Landrover. She thought, *'I'm glad his leg is getting better.'* They set off into the desert following a bit bigger track going due West which they hoped was heading for the Nile. Charlie kept an eye on the compass as he wanted to get to the Nile and not via round to aim North and just follow along, with it running out of sight on their left. They soon stopped for brunch. Anna made a good fry-up on their little gas fire and they washed it down with mugs of tea. While Charlie was washing up she went behind the Landrover and took off her bra and undid the top buttons of her shirt. He thought she had just gone for a wee. It was only half an hour into the drive when she noticed him look down at her chest. She laughed,

"I have just caught you out. I knew you were 'all talk and no trousers'. As we were driving over smooth sand, I took my bra off after lunch. It has taken you half an hour to notice. It only took the Ethiopia Police Chief one second!" Charlie blustered,

"That's not fair. Of course I noticed."

"You are a bloody liar, but you could make it up to me." She opened the button on her shorts. Soon she stopped the vehicle and let the lovely feeling wash over her. She gave a deep sigh.

"Thank you Charlie, I'm glad you haven't lost your touch. That was very satisfying. I hope your ankle keeps improving. Now we are in the hot country I think it would be much cooler if we slept on top of the Landover. I could help you up the ladder by putting my head between your thighs and giving you a lift up, taking your weight on my shoulders."

That's what they did, after cooking and eating supper, which was delicious. Charlie showed her how to use an old rectangular tin aviation fuel carrier with its top cut off as an oven over the hot coals. He also found some dried rosemary stalks and garlic cloves which they pushed into meat. They mixed some dried mint with vinegar and sugar. The roast meat was delicious and none the worse for having bread as a carbohydrate rather than potatoes.

The following day they left the wilderness behind and entered the massive cotton growing area around Wad Medani. They soon reached the Nile. They stopped in the middle of the afternoon, as they found a good tree covered spot with no one about. However they put their swimming costumes on to swim, as they were not totally sure they were alone. They doubted if there were crocodiles.

Next morning Anna found the grapefruit which they had forgotten about for breakfast. They turned out to be 'uglies' which are really large lemons with very thick skins. They were a little sharp, but quite edible.

Wad Medani was a large sprawling town. Using the Nile for guidance they navigated their way through. Initially they were pleased to see Tarmac. However in stretches it was so bad that it was worse than the sand. The Tarmac ended as they left the town. After about seventy miles they stopped to buy food before heading directly East away from the Nile as it was now populated all along its banks. They did not have to go far until they were completely alone, but of course there were no trees, as they were now in the Sahara.

Charlie's ankle was improving all the time. That night they were both naked at the back of the Landrover ready to climb. Anna said,

"I think you can easily manage on your own. I am sick of your hairy thighs rubbing my ears."

"Oh," said Charlie, "OK, I will lift you. Legs apart." Anna did what she was told expecting him to come from behind her. Instead he lifted her with his face in her groin. She had a fit of the giggles and they both would have fallen if Charlie had not been so strong. When they both got on to the mattress Charlie continued with his face in her bush. She stopped giggling and lay back gasping as he brought her to an orgasm.

They slept really well as the temperature was just right for them to lie on the top of the bedding in the nude. Just as it was getting light, Anna awoke as there was a lovely gentle warm breeze. She moved slightly, without waking Charlie, so with her legs apart and her knees bent, she got a wonderful sensation. She felt very sexy. She did not want to wake Charlie, but she wanted him so much. She just could not wait. He had rolled on to his back. Very carefully she got her leg over him so she was poised above him. She was certain he would wake, but as he was on his back he started to snore softly. She smiled, as so often in the night he would snore and she would push him on to his side to stop him. She gently dropped all her weight on to him and before he could make a noise she fell forward and started kissing him. As they stopped kissing, Anna straightened her legs and just lay on top of him, gasping. Charlie said,

"It was the best wakeup call that I have ever had."

They drove back due West to reach the main tracks which ran near to the Nile. Soon they were heading North again towards Khartoum. Charlie was driving. Anna looked down at the front of his shorts and laughed,

"You cheeky monkey. What were thinking about?"

Charlie blushed and stammered,

"My wake up call." She casually squeezed his swollen front,

"You don't need to be embarrassed I'm pleased. You can't see, but my nipples are hard thinking about it." She reached over and kissed his neck.

"We will have some high jinks in the hotel in Khartoum tonight. I can't wait." Charlie laughed,

"You might have to. Remember we have got to go to Immigration first. We may be locked up."

They were on the outskirts of the city and stopped at a garage to fill up. As usual after they had paid they were stopped by two secret policemen. As they were looking at their passports, Charlie asked them the way to immigration. They read the Arabic and immediately saluted. Then they waved down two policemen on motorbikes.

"These men will escort you to immigration."

They set off in a motorcade, one policeman in front and one behind. Anna said,

"Do you think we are going to be arrested?"

"No, I don't think so, as they saluted. I just think we have been bloody lucky finding that chap in Gedaref."

When they arrived at the big imposing building which they assumed was immigration, they were shown where to park and were ushered inside. They were given some forms to fill in at a reception desk. Their passports were then taken away with the forms and they were asked for £2 each. Within in five minutes their passports were returned, containing visas and a receipt for the money. They had said on the form that they would be staying at the 'Grand Hotel'. The policemen on the motorbikes were instructed by a secret policeman to escort them. Anna whispered,

"I like the Sudan. They are so polite and efficient a far cry from Ethiopia." Charlie laughed,

"Very boring for you. You only need expose yourself to me!"

"After a remark like that, Charlie Ferguson, I have a good mind to ask for separate rooms when we get to 'Grand Hotel'."

When they had parked in the hotel car park. The policemen saluted and roared off on their bikes. They felt very scruffy when they walked into the massive entrance hall to the 'Grand Hotel'. However they walked up boldly to the desk and checked in. Anna did not ask for a separate room! They had difficulty persuading the porters that they were quite happy to carry their own rucksacks. Their room was on the top floor. It was very large and commanded a wonderful view of the city. Charlie said,

"I feel like Chinese Gordon." Anna asked,

"Wasn't he gay?" Charlie replied,

"I'm not sure. He was certainly very strange. I just meant I felt like him, as we are in such a luxurious room." Anna had been investigating the bathroom,

"Even the loo is like a throne!"

Charlie turned on the massive ceiling fans which clanked into action. There was even one in the bathroom. It was hot but no oppressively so. With the fans it made the temperature very pleasant. Anna said, "In spite of your cheeky remarks about me exposing myself. I feel sexy. Are you going to continue to play with the fans or are you going to ravish me?" She did not realise that he had come out of the bathroom and was right behind her. He grabbed her and lifted her with ease. He pushed her on her tummy on to the bed.

"I am going to ravish you. I don't think I can wait to get your clothes off. He was lying on top of her, with his legs between hers and holding her arms out spread-eagled. Anna giggled,

"Well, I don't think you will get very far. I have got my bikini bottoms on under my shorts! You are welcome to try but don't you dare rip anything." Anna had forgotten that Charlie knew she was very ticklish. Charlie started to tickle her. She started to giggled,

"It's not fair. Please stop. I will do a strip for you. Anything. Please stop."

So it was that she did a very sexy strip for him, as he sat on the bed. She sat on his knees naked,

"I'm a lap dancer you are not allowed to touch me." She sexily took off his shirt. They ended up having a lovely relaxing bath with Anna sitting with her back to him in his lap. They washed the clothes they had been wearing and then lay back enjoying the bath. After their bath they went out into the city and went into the 'Suk'. They were measured so that they each could have a galabier made for them. They thought they would be useful garments as they had various deep pockets. They made a real effort to dress for diner in the hotel which they rightly guessed would be very formal. Anna looked very glamorous in a long black dress. Charlie had never seen her dress up before. He was most impressed and said so. Anna was delighted. He managed to get a pair of trousers pressed so in his dark blue blazer he actually looked quite dashing. In Anna's eyes he looked very manly. However they were very tired and were quite soon in bed cuddled up together under the clanking fans which did not stop them sleeping.

Anna was pleased in the morning as Charlie suggested they had another night of luxury before setting off into the Sahara. They bought both fresh food and also dried food for the journey. They knew initially they would be travelling beside the Nile. However the Nile turned a right angle going Westwards at Abu Hamud. They intended to carry on due North beside the railway line and meet the Nile at Wadi Halfa. They took a felucca so they could see the colours of the Blue Nile from Ethiopia where it met the White Nile from Uganda. They continued by boat to Obdurman on the opposite side of the Nile. Charlie regaled Anna with a description of the last cavalry charge carried out by the British Army. It seemed amazing to Anna that Sir Winston Churchill had taken part.

They walked down the Western bank of the Nile along the corniche in the fast fading twilight before collecting their galabiers. Anna surprised Charlie by wearing a second long dress for dinner. It was white and had a halter neck so it showed off her tanned back beautifully. They had a lot of laughs trying on their galabiers before going to bed. Anna purposely stood in front of the light from the bathroom, as she knew Charlie would see her naked body though the material. You could not actually see through the garment, although if they did not wear pants you could see they were naked. Anna looked fine in white lacy knickers but she thought Charlie looked gross in his old white pants which were now distinctly grey. They took them off before making love and falling asleep. Charlie was captivated, when Anna woke him before dawn to make love again.

They enjoyed the big breakfast which included individually made omelettes at their table, before loading up and heading North out of the city on the Obdurman side. It was much easier finding their way out of the city. They did not need their police out-riders. Initially they were driving in multiple deep tracts in the sand between the Nile and the railway line so they knew they could not get lost. There were no trees except right near the Nile which was probably two miles away to their left. They stopped for lunch. For the first time Charlie rigged up an awning which he had made up in Kenya when he was planning the trip to give them some shade. There was just enough room for the camp table and two camp chairs. The fresh food was good but they were both too hot to be really hungry. Anna was pleased that Charlie's ankle was so much better. He was doing half the driving which was very hard work in the deep sand ruts made by all the other traffic. Not that they actually saw any traffic. The ruts obviously remained, as it never rained in the desert. It would require a very strong wind as the sand set like concrete with the dew which formed during the night.

That night they decided to camp out in the desert. They thought they were about half way between the Nile and the railway line. Anna had imagined that the Sahara would mainly be flat sand but the terrain varied enormously. Sometimes indeed it was flat with soft sand covered by a crust which did not take the weight of the Landrover so they had to grind along through the soft sand. Other times it was hard shingle/sand mixture which would take the Landrover's weight. Then they made better speed. Then a lorry would have gone ahead of them and broken the hard crust and they were back grinding along in the soft sand. It was very frustrating. There were sand dunes and there were small hills of shingle. There was very few other vehicles which they rarely saw, but heard in the distance. There were none at night. Rarely they heard a train.

They found a hollow to give them some sort of privacy. Charlie stopped the Landrover and backed up to a flat place with the front of the vehicle pointing out of the hollow. Anna got out of her side and just took all her clothes off and threw them on her seat. She walked around the back of the Landrover. Charlie was opening the tail gate and did not see or hear her. She leant against the Landrover in a very provocative pose and said,

"Hullo sailor!" Charlie turned and laughed,

"Anna, you are truly wonderful. I was feeling very tired and slightly irritable and now I feel wonderful."

"I'm glad of that. If taking my clothes off is all that is required to cheer you up. I will do so at every possible occasion."

"You might regret that statement when we get to cold old Europe. May I wrap my arms around you. I know I am filthy?"

"So am I. Go for it." After they had kissed Anna asked if Charlie had an apron. He rummaged in the back of the Landrover and supplied a water proof one which he normally used when he examined cows in Kenya after he had taken his shirt off. After complaining about the smell of cows, Anna put it on to do the cooking, saying she did not want hot fat, from the frying pan, to spit on her tits. The meal might not have been Cordon Bleu but in Charlie's eyes the cook was spectacular.

The next morning after breakfast they drove to the Nile and after 20 minutes driving parallel to it they came to a village. They got some fresh food, lamb or goat chops, Charlie wasn't sure which. They also got tomatoes, aubergines, eggs and flat bread. Then they found some more uglies. Charlie insisted on buying them. He said he didn't want Anna to get scurvy! The desert near to the river was a mass of tracks and very heavy going. They went at an angle to the Nile and found some much harder sand. There were more hills which was probably why others had not been that way.

Charlie was driving which meant he had to keep looking in the near vicinity, so it was Anna who saw them first. "Bloody Hell, Charlie, we must be in Egypt! There are the pyramids." Indeed there were several. They looked large as they were some distance away. However they actually were much smaller that the famous pyramids at Giza. There were five varying in height between twenty and forty feet. Charlie stopped by the biggest one which had opening about ten foot up. He helped Anna to scrabble up. The opening led to a small empty chamber. Anna held his hand. They both felt like tomb robbers. When then were back out in the sunshine Anna insisted on taking his photo with him standing by the entrance. It was time for lunch so they sat on the bottom blocks of the pyramid eating flat bread and apricot jam sandwiches.

The afternoon was uneventful. As they were both tired with the hot drive they stopped earlier than usual. Anna dosed on the top of the unopened tent on the top of the Landrover in the nude to improve her tan while Charlie read a book in a chair under the awning. He was delighted he could find a reference to these pyramids in the guide book They were at a place called Shendi.

Anna went to sleep. Charlie realised how tired she must be. He was so relieved his ankle was better, so he could do more around the camp. The driving was tiring, but actually both of them found being a passenger was more wearisome, as the passenger had no warning when the bumps were coming and had nothing to really hold on to. At least the driver had the steering wheel.

Quietly he got the camp organised and started the food preparation. He had the kettle boiling when Anna woke and came down the ladder. He made her a cup of tea. She stretched languorously, put arms around him and kissed him. She sat down and said,

"I had a wonderful sleep. Thank you Charlie."

"I was worried that you might get burnt but I thought the sun had lost some of its power and I noticed you have not put on sun cream for weeks. Your tan looked stunning at the Grand Hotel."

"It is so lovely, you cannot see any tan marks on my back or breasts, only a faint mark where my bikini bottoms come. You are the only person allowed to see that."

"That mark actually is even more sexy than having an all over tan."

He told her all his reading about Shendi. "Apparently they think one pyramid was the burial place of a princess. You must be her reincarnation. I can imagine you riding in a chariot with your beautiful hair blowing behind you."

"Surely I would be dark not blond and I suspect I would have been much shorter?"

"You are right, but I still think you are bloody gorgeous."

"Do you prefer blondes? Most men are meant too."

"Yes, I do, especially real blondes like you."

"You claimed to be a virgin before me. Have you seen many real blondes?"

Charlie went very red. "I had an affair with a real blond, but I never actually made love to her." Anna laughed,

"You must have got very near to it, if you knew she was a real blond. I think she taught you a thing or two. Is that why you are such a good lover?" Charlie replied,

"Yes we had some good times."

"I don't want to know who she was, but I am grateful to her. One day I bet we meet her and I will realise you had an affair with her. Girls pick up on those sort of vibes."

No more was said, but Anna thought Charlie was particularly loving and gentle with her that night. She thought how lucky she was to have a great big strong rugby player who had jumped into a crocodile infested river to save her, but who was also gentle and kind. She smiled to herself, as she also remembered, when he had been more dominant in their love making. She had enjoyed that as well.

The following day they were travelling in a much narrower sandy strip as the Nile was much closer to the railway line. Charlie was driving. He seemed to have been grinding along in low range, four wheel drive for ages. The sand was all soft. He could not seem to get any traction.

"I am getting bloody sick of this. The sand looks much harder on the other side of the railway line."

Anna laughed, "Now Charlie remember you signed that you would never drive on a railway line in the Sudan!"

"I won't actually drive on it, only across it."

"I should go for it then."

So they bumped over the single track of the railway and turned North again with the railway track just visible on their left. Others had crossed, but because there was a much bigger area, Charlie could find areas of shingle so he could get out of four wheel drive and make better time. When it came to time for them to camp, Anna was driving. She headed out into the desert at right angles to the track. The area was totally flat. She could not find a small hill to hide their camp. She just stopped the Landrover and said,

"This will have to do. I'm hungry and really ready for a cup of tea."

"Let's have a piece of fruit cake which Kim gave us?"

"Great idea, Charlie. I will make the tea if you can find the cake." Soon they were sitting in their camp chairs watching the sun set. For several camps when there were no trees, Charlie had rigged up a pole off the roof rack so they could crouch under the rose below the canvass bag for a shower. That night, Anna had a good idea. She got the old camp bath under the shower and knelt for her shower. "If you are careful Charlie you could join me." So they had a lovely shower together. Anna thought it would be really unlucky if a lorry, full of Sudanese drove by. Anyhow what the hell.

The next day when they joined the tracks near to the railway line they kept right to the outermost edge where there were fewer tracks and the going was better. They stopped for lunch and Charlie rigged up the awning. Among other things they ate some uglies. As Charlie threw the skins into the desert he said,

"I wonder how long they will take to biodegrade."

"A bloody long time as it is so dry. You ought to pick them up."

"I shouldn't think anyone will come this way for a hundred years." That was a statement he was going to regret!

Anna drove after lunch. Charlie dosed off. She kept following the tracks, but after a bit she was sure she was driving more to the East instead of driving North. Eventually the tracks became fewer and fewer and she was sure she was driving East. She stopped which woke Charlie.

"Sorry to wake you, but I'm sure we are now heading East. The tracks I have been following have become fewer and fewer."

They both got out. Charlie looked at the setting sun in the West which was almost directly behind them. He then found the compass to double check. He said,

"Well done for stopping." She flung her arms around his neck.

"Charlie, you are so kind. Thank you for not being cross with me. What do we do now? Are we heading towards Port Sudan? You are so lovely. I have made a complete cock up and got us lost in the Sahara and you find something good to say, like, well done for stopping!" Charlie just laughed,

"Let's camp here? No one else seems to want this spot!"

So they set up camp. The sun was still hot so Charlie rigged up the awning. Anna made them a mug of tea each and they had a piece of fruit cake. She asked,

"What now? Do we just set out on a heading due West until we cross the railway line?"

"We could do that, but it is a little risky. We might meet a donga we couldn't cross or get stuck in some soft sand. I think the safest thing is for us to just follow our tracks back to main drag and then go North again, going slightly west all the time."

So that's what they planned to do. They had a good supper. They cleared everything up ready for the morning and climbed the ladder up on to the roof rack. They did not need the tent but although initially they were hot enough to just lie on the sleeping bag they knew that by the early hours of the morning there would be a chill in the air and they would crawl into the sleeping sack and cuddle up. Anna was lying naked on her back. She reached for Charlie's hand.

"I am the luckiest girl alive." Charlie drew her hand to his lips.

"Well, I am also the luckiest man alive, even if the girl I am lying next to gave me the rudest present, I have ever received!"

"Well that girl would rather enjoy it if that lucky man would like to prove that size really doesn't matter." Charlie stopped her giggling with his kisses.

Later she rather dreamily asked,

"That was lovely. If we break down out here. What do we do? Can I die in your arms, like the couple in Pompeii?" Charlie replied,

"Actually they say the best thing is always to stay with your vehicle, as a vehicle is much easier to see than a man walking. However no one knows we are here and therefore no one will be looking for us. I reckon we have enough food and water to last us for three weeks. If no other vehicle comes along in a week, I suggest we set off one evening walking due West on a compass bearing carrying as much water as we can and a little food and make a dash for the Nile. I think we would make it?" Anna replied,

"With that happy thought, let's have another shag and go to sleep?"

Charlie drove first thing in the morning. Initially it was easy to see their tracks but then they came to an area of shingle and Anna had to get out and run ahead and show him the way. She tried sitting on the bonnet of the Landrover, but she could not see the tracks well enough. Luckily there were more areas where the tracks were visible. Then she would hop back in the cab and they would make better time. They kept swapping every hour. They were getting pretty weary when Anna suddenly laughed and said,

"It's time we stopped for lunch." She stamped on the brakes. Charlie said,

"Why the haste?"

"Look over there. Some numpty threw some ugly skins on the ground. I have brought him back to pick them up." They had arrived back, where they had had their lunch on the previous day. After Charlie had rigged up the awning he, rather sheepishly, went and picked up the ugly skins. That evening they were back in the large number of tracks in the desert near to the railway line. They drove for an extra half hour so that they really had their bearings for the morning and then made a camp only a couple of hundred yards eastwards into the desert. They were determined not to get lost again.

They journeyed on northwards, never really letting the railway line out of their site, except in the evening when they drove a few hundred yards out in the desert to camp. Most days they crossed over the railway when they saw a village on the Nile to buy food. They varied their purchases as much as possible. Sometimes they bought some sheep meat. They often bought eggs, aubergines, okra and always bought tomatoes as they were so good. The flat bread went stale in just a few hours so they only bought one flat round loaf each day. Anna loved the little shops and picked up some Arabic. Once she found some potatoes and another time she bought two small lettuces.

She was sad when they reached Abu Hamud, when they knew they would lose the Nile, as it did an enormous loop round to the West. They had no way of keeping things cool so they could not stock up.

They still had the railway which went due North in a dead straight line. On their second night, Anna wondered what Charlie had up his sleeve in his old school, tuck box. It had been hidden under everything else behind the partition separating the front seats from the back of the Landrover, together with the Landrover spares and tools, which luckily they had not needed.

He teased her, as he said she was like a wife receiving a Fortnum and Maison hamper. Actually she was pleased, as there were all manner of tins and packets of food. The first night she made a risotto with the remainder of the fresh vegetables and a tin of corn beef. From then on she planned the menu when she was a passenger and Charlie was driving. Charlie thought she was very inventive, and said so, which secretly she was thrilled about. She remembered her Granny saying, 'the way to a man's heart is through his stomach.' She also thought that with Charlie sex played quite a part, but her Granny would hardly have said to her, 'the way to a man's heart is through his cock!'

Her musing must have shown through her face and Charlie noticed,

"What is amusing you?" She told him what she had been thinking about. He reached over and slipped his hand down the front of her bikini bottoms.

"No Charlie, that is not the way to my heart, even if you do get me seriously excited. I think you had better pay attention to the sand conditions or you will get us stuck in the soft going. In fact it was a few hours later when, through no fault of Charlie's they very nearly got stuck in a sea of deep soft sand. Charlie just managed to grind them through it on to some harder going.

The following evening when they were thinking about stopping for the night, disaster struck when Anna was driving. The sea of soft sand just seemed to go on forever. She had started in two wheel drive and gone into four wheel drive as soon as she felt she was in trouble and then had pulled the red knob back, when she knew she needed more torque, but the sand was just too deep. A lorry with bigger wheels would have managed it.

"I'm sorry Charlie, I've seriously mucked up. Look ahead we only have about twenty yards to get to the hard sand."

"Rubbish you got the best out of the old Landy you could, she is just too over laden. You are a star getting us this far."

"You are so lovely. Why didn't you say. You silly bitch you have got us stuck?" Charlie laughed,

"Because you didn't get us stuck. We will get ourselves out of it. Honestly it was not your fault."

She squeezed his hand. "I don't deserve a lovely bloke like you." No more was said. They started lightening the Landrover and carrying the stuff on to the hard sand. Even though it was evening it was still hot. Anna took off all her clothes and carried as much as she could. She just wished she was as strong as Charlie. She could hardly carry one jerry can of petrol and Charlie could carry one in each hand. "I wish I was as strong as you."

"Each to his own, I wish, I could be like you. You will make a marvellous vet. You are so good with your little hands. You will make a great surgeon." Whether it was exhaustion, dehydration or her time of the month, Anna burst into tears.

"Hug me Charlie. I love you so much." Then with new determination she turned and headed out into the deep sand to carry some more. When they had totally emptied the Landrover, Charlie showed her the sand ladders. There were four pieces of weldmesh under the mattress on the roof rack. They got them down after they had carried the mattress to a flat bit of hard sand.

"I suggest we make ourselves some tea and some supper, then have a body wash to save water and get some rest. In the morning we will both be stronger for the big push." Anna replied,

"That has my vote."

It still had not got cooler when Anna lay, naked on her back on the two sleeping bags zipped together. "Take me, Charlie. I'm bone tired but I still want you. Unless you are too tired." She drew her legs up as Charlie started kissing her between her thighs. Then she started panting. "I didn't deserve that. I must stink."

As Charlie entered her he said,

"You do but it is your smell and I love it."

Anna could not remember when she rolled on to her side and he cuddled her back.

It was just getting light when she woke and felt him hard between her thighs. She knew he was still asleep as his breathing was very slow and steady. She marvelled that he was still aroused. Somehow that made her want him. She knew most normal men wanted sex virtually every few minutes, but she wanted sex as often as he did. She hoped she was normal and just had met the right guy. She thanked her lucky stars she had bought plenty of pills in Nairobi. She rolled away from him, which she knew would wake him. She kissed him as she pulled him on top of her.

"You lovely old, dume. I want to give you encouragement to push us out of the sand. I don't think I will weaken you." Then she laughed as with three or four thrusts she knew he had come deep inside her. "You are amazing anyone would think you hadn't had sex for a month. I will wait for my orgasm this evening."

They had a cup of tea and some cornflakes with UHT milk as the sun came up. They jacked up the front of the Landrover onto the weld mesh with the high-lift jack. Then Anna started the engine and with the vehicle in the lowest gear waited with her foot on the clutch until she heard Charlie's shout. The Landrover shot forward. Now it was so much lighter it seemed to float over the sand and she was up on to the hard shingle. She ran back to Charlie who was lying in the sand, laughing.

"I think I have given it my all this morning."

"I think you will be able to give it your all again this evening."

They packed up the Landrover with everything in its special place and started off again. Half way through the morning a train came chugging by. She looked at Charlie. He was grinning.

"Charlie you signed that you would not drive on the railway line."

"I know but if we see anymore large areas of deep sand, I am going to have amnesia!"

In the 310 miles to Wadi Haifa they actually only drove on the railway twice. Anna was glad they never got caught. She certainly did no relish going to a Sudanese jail or even worse ringing her parents to come and get her out.

Actually they did not get to Aswan but came to a village on the Nile as it came in from the west. They bought some provisions and went about ten miles along the shore to find the ferry which would take them out of the Sudan into Egypt across Lake Nasser which had been formed by the building of the 'High Dam' by the Russians. They knew a ferry left twice weekly. When they got near they could see a boat, painted green and white. They were delighted, as they seemed to have hit the right day.

Their pleasure was short lived, as they were told that the Landrover was too large to go on this new ferry. They would have to wait for four days until the old Sudanese ferry arrived which was big enough to accommodate the Landrover. There was nothing to it but to wait, so they drove on the hard sand close to the shore of the lake a few miles away from humanity. They made a more permanent camp and in fact had a wonderful time. They did all their washing. Anna cooked some interesting meals. Charlie did some serious sewing. He made six old woollen blankets which he had brought from Kenya into a giant sack so they could put the two joined, sleeping bags in it as he knew they were in for really cold weather when they reached Europe. Initially they thought local people might come to bother them, but they were left entirely alone. They spent the whole time naked. The lake was lovely and blue, and was very clean fresh water. Swimming was wonderful both early in the morning when they woke, in the middle of the day when it was hot and in the evening before supper. Anna was delighted as although she was already very brown she lost all her tan marks. She marvelled as she did not wear any sexy clothing but Charlie seemed to want her all the time. Actually she seemed to want him just as much.

It was with some reluctance that they made their way back to the make-shift docks to get on the ferry which was very old and dirty. It was really only a glorified barge and had to be towed by a tug. Loading the Landrover was a nightmare, as Charlie had to drive it across two planks. Anna wanted to get in the cab with him, but he very firmly forbade her, saying if the Landy went in the water he would only have himself to think about and therefore would be more likely to survive.

There were numerous forms to fill in about the vehicle for the Sudanese customs. Then the customs would not let them take twelve Sudanese pounds out of the country. Charlie waved the magic writing in his passport. They would not back down, but would allow him back on the shore to purchase goods in the Sudan. Anna was not too impressed with the food. It was all tins of sardines and pears from Yugoslavia. However it was better than having the money confiscated. Charlie just wished he had hidden it.

Most of the passengers made camping spaces on the two decks of the barge. Charlie managed to get them one of the four cabins, so at least they had some privacy and were able to lock the door with a padlock. The cabin contained two bunk beds and a chair which was fixed to the floor. There was a window with bars and a shutter. It was all rather primitive, but they knew they only had to put up with it for two nights. They could reach some stuff in the back of the Landrover but it was in such a narrow space that they could not open the doors either on the driver or the passenger side. When Charlie had got out after he had driven it on, he had to clamber over the kit in the back and out the back door.

Anna was apprehensive after they set off, as several groups were cooking on stoves on the wooden deck. The fire in the DC 3 was still fresh in her mind. She was relieved that there was a pump which could be worked by hand to bring up water from the lake. They had a washing-up bowl so she could have a wash in the cabin. With the shutter closed it was stifling hot. There was no electricity so Charlie had to hold a torch. They both had a good cooling wash and then with the torch turned off they opened the shutter. With the barge being towed along there was a pleasant cooling breeze. They put on their galabiers and went out on deck. They walked to the stern and held hands in the moonlight. Even with the other passengers it was still very romantic. At about ten o'clock they decided to turn in. To make the most of the breeze through the window they both had their heads on that end of the bunk. Anna was on the top bunk and was a little apprehensive as her head was right near the open window. She knew they would be too hot but she persuaded Charlie to come up and join her. She got him to lie on his back and she went to sleep lying on top of him. They had put their sleeping bags under them to act as a mattress. They were naked under their galabiers. Anna was a little monkey and fondled him before dropping off to sleep. Poor Charlie took some time to drop off as he was so aroused. Eventually the throb of the tug's engines lulled him to sleep.

The rising sun woke them, so they went out on deck which was quite cool, to use the garderobe. They mused that the galabiers were very sensible garments for this type of climate.

The day was hot and boring. Their arrival at Abu Simbal in the evening was an experience not to be missed. When the Nile was blocked by the high Aswan dam, the water would have flooded the temple so the temple had been moved above the water level. It was amazing spectacle. The tug chugged on pulling the barge through the azure blue of the lake. How Anna and Charlie wished they were back at their idyllic campsite. They made themselves a very mediocre supper followed by a tin of pears. Anna thought she would have to start enjoying them, as them had many more tins to get through.

The moon was still beautiful although it rose a little later. Anna always loved the bright stars in Africa where there was so little ambient light. They went to bed after Charlie had made her promise not to get him excited.

"I promise, Charlie. Making love on this top bunk would be like making love in a coffin!"

It was past 2 o'clock when the change of motion of the barge woke Charlie with a start. This woke Anna. They did not need to say anything they both were up immediately and slipped into their shoes. Luckily they still had their galabiers on as they went on deck. Amazingly everyone else seemed to be asleep. The hawser had parted and they were drifting and the tug was chugging off into the night. Charlie ran to the bridge of the barge and woke the befuddled captain, who although he was a Moslem had obviously been drinking. He worked the big old blow horn which of course work everyone on board.

Anna in the meantime had managed to get some men to pull in the broken hawser. Lights were lit and torches were turned on. Charlie could see the wake of the tug which was obviously turning.

The commotion lessened, as the crew of three established some order. Charlie put his arm around Anna,

"I think we will leave it up to them now. Let's go back to bed?"

That's what they did and they were soon asleep as the rumpus died down. In the morning the captain came to Charlie and thanked him for his prompt action. Anna hardly could contains herself when Charlie said, "Think nothing of it old boy."

Chapter 7

Egypt December 1970

When they docked later in the day, Anna thought the crew were much more helpful than they had been when they loaded the Landrover. Once again there was a lot of paperwork to be completed for the customs, as of course they were entering Egypt. One crew member was sent with Charlie and Anna to guide them into Aswan. They were slightly concerned, when he told them to wait by a very shabby office. He entered and came out with a set of Egyptian number plates. He helped Charlie tie them on and then saluted. His job was obviously done. He disappeared into the gathering dusk.

Anna then drove around Aswan looking for somewhere to camp. Charlie shouted, "There's an old quarry. That will do."

She stopped and parked up in the quarry near an unfinished obelisk. She made tea while Charlie unpacked the Landrover and put up the tent on top. She had just started cooking supper when the first 'combi' load of Japanese tourists' arrived with a guide who started his spiel in English. It was then that Charlie realised where they were. They were in the famous 'Quarry of the unfinished obelisk'. The other obelisk is in London! Luckily Anna had finished making supper and Charlie had struck the camp before the next 'combi' arrive. They made a hasty exit.

In was now dark and they could not find anywhere to camp so they had to go to a hotel. There was not any choice. They were all posh tourist hotels. They picked 'The Nile View'. Their room was very luxurious. Anna was delighted.

"I know this is costing a fortune, but thank you so much, Charlie."

"You jolly well deserve it after those two nights on that grotty barge. You are a marvel. I don't know how you do it. You got the crew working for you, as if you were the Captain." She kissed him,

"You are my Captain but can I entice you to share a shower and wash my hair. I still remember you washing it so beautifully the day we met. I have a lot to thank that old croc for." Then she gave him a cheeky smile,

"I kept my word and never told Des what a good ladies' hair dresser you are!" As he was washing her hair, Charlie told her how the rugby crowd were always teasing him. He told her how one day he was flying down from Turkana to Nairobi. He said he must have eaten something bad, as near Naivasha he realised he was desperate for the loo. He did not want to land at the main Naivasha strip, as it was in the middle of town next to the road, so he picked the strip on Crescent Island. He did not see the telephone line at the near end of the strip. He caught it with his wheels. It had frightened him, as the plane seemed to stop in mid-air before the line broke. He was worried that the plane would flip but he managed to land OK. He jumped out, grabbed the panga and loo roll and went behind a bush. What he did not know was that one of the rugby crowd had been driving on Crescent Island. He had seen him hit the wire and then rush to the loo! When Charlie had gone to rugby training that evening he was greeted with,

"Who frightened himself so much hitting the telephone wires that he had to go to the loo?" He said he never could convince anyone that he had actually been desperate before he came into land! Anna said,

"Poor you, I believe you, Charlie. I know what a delicate stomach you have." Then she laughed,

"You are a real hairdresser! They always talk when they are doing your hair. How much has that shampoo cost me?"

"Actually you have no need to tell me. I can feel him hard between my thighs." They made love standing up in the shower. Charlie was given another treat as Anna found a sexy pair of shortie pyjamas at the bottom of her bag which he had not seen before.

The next morning they set off to drive the 800 miles to Cairo with their Egyptian number plates. The road was good Tarmac. Charlie said,

"This is a bit of alright. I don't think the Egyptians need worry that we will drive on their railway lines!"

They came round the corner and there was a police road block. The policemen were very friendly and seemed pleased with the number plates, but they were insistent that they could not pass without authority from the Chief of Police in Aswan. Anna persuaded one policeman to come back with them to show them the way to the main police station. She moved over to the middle seat and was surprised that she still had a nice feeling when her thigh touched Charlie's.

They were not kept long at the police station and were soon off with the policeman back to the road block with their stamped piece of headed paper. There was a lot of waving when they dropped him off and the barrier was raised. After another ten miles there was another road-block, this time manned by the Army. The soldiers saluted smartly. Charlie showed them the piece of paper. The Captain of the guard was summoned from his wooden hut. He explained that they could not pass without permission from the Colonel in Aswan. Anna moved over to make room for a good-looking Lieutenant to accompany them back to Aswan. Charlie turned around. There was more waving at the police barrier.

Once again they were not kept long at the army HQ. They set off again. There was more waving at the police barrier. They dropped off the Lieutenant and they were on their way. Charlie laughed,

"Cairo here we come." A further few miles and he was regretting that statement. They were stopped by a large barbed-wire barrier manned by the Ministry of the Interior. A man in a suit was summoned who explained that there was no way non-Egyptians were allowed to drive between Aswan and Cairo. Charlie was exasperated, but the man was adamant. One of his men was sent back with them to the office in Aswan. There was more waving from the army and the police. The Interior Ministry building was rather sinister. They were told to sit in the shade outside. After over an hour they were ushered in. Anna squeezed Charlie's hand.

"Keep cool my love!"

The man in charge was seated in a large cool office behind a massive desk. He got up and immediately apologised for keeping them waiting. He waved them to a couple of chairs, as Charlie asked how they could get to Cairo. He suggested they would have to go by train, which he said were very fast and efficient. Charlie explained about the Landrover. He responded by saying he would give them a letter to the railway superintendent who would put the Landrover on a 'flat-car'. A clerk was instructed to get this prepared while Charlie and Anna were given a cup of tea. He also drew them a map to help them get to the train marshalling yard.

They found the marshalling yard. The station master was very pro-British having worked in Crewe. Once again Charlie had to drive on planks to get the Landrover on to the flat car. It was secured with chains and chocks. The station master did not know when he could get them hitched up to a goods train, but he said they were welcome to camp with the Landrover. He said it would be safer, as there were thieves about. Then he left them saying he would return, when he had more information.

Once he had gone, Anna said,

"Well this is going to be an experience. It is going to be like the trains in the cowboy films. You know with all this messing about it is half way through the afternoon. Shall I make us a late lunch I am starving?"

"Sounds good to me. I will rig up some shade. I will have to move the awning from the side to the back of the Landy."

They were halfway through lunch when there was a loud bang. A stone had hit the side of the metal Landrover. Charlie said,

"It came from the direction of that wall. I will wait until I see the culprit and throw it back at him."

"I don't think that would be a very good idea. It is a battle you won't win and I am worried you will be hit on the head. Let me try my way."

She jumped off the flat car and ran to the wall with some wrapped boiled sweets which they were going to have with their coffee. She heard voices behind the wall. There were obviously a group of young boys behind the wall which she noticed had glass in the cement on top. She threw over a sweet. She heard some whispering. She threw over another one, there was more whispering. She beckoned Charlie over so she could climb up on to his shoulders. She threw over two more sweets and climbed up him, as he had his back to the wall which was about eight foot high. She came face to face with a cheeky young boy. They both smiled. She pointed at the glass to indicate that she could not pass the sweets. Then she threw the rest of the bag over. The face disappeared but five boys moved from close under the wall to the stand further away. They picked up the bag, waved and ran off. Anna jumped down off Charlie's shoulders.

"Hopefully they won't give us anymore trouble."

They spent the rest of the afternoon reading whilst sitting under the awning on the flat car. Anna cooked some supper and they were soon in the tent on top of the Landrover which now that it was dark was not that hot. They were rudely awaken in the morning by a shout from the station master. When Charlie put his head out of the tent, the man said he had bad news. They would have to unload the Landrover as the army needed all the flat cars to move tanks. Charlie cussed. However there was nothing they could do, but pack up and drive back to the Ministry of the Interior after they had unloaded the Landrover off the flat car. They were sent away and told to come back the next day, as there was no one was available to speak them that day.

Charlie was cross, but calmed down when Anna suggested they hired a small rowing boat and he rowed them out to the Temple of Philae which had been partially submerged by the Nile. She made them a picnic. Then she sat in the back of the boat in her bikini, while Charlie rowed and told her all about the Temple which for Egypt was not that old, dating 300 BC. In fact it was a good fun afternoon. They had to check back into the posh hotel. Anna enjoyed putting on a dress so they could eat in the hotel.

The following morning they were shown into the same man's office in the Ministry. He greeted them affably. He had obviously heard that they had been kicked off the flat car. He said he had a suggestion. They could hire an Egyptian driver. Charlie said he would be happy with that. However he was not happy when he was told that they would have to travel by train. The man said he would vouch for the driver. Charlie had to agree, as it seemed to be the only way forward. They were given more tea while a suitable driver was recruited. They got their small rucksacks out of the Landrover and showed the driver the vehicle and the spare tyres etc. He gave them his driving licence and agreed to meet them at noon in two days time at the Cairo Hilton. Charlie gave him money for fuel and a sum of money was agreed which he would receive when the mission was completed. With considerable reluctance they watched him drive off. They then walked to the train station to get their train tickets. They decided to break their journey with a day at Luxor to view all the antiquities.

They had a sleeper on the train for two nights which was great fun. Anna told Charlie making love on a moving train was very erotic. He felt the same, so they at least, forgot their worries for a time. They definitely returned, when they arrived in Cairo. They were late at the Nile Hilton. The driver was not in the lobby. They both began to panic as Charlie approached the reception desk. Then they relaxed as the receptionist told them that the driver was around the back of the hotel. Apparently he had started shouting, as the receptionist had told him that Charlie was not on the hotel list. He was upsetting the other guests, so security had escorted him around the back of the hotel.

The driver was delighted to see them. He insisted on showing Charlie the Landrover, and that all the contents were inside. Charlie asked what had happened to the wing mirrors. The driver said he had taken them off and showed Charlie where he had put them. He said he was concerned that they would get stolen! He had driven 800 miles without mirrors. Charlie thought it was a total miracle that he had arrived at all! Charlie gave him back his driving licence and the money he was owed. He seemed pleased and disappeared into the crowd. Anna and Charlie then drove off to try and find a couple who were friends of Charlie's in Kenya, but had moved to work in the Veterinary Laboratories in Cairo.

Eventually they found their house in the suburbs. They were a young couple called David and Janet. They were very welcoming. Janet was particularly pleased to meet Anna, as she had expected Len. Charlie had not bothered to tell her in his letter! In fact they were delighted to see pals from Kenya, as they had found making friends in the expat community in Cairo quite difficult.

Anna was pleased as they seemed very relaxed. She was taken at face value as a girl friend. There were no problems sharing a room with Charlie, as they only had one spare room. It caused a lot of laughter in the morning when Janet knocked and bought them in cups of tea and they were in the same bed. Janet said,

"Did you spend the whole night together in just a single bed? David would drive me mad if we weren't in a big bed." Anna laughed,

"Whether we are in a big bed or lying in hundreds of square miles of desert, Charlie always seems to be on top of me. I have a lot to put up with Janet. He is just so big, except where it counts!" Charlie gave her whack with a pillow. Janet said,

"I won't comment on that and leave you to sort out your differences. David and I are off to work. There is plenty of food in the fridge so just help yourselves for breakfast and lunch. We will be home about six. I have booked us all a special meal out in the desert for eight. There is a floor-show. Have fun."

They did have fun and then had a leisurely breakfast. They made themselves a picnic with some of Janet's food and some of theirs. They spent the day out at the pyramids at Giza. Charlie told Anna all about The Emperor Napoleon's appalling behaviour of using the Sphinx as a target for his artillery practice.

The floor-show was quite amusing as it was two Whirling Dervishes. Anna was convinced they had taken drugs and thought at any moment they would be sick!

In the morning Charlie and Anna got up before Janet and David as they had to pack up and drive to Alexandria to catch the evening boat to take them to Beirut after breakfast. Anna felt sorry for Janet as she was tearful when they said goodbye. It was obvious that she at least regretted the move to Cairo where they made more money but we're not as happy as at Kabete in Kenya.

The journey to Alexandria was uneventful. The Tarmac was excellent and there were no road blocks. They drove along the Corniche before driving into the docks at the port. Anna knew her role which was to stay in the Landrover, move it if told to and to guard it. Charlie set off to sort out all the documentation with the words,

"Don't speak to any strange men!"

"I should me so lucky." Was her reply as she settled into her book.

Two hours passed before Charlie returned to collect the Egyptian number plates. He said the port office was a complete shambles, but hopefully someone would come to tell her, where to drive to soon. Another hour went by, before two scruffy stevedores arrived, saying they would drive the Landrover to the loading place, but Anna could stay with the vehicle. Anna smiled very politely and said she would drive and they could have a lift if they wanted to show her the way. Obviously this was not what they expected, but Anna's look which would have made the 'Light Blues Rugby Squad' stand to attention made them acquiesce. She stayed in the driving seat when they reached the dock where a ship was being loaded. Strong strops were placed under the front and rear of the chassis. Obviously word had got round that she was a women not to be tangled with. She was left sitting in the driver's seat.

Suddenly there was a shout and the Landrover was airborne. She was a little scared, but there was little she could do. As her Grandfather would say, 'She had made her bed and now she had to lie on it'. The Landrover was gently swung over on to the deck of the boat and the wheels were chained down to metal eyes in the metal deck. She was then left alone. She got out and locked up after she had collected their two over-night rucksacks. She walked up to a very important looking man in a blue uniform with plenty of gold braid, and asked him, if he was the Captain. She knew he wasn't but she thought a bit of flattery would work wonders. He smiled and said he was the deputy purser and could he help her. She replied saying, "That would be very helpful if he wasn't too busy. Perhaps he could show her to her cabin which had been booked in the name of Ferguson?"

He summoned a steward dressed in immaculate white who consulted his clip-board. He said Anna should follow him. He insisted on carrying the bags and showed her to a cabin which she was pleased to see was a hundred percent better than the boat on Lake Nasser. She was not sure how big a tip to give, but what she gave him elicited a small nod of the head so she guessed it was about right. He left and shut the door giving her the key. She unpacked her things and bagged the bottom bunk. She smiled as she guessed Charlie would be on top of her whichever bunk she was in!

She locked the door and went up on deck. All seemed well with the Landrover. She walked round, but there was no sign of Charlie. She wondered about immigration. Charlie had her passport so she hoped he would fix it. She went back to the cabin, as she thought Charlie was bound to come there once he had done the paper work. The cabin was quite cool, as there were jets of air coming in from the ceiling. She felt sticky and dirty so she decided to have a wash and was delighted to find there was a tiny shower. She was just coming out of the shower when there was someone trying the door. Then there was a real thump on the door. She just knew it was Charlie in one of his impatient moods. She threw open the door. Charlie fell in saying,

"Oh it's you."

"Who did you expect, Queen Hapsetsut?"

"Cleopatra bathing in asses' milk at least."

"I'll give you Cleopatra!"

Still wet and naked, she jumped at him, putting her arms around his neck and her legs around his waist. His clothes were soaking. He laughed,

"However did you get on board? I have been looking for you in the docks for hours."

"I came in the Landrover. I was told to guard it." Charlie's eyebrows shot up.

"You mean you came when they craned it aboard? That was hell of a dangerous thing to do. They might have dropped it!" She bit his ear lope.

"Which would have worried you most, them dropping the Landy or me?"

"Well if it had been the Landy it would have been a real pain we would have to have flown home!" She was just about to bite his ear lope really hard, when a voice said,

"We thought we had better introduce ourselves we are in the next door cabin." Although the man had come through the door, he could really only see Anna's face, her naked body was shielded by Charlie. Anna with great presence of mind said,

"I'm Anna and this guy with his back to you is Charlie. He found me naked in the shower and decided to take advantage of me. Can we meet in the lounge in ten minutes for a drink?"

The man spluttered,

"Of course, of course. I'm Peter and my wife is Glynis. He reached out his hand. Anna shook it over Charlie's shoulder. Peter then backed out of the cabin. After the door closed, Anna had a fit of the giggles as Charlie put her down.

"Lucky you are strong chap, Charlie. If you had dropped me, Peter would have got a real eyeful. Get those wet clothes off? I need a drink, and no we have not got time for a shag!"

Glynis was effusively apologetic when they met in the bar. To try and put her at her ease, Anna told her about having to take her bra off and unbutton her shirt to get them out of Ethiopia. Glynis was obviously appalled. Peter did not help by saying,

"I am going to change jobs and become an immigration man."

Glynis could not hide her fury, but Anna just laughed saying,

"If you had come to our Cabin two minutes earlier. I would have opened the door thinking it was Charlie and given you a full frontal. You could then have stamped my passport." Peter did not dare to open his mouth, as he knew anything he said would infuriate Glynis. In fact they were good company and, Charlie and Anna, met them for breakfast.

Things did not go well after breakfast. They packed up their small rucksacks and put them in the Landrover and locked it. Then they stood at the rail and watched the ship dock. There was a lot of shouting as the hawsers were made fast. Then the crew started to put the slings under the Landrover. Charlie was cross as he was not allowed near. He was nervous and wanted to make sure it was properly secured. Anna tried to reassure him,

"It will be fine. They got it on board OK and it had my great weight inside." She leant forward and whispered in his ear,

"Sometimes you enjoy my weight on you!" Charlie squeezed her hand.

The crane on the dock lifted the Landrover off the boat and swung it precariously over the side. There was a shout from a stevedores as the vehicle started to pendulum. Anna did not complain but Charlie was squeezing her hand like a vice. The Landrover was now swinging about three foot above the ground. Everyone was shouting, but no one dared to grab hold of it to steady it. Anna was relieved that Charlie was with her on the boat and could not rush forward to stop it swinging.

The crane driver must have released something, as the Landrover was suddenly dropped like a stone and bounced two feet in the air. Anna's hand was crushed, as if it had been under the vehicle. She kept her cool and said,

"I won't run away. You can let go of my hand?"

Charlie saw her massaging it with her other hand,

"My darling, I am sorry. I was thinking about the Landrover." Anna managed to laugh,

"You have never called me darling before and then you spoil it by saying you were thinking about the Landrover! What are you like? Perhaps you will remember me tonight when you want to bounce up and down on me like a rubber ball!"

There was a discreet cough behind them. It was Peter who must have heard their conversation.

"Don't worry Charlie, these old girls are pretty tough." Anna chipped in,

"I assume you are referring to the Landrover not to me, but I am equally as resilient!"

All Peter could manage to stutter was, "I'm sure my dear."

They could see Glynis approaching. In a low voice Anna said,

"I think it would be as well if you didn't let Glynis hear you say that you thought I would be a good lay!" Peter just went very red.

Charlie's worries were not over yet. The strops had been taken off the Landrover and there was a lot of pointing up at the boat. Then it was obvious they were all pointing at Anna. She whispered to Peter,

"I'm a bit nervous, it would appear that you aren't the only man to think I might be a good lay."

Peter looked and just mumbled. Then the deputy purser came over to Anna.

"Madam, disembarkation is not yet allowed yet, however if you would follow me with the keys of the vehicle, together with the Carnie Du Passage."

She looked at Charlie who nodded and handed her the keys, and papers, saying will you be OK?" She laughed,

"I'm sure I will unless they heard what Peter said!"

Anna was escorted down the gang-plank. Glynis was appalled,

"Will she be OK. A young girl totally on her own?" Charlie said,

"I have every faith in her. She is jolly tuff. When I first met her she was rescuing a zebra foal from a crocodile in a river." Glynis turned to Peter,

"Was that what you were referring to?"

"That's about it dear," replied a relieved Peter.

They watched, as Anna unlocked the Landrover. She got in the driver's seat and two men got in with her. She drove out of view into a big shed.

Inside the shed she was told to take everything out of the vehicle to be checked by the customs. Anna was pleased, as it also meant she could check to see if anything was damaged. They had not been carrying any glass bottles and eventually Anna had got everything out into an orderly pile and was satisfied that everything was OK. She looked under the vehicle and under the bonnet. She did not really know what she was looking at, but thought it looked normal.

A very smart customs man arrived. He stamped the Carnie and gave a cursory look at the pile of baggage and said,

"Are these all personal effects?"

"Yes." Anna knew to say as little as possible.

"Good, welcome to Lebanon Madam. You may leave the dock with this pass."

He gave her a very official looking paper and left. She then loaded the Landrover. All this took a considerable time. She wondered what Charlie was doing, but got on with the job, expecting him to arrive at anytime. He did not, so when she had finished she drove the Landrover out of the building along to the gang-plank. Charlie was looking away from her, helping Glynis. She called out,

"Your driver awaits further orders!" Charlie swung around.

"Bloody hell we have been worried about you. We gather getting the Landrover through customs needs a considerable bribe." With a smirk she replied,

"It did, you owe me." Glynis butted in.

"You poor girl you must have been terrified. Charlie, you must look after her. This is The Middle East, young girls are not safe on their own. I do hope you find your friends. Good luck. They all embraced. Anna and Charlie drove out of the port into the chaos of Beirut.

Chapter 8

Lebanon January 1971

It was a nightmare journey, as it was now dark. Anna was driving and Charlie was navigating but he did not really know where he was going. Eventually in exasperation, Anna stopped and parked in front of a bar.

"Let's ask? This is hopeless."

Charlie went into the bar and Anna stood outside, beside the Landrover, looking at the street names which luckily were in English as well as Arabic. She laughed as she realised they had parked directly in front of the apartment block that they were looking for. She locked the Landrover and went into the bar. She was the only girl. Heads turned. Charlie had been given a large glass of beer. Anna went up to one of the men standing next to Charlie,

"Since you appear to be shouting, mine's a beer as well please?"

The guy looked around in horror.

"Who are you? This is a men only bar."

"Well it isn't now is it. Charlie will vouch for me. I have just come with him from Kenya. I'm Anna, his driver, cook, camp organiser and a few other things beside."

"For God-sake shield her, guys. She will get us all thrown out." Charlie came to the rescue.

"Sorry I was about to explain. Len got hepatitis and flew back to the UK. Anna came instead."

The first guy held out his hand.

"I am sorry, I'm Greg. We are all rugby friends of Charlie's. This is Daren, Reg, Johnny, Dave, Chris, Steve and Rich."

Anna nearly did her rugby training regime, but instead shook each offered hand and repeated the name. It was not lost on any of them that she always called each by his name and never made a mistake. She drank with them pint for pint. They soon stopped looking at her, as if she had arrived from Mars and just accepted her. They also noticed she paid a keen interest in all the rugby conversation and occasionally asked a question or queried something. She realised, as she was a girl that for all their bravado most of them were quite shy. Plates of food appeared which Anna was grateful for. She knew she was getting pissed but was determined not to let Charlie or indeed herself down. Eventually the party broke up. All Charlie and Anna had to do was pick up their overnight bags from the Landrover and stagger across the road with Greg and Daren.

Although she was pretty drunk and therefore she realised her judgement might be suspect, She liked them both. They obviously were not gay and Greg particularly could hardly take his eyes off her. She made a mental note in her drunken haze to be very careful and not get into an 'Ian type situation'. There wasn't a spare room in the flat so Anna and Charlie had to go back to the Landrover to get their mattress and bedding. It was quite bulky and they were giggling like school kids getting it up the stairs. Greg and Daren had already gone to bed.They both had mugs of tea and pints of water before got themselves sorted out and they settled down. They could hear snoring from one room which caused more giggling from Anna. She said,

"Sorry Charlie, no bouncing on me tonight. I will be sick, but my back would love a cuddle."

So they slept.

They were woken by a groaning Daren walking naked through the living room, where they were sleeping, to get to the bathroom. He came back through, still naked, totally obvious of Anna, who as soon as he had gone scuttled to the loo and came out in shorts and a top. She went into the kitchen and made mugs of tea. She sipped one herself and brought one to Charlie. He sat up holding his head. She said,

"Man up Charlie, slap on a pair. I have a mission for you."

Through his pain he managed a smile,

"You were marvellous the whole of yesterday. You never got cross and I deserved a severe reprimand. Do you forgive me?" She kissed him,

"That says I do. At least I have cleaned my teeth. That kiss left a lot to be desired! Your mission is to sip some tea and then take these mugs through to Darren and Greg. They have got to get to work. I will get some breakfast ready for all of us. We can sort out our bedding when they have gone."

Greg and Darren soon came through. They were obviously impressed with breakfast even in their weakened state. When they returned after work they were even more impressed. There were cold beers in the fridge and Anna was cooking supper.

"Where's Charlie? " Darren asked.

"He has gone out to get some wine for supper. We forgot when we did our shopping. I hope 'spag bol' is OK for supper?"

"That's great. I hope he gets red. The local red is quite good, but we don't go for the white, as it is too tart. Let's have a beer for now?"

The lads had two beers before Charlie returned. Then they felt a little better. Anna just said she would wait for the wine. Greg said,

"You were amazing last night, Anna. I watched you. You matched us pint for pint. Wherever do you put it?" She laughed and was pleased he had been watching her drinking, rather than lusting after her, as she had thought.

"I was under a lot of pressure not to let Charlie down with his friends."

"Well you are our friend as well now. Thank you for tiding up. I'm sure Charlie helped a little but I definitely see a 'woman's touch', here in the flat."

"Thank you Greg, I am very conscious I am not Len." Greg went a little red.

"Daren and I are a little bit embarrassed, as we thought Len was coming, but knew he and Charlie were only here in Beirut for three nights. We have fixed an all boys night at the Casino tomorrow night. I have tried, but the Moslem management will not allow you as a girl to enter. I'm really sorry."

"Honestly, pleased don't worry about it. I have had to be very careful in the Sudan and Egypt. I know the form, but do tell me what happens at the Casino?"

"Well there is a floor show including horses pulling a chariot on stage. The girls wear wonderful hats!" Anna answered,

"My guess is that is all they wear?"

"Well yes, that's what I understand."

"At least you have warned me. I will have to be wearing something pretty exciting for Charlie when he gets home after that. I suppose I'm like a 'live in' girl friend. Charlie has me day in day out, 'warts and all' so to speak."

" I shouldn't say it, but I think you are bloody gorgeous," replied Greg. Darren raised his beer,

"Here, here'"

Charlie returned with the wine and no more was said.

In the morning Anna said at breakfast before the lads went to work,

"I'm going out shopping on my own after breakfast, Charlie. Greg and Darren have told me what's happening tonight. I will see what racy underwear Beirut has to offer. I want to look my best when you come staggering in the early hours. I don't want you lusting after some Lebanese lovely for the rest of the trip. Is the Casino far away?" Darren answered,

"Only a mile or so up the coast. We will get a service taxi outside of the door. The others are making their own way there."

When they had cleared up, after the others had gone to work, Anna left to go shopping saying she might not be back until after they had left, but Charlie was not to worry as she had a key. She gave him a big kiss saying, "Have fun."

Anna had a plan which she knew was unlikely to succeed but she would give it her best shot. If she failed she could always buy something. In reality she knew Charlie so well now. She knew the less she wore the happier he was! She also knew that wandering around as a blond in a Middle Eastern city was not very sensible, but it was broad daylight and Beirut was said to be pretty safe.

She got a service taxi to the Casino. She was familiar with service taxis from Cairo. You wait on the side of the road. The taxi which might have people in it would stop. You got in and said where you wanted to go. Others might get on or off, but you paid only your share of the fare.

The Casino was obviously closed, but there was a big gate to the side which she guessed was a service gate. She walked boldly through, as if she owned the place, and asked a man directions to the horses saying she was a vet. He pointed around the back. Then her boldness paid off. A grey Arab horse came cantering around the corner dragging a screaming girl. Without a thought for her own safety she grabbed a trailing rope from its head collar and pulled its head sharply round. It was unbalanced and nearly fell on her but at least it stopped. Men appeared from everywhere and rescued the girl who had stopped screaming, but was obviously very shaken. Anna gentled the horse which stood for her quivering. Anna was relieved the girl could stand, but she was only weight baring on one leg. She was very badly scratched and there was some bleeding, but Anna guessed there was nothing life-threatening. Anna thought she was not likely to be Lebanese as she was blond.

An older woman who was obviously in charge arrived. Anna could see she was both concerned and angry. There was a lot of Arabic and Anna recognised some French. She was hopeless at languages and so could not understand a word. No one paid any attention to her. She kept talking to the horse which had begun to trust her and relaxed. Eventually after the injured girl had hobbled away, the older woman looked at Anna and said something in French. Anna replied in English saying she was sorry she did not speak French. The woman looked perplexed, but asked in English if she was the new girl called Claudia. Anna said she wasn't, but that she was an English vet who had just grabbed this runaway horse.

"Well you certainly seem to have a way with horses. From what I understand you have not only saved Elisabeth serious injury but also have prevented any injury to Herecle, my best horse. Have you enough control to lead him back to his stable?"

"Yes, I think he will be fine."

So Anna led him following the woman round into a very smart American Barn. The big doors were closed and Anna realised the whole barn was air conditioned. Apart from the normal horse equipment there were four very large stables. Anna led Herecle into the empty one. He immediately started on his hay net. She helped the lady remove the tack. Then Anna felt down all the horse's four legs like she had seen Charlie do in Kenya. She felt a fraud, but she thought if there was a problem she could always say she was confused by the language. At least she had got her place at vet college! She turned confidently to the lady and said,

"He seems fine. I can't feel a wound on him."

"Thank goodness I need him tonight. Can you come with me to the groom's quarters and we will find out how Elisabeth is and make plans for tonight.

There were four grooms including Elisabeth who was obviously feeling very beaten up. There was a lot of French which Anna did not understand. The girls all shook her hand and Elisabeth very gingerly hugged her. She was given a strong cup of black coffee and a glass of water. Eventually the older woman who Anna gathered was called Lillianna, turned to her and said,

"Are you familiar with driving horses?"

"I think so, I have driven horses often enough, but never a chariot." This was far from truthful. She had driven a pony and trap on holiday in Ireland, when she was in her early teens. Elisabeth butted in,

"My guess is you might have done, but not in the nude on a stage!"

Anna tried a Gallic shrug, " You guessed right, but I will have a go. I came to get a bit of money doing some horses teeth, but I imagine going on stage pays better?"

Lillianna laughed. "If you can get us out of a muddle tonight, I will make it worth your while. You seem to have a good figure. Are you a real blond?" Before Anna could answer, Elisabeth said,

"You can easily shave. I have to, as I am fair but not a true blond." It was Anna's time to laugh,

"I'm a true blond, OK."

Anna's plan was to have somehow got back-stage looking after the horses. In some ways this was beyond her wildest dreams. Would Charlie be cross? She had not blamed him for wanting to go out with his chums, she just wanted him to know she was not a 'sit at home' type of girl. Now she was in really deep water. She knew her mother would be furious.

It appeared that Lillianna had promised the management that, as tonight was a total sell out she would have two blond girls and two grey horses. For a few other nights she could use the two bay horses and the two brunettes until Elisabeth had recovered or the new girl Claudia had arrived. Being an Arab country, blondes were more in demand. The other blond was called Margeit and took Anna under her wing. Margeit knew it was important that Anna really did know the ropes, so to speak, in more ways than one.

They did a lot of work with Herecle and Adonis, the other grey. They were both well trained and seemed to enjoy the treadmill which was on the stage. This was required so they could give the impression of the horses cantering actually on the stage. The tricky part was for the horses to match the speed of the tread-mill which was controlled by Lillianna just off stage.

After lunch they were given time to rest. Margeit told Anna to take off all her underwear and wear loose clothing. It was important that her skin showed as few blemishes as possible. Margeit teased Anna as she now had an 'all over' tan having spent so long in the nude in the desert. Margeit said she had to get rid of her tan marks with a chemical called potassium permanganate.

Then they had to get themselves ready. There were local grooms to get the horses ready under Lillianna's close supervision. Anna thought getting ready would be simple. She thought she just had to take her clothes off! She hoped she would get a chance to see where the boys were. She was wrong. Margeit helped her, but there was masses of makeup and of course the very glamorous hat had to placed on her head on top of her long hair. In fact it was a sort of mock helmet with lots of white ostrich feathers. She suddenly got stage fright. To steady herself she tried to remind herself of coaching the potential 'blues' squad.

She had never worried about being naked, mainly because her four elder brothers had not been really bothered about clothes even though her mother had often scolded them. They lived in a big house but only her parents had their own bathroom. Her brothers often seemed to blunder in on her when she was in the bath. She had rather got used to it. However being on stage was something very different. Again she worried about Charlie being cross. It was too late to worry about that now.

Their act was the finale, but they were not allow to leave their dressing room until they were called. They had to wear dressing gowns until the last minute. The horses stood on the treadmill stamping their feet, as she and Margeit got in the chariot and were handed the reins. Initially the horses were held by the grooms as Lillianna's slowly increased the speed of the treadmill, first to a walk then to a trot and then to the canter. The grooms let go and moved off stage. Margeit and Anna now took control with the reins. The curtain went up. The audience gasped and then cheered. Margeit and Anna both had to smile. All Anna wanted was for it to be over, but she knew the audience had to be given their money's worth.

Charlie and the rugby boys had a good table near the front. Greg shouted,

"Wow they are stunning girls. Charlie, the one on the left looks just like Anna!"

Charlie looked rather carefully at the one on the left. The girl was heavily made up but she had a body as beautiful as Anna's. He thought what a lucky man he was to have such a gorgeous girl friend. He felt guilty that he had left her behind. He had been slightly concerned that she had not been back when they left, but he knew how independent she was and she had said that she was not going to rush back. The curtained closed and they all had more drinks.

Back stage Lillianna was pleased. She thanked Margeit and Anna. She came into their dressing room as they were getting back into normal clothes. She said she was delighted and she gave them both extra money. Margeit lived with the other girls on site, but Lillianna organised a reliable driver who worked for the casino to take Anna home. Elisabeth was still up and kissed Anna goodbye and gave her a Polaroid photo of her on the Chariot. She was actually laughing as the horses had begun to canter before the curtain went up. So Anna got home before the boys returned. She had a good shower. She had not bought any underwear, but she had a pair of quite risqué shortie pyjamas which Charlie had not seen which she had kept for a special occasion. She smiled to herself. How she loved him. He was so lovely and down to earth. Just get naked and then have a damn good shag!

She put her galabier over her pyjamas. She knew it was only see through if the light was behind her. She was just laughing to herself that Darren and Greg had seen a lot more only two hours ago, when she heard them come in. She had just made herself a mug of coffee and was in the kitchen. She knew it would not take long for her and Charlie to roll their bed out in the sitting room when the others had gone to bed. She called through,

"Who wants a mug of coffee? The kettle is hot I have just made myself one."

They all had obviously had some drinks but they were not nearly as drunk as on the first night. Charlie was all contrite,

"Anna, I did not expect you to be up. You could easily have gone to bed in the living room and we could have stepped quietly by you." Anna just laughed. Greg said,

"It was quite an amazing floor show. The girls were stunning. In fact the most beautiful one looked just like you. They were in a chariot, the horses were galloping and the girl who looked like you was laughing. She should have been terrified." Anna laughed again. Greg did a double take. His jaw dropped open.

"It was you!" Anna blurted out,

"Actually they were only cantering"

She wrapped her arms round Charlie who still did not really believe what he was hearing.

"I hope you won't be cross Charlie?"

"Of course I'm not cross. I am flabbergasted. However did you manage it?"

Anna told them the story and passed him the photograph.

"That's for your eyes only. Don't you dare show it to anyone else."

"Go on let's see Charlie." Chorused Greg and Daren. Anna chipped in,

"No you will just have to remember the real thing. Anyhow Polaroid pictures fade very quickly. Come on drink your coffees it's time we all got some sleep."

Charlie and Anna did not actually go to sleep right away as not only did they have to get their bedding ready but also Charlie had to see the sexy pyjamas. Then they very quietly made love which was just as satisfying, as they felt like naughty children. Charlie had to be really gentle as he had to be quiet and slow.

They all slept in, in the morning, as it was the weekend, and Greg and Darren did not have to go to work. When they got up, Anna teased them, as because half the populous were Moslem and half were Christian they always got a three day weekend. They gave Anna and Charlie a big send off. There was no doubt they both really rated Anna.

Charlie and Anna were not actually leaving the Lebanon, but we're going to see the Roman ruins at Baalbek and the famous Cedars, before going up in the mountains to have two days skiing. Greg had a Lebanese friend who was renting them a self contained flat at the back of his house in Fargo. In fact they had a job getting up into the mountains, as there had been a very heavy fall of snow. Charlie was glad of the wheel chains.

Anna was delighted with the flat as she did not enjoy camping on someone's floor, however hospitable they were. She realised now how she loved the desert and the bush. She was talking to Charlie about it and by mistake said,

"I just love being myself and walking about with no clothes on." Charlie observed,

"So I found out yesterday!"

Anna jumped into his arms. Wrapped her legs round his body and kissed him, with her arms around his neck.

"You can tell me now we are alone. Were you really not cross with me?"

"No I was extremely proud of you. You are bloody marvellous, but I suggest you wear some clothes up here as even with the heating it is bloody cold. It is too late to go skiing now. At least we have got some gear. Let's go to bed?"

That's what they did. They not only had a double bed sized duvet but also their sleeping bag sack so they weren't cold at least after they had got warm in the time honoured manner.

They had a fantastic day of skiing the following day. There was deep fresh powder. They had the two slopes virtually to themselves. Obviously the Lebanese were not early risers. Also they guessed that the majority hadn't been able to get up the mountain. They were really grateful for the Landrover and the wheel chains. There were two lifts which were working. The owners were hoping punters would eventually arrive. They bought lift passes for the two days. There were no queues. What was really wonderful for both of them was that they were both of a very similar standard. Anna was more stylish and made beautiful tracks through the powder. Charlie was a very strong skier and attacked the slopes with a passion. They both rarely fell, but when they did, the falls were usually spectacular, but not painful as the deep powder was very forgiving. They both had skied in powder before. Charlie loved doing 'jet' turns leaning well backwards to keep the tips of his skis just above the snow. Anna was like a ballerina, jumping on the turns. It was half way through the afternoon when she fell in a patch of very deep snow. Charlie helped her up. They kissed. Breathlessly she asked,

"You know I was given quite a large amount of money by the lady at the Casino. Can I ask a big favour? When we go through Europe, can we have two weeks skiing in Wengen in Switzerland? It is my most favourite place in all the world. It will be expensive, but I will pay."

Charlie kissed her again.

"I would love that. I also have skied in Wengen. That's a marvellous idea, but with one proviso, you will take all your clothes off tonight and I will pay!" She kissed him again,

"You know bloody well that I'll take off my clothes anytime for you but I'm going to pay!"

"Anytime?"

Anna unzipped her ski jacket and replied,

"Anytime, but I pay."

"OK, you win but only because I am worried you will catch your death of cold!"

There was a large amount of further snow over night. The slopes below the top of the two lifts were very treacherous. There was a lovely layer of soft powder on top and then a crust below. Most of the time the skier glided over this crust but sometimes the skier went through. This happened more often with Charlie as he was heavier. Anna was worried, particularly as the bindings on the skis they had hired were not the most modern. She persuaded Charlie to stop skiing downhill, but to climb up from the top of the higher of the two lifts. It was hard work, as they did not have either skins or cross-country skis. They tramped steadily zigzagging across the slope. Each time they stopped, Anna would tell him a story about her Grandfather who had skied at Wengen so many years before. Charlie was fascinated. When they stopped for the final time, Charlie said,

"I can't wait to get to Wengen." They kissed and decided to ski down in the virgin fresh powder now before the weather closed in. They skied down in parallel, so when they got to the top of the ski lift where they had started, they could see their tracks curving down. Anna laughed as hers were much more regular than his.

"I'll have to teach you better rhythm in bed tonight."

"That will be fun."

"Only if you now do what I say on this last run over the dangerous crusty snow. You are a bloody strong skier, but even strong skiers can get hurt." She smiled at him,

"This is Anna, your coach talking. I want long careful traversing, no speeding and an unhurt Charlie at the bottom. Got it?"

Charlie nodded and they both got down safely. Skiing had been great. The love-making even better.

There was even more snow in the night. They both thought they might be stranded up in the mountains, but with the chains, the Landrover with Charlie driving very carefully, managed to get them down. It was miraculous that as they got down to sea level near the Mediterranean, the sun shone and it was really warm. Charlie said,

"I can see how you can snow ski and water ski here in the same day." Anna added,

"I don't think I will try it. The water looks beautiful, but I have been to Greece in early June and the sea was freezing. I bet it is even colder now."

They left Lebanon after they had camped that night near to the Syrian border. After dark it was cold and they were soon in the sleeping sack in the sewn blankets in the tent. They both had several layers of clothes on. It was too early to sleep and they just talked about all manner of things. Slowly they got warmer and Charlie loved helping Anna out of her clothes. Although they were snuggled in the sack it was the bottom half of her attire which was removed first. She teased, Charlie,

"How is it that I have two sweaters, a shirt, a bra and even a woolly hat on and yet my knickers have to come off?"

"You could easily get prickly heat in your groin."

"My guess is, it is going to be your prick in my groin now that my knickers are off. I suppose it's too cold for foreplay. Come on Charlie remember last night you were so slow and controlled."

"Am I that bad?" She giggled,

"Yes often, but I know it is difficult for you as my desires are so variable. Sometimes I want you to be hard and demanding and just take me. Other times, like now, I want lots of kissing and fondling."

Charlie got the message. In fact it was really exciting stimulating her. Initially she just lay on her back and seemed to let good feelings just wash over her. Then suddenly, as if he had switched a switch he could tell she really wanted him. He teased her then and she became more and more excited. He was naked but she still had on layers of clothes on her top half. She let him continue to rub her, but she started to take her clothes off. As her bra came off he started sucking her breasts. She was breathing hard, in fact she was gasping. She suddenly rolled him on his back and straddled him. She tried to guide him inside her but he kept moving and teasing her.

"You bastard, you know just what I want, but you won't let me have it. OK, two can play at that game."

She reached for his wrists and held them above his head. They both knew he was so much stronger than her and that at any stage he could move his arms, but he went along with the game. He did not make it easy for her and kept trying her strength. He wondered what she was trying to do. Then he found out. She had somehow managed to get his erection under her. She undulated her body and he was inside her. She ground down on him and would not let him come out of her. Also she would not let him move in and out as he wanted. She took a deep breath and kissed him hard so he could not breathe. Somehow she had got her legs around his waist. She locked them behind him. However he was stronger and slowly although she held his wrists, he brought his arms down and grabbed her wrists. He held them easily then and started to thrust as he wanted. She met him thrust for thrust. She gasped,

"I enjoyed that fight. Now take me." She laughed and gasped,

"I am so bloody juicy, you are not being stimulated enough."

She was right. They kept thrusting together until she had another orgasm. He reached and sucked her breasts really hard. She came again.

"That was magic."

Charlie released her wrists and her arms came round his neck, as they kissed he came.

It was minutes until their breathing came back to normal.

"I'm sorry to be so contrary. Initially I just did not want you but suddenly I did. Thank you for persisting. I love you so much."

"Anna, you are so bloody sexy and wonderful. I love you with all my heart, my darling." She giggled,

"What even more that your Landrover." He started kissing her neck.

"No more Charlie. I should not joke. I am totally spent."

He knew she was telling the truth as she was instantly asleep in his arms.

Chapter 9

Syria and Turkey January 1971

In the morning they crossed into Syria. They were surprised how simple it was. Once in Syria they drove towards Krak des Chevalier. Charlie told Anna all he had read about the castle. It was the biggest Crusader castle and had never been taken in battle or by siege. Once it had been taken by treachery. It was high on a hill and commanded the whole area. They could see it from miles away, as they approached. The weather had deteriorated and it was lightly snowing. They both wished they had better warm weather gear. They had hired their ski clothes. There was no heater in the Landrover. In hot climates the exhaust which ran close to the passenger foot well, made it unbearably hot. Now the cold and the wet outside cooled it rapidly. Where in the heat they had every window and vent open, now they tried to block up every crack. They had bought two blankets in the flea market in Beirut. Before they got in the Landrover they wrapped them around their bodies over their clothes under their armpits. They were not worried that they looked like a couple of old grannies with car rugs. They could still drive in this garb.

There was a car park near to the main gate of the castle. Their entry fee was a pittance. Charlie told Anna as much as he could about the castle. It had eight walls and the only way in was to walk around the wall until you came to a gate into the next wall. None of the gates were opposite each other. Within the outer walls were stables for 1800 big horses able to carry a man in full armour. Charlie counted 26 smithies. There were wells and giant cisterns, throughout the castle, to supply fresh water. There were enormous granaries for food, not only for the defenders, but also the horses.

Charlie was very enthusiastic. Anna guessed it was a boy's thing. She could just imagine the bitter cold in winter and the blazing heat in summer. Now it was the cold which she hated. Camping was such hard work, but she knew they should save money and anyway the odd hotel in a town they saw did not look encouraging. They no longer lit a fire, as there was no dry wood. They had taken the tent off the top of the Landrover, as if there was any wind at all, it made the inside colder. They now put the awning on the ground as a ground sheet and then put the tent which had an attached ground sheet on top. Anna smiled to herself. The good thing about the cold was that their love making was really great. She loved Charlie wrapping his strong arms around her. She did not even mind his snoring when he slept on his back as that meant she could sleep on top of him. In fact she noticed, when he had nothing alcoholic to drink he did not snore at all even on his back. Charlie also noticed the different sleeping arrangement so he suggested folding the mattress to give them a greater distance from the cold earth beneath the tent. They now folded the sleeping sack so that they had yet more covering. This also gave them more room in the tent so that they could keep their clothes handy and could get dressed in the bed. Anna knew, Charlie loved her wriggling about. The only annoying thing was having to get out in the cold to have a pee. They both were always as quick as they could be and then they often made love to warm up. Anna would not let Charlie get away with being too quick saying,

"You are so lovely I could not stop!" She made him slow down. He would laugh and say,

"I feel like a dog being trained," she replied,

"I know by your reaction that you actually find it more fulfilling if you are made to wait. Am I right?"

"Yes you are right but now I want you again!" He heard a giggle,

"What's the bloody delay. I want you again as well."

So now they were not quite so early getting going in the Landrover. In fact because it was so cold they ate breakfast and drunk their mugs of tea quicker, while they were packing up, so the delay was actually minimal. Also the Landrover was becoming increasing difficult to get started in the morning. It began to worry them both. Charlie had brought a spare battery which helped, as he changed it each day, to always keep them both fully charged, but he knew deep down there was something not quite right in the engine, as they did not seem to have quite as much power.

Leaving Syrian immigration and customs was as easy as coming in. However something seemed to be wrong at the Turkish side of the border. No one spoke any English and obviously Charlie and Anna did not speak any Turkish. They wondered if the trouble was that it was lunch time. You would not have thought it was the middle of the day. There was quite a thick mist. It was very gloomy. The temperature was still below zero. The officials kept showing them all the ice on their hut. They kept pointing at the road and at their tyres. Eventually they lifted their arms up in resignation and lifted the barrier. Charlie drove off. The road started to climb in a series of S bends. The engine was warm and the Landrover seemed to be coping well. Anna asked,

"I wonder what that was all about."

"Thank goodness they let us go, you would have been frozen to death if you had to open your shirt."

"Too bloody right. You are a very good boy when you come back into bed, when you have been out to have a pee outside. You always warm your hands before you touch me." She gave his neck a little kiss. He rubbed her trousers on her thigh. She kissed him again,

"I love you, you great big bear, I can't wait for tonight."

They were still climbing. Although it was misty it was magical, as the pine trees were clothed in snow, and frost covered their trunks. They stopped and continued on the flat for about a mile, before they started to descend. At the first S bend, as Charlie started to turn nothing happened, it was if the steering wheel was disconnected. He touched the brake. Nothing happened.

"Shit, black ice! Hold on!"

Luckily they did not hit any rocks but came to rest with a sharp jolt as they hit the bank. Mercifully the strong bumper of the Landrover which was wrapped by a thick tow rope did not buckle. Charlie asked,

"Are you OK?" His shout had alerted, Anna, who had held on to the handle in front of her.

"I'm fine."

He turned off the engine and got out. He slipped straight down on to his bottom. The road was just a sheet of black ice. Anna got out carefully, holding on to the Landrover. Charlie had got up unhurt and holding on to the vehicle came around to her side, saying,

"Now I know what they were on about at the border. It is also why we have not seen another vehicle. We are on our own. I suggest we both get back in the Landy and I try to back up a few feet so we can get the wheel chains on. At least going in reverse we will have the best chance of getting up the slope."

Initially the wheels just spun but the friction created some heat and the vehicle slowly inched backwards. Charlie stopped, leaving it in gear with the handbrake on. He got out and carefully moved around so he could reach a rock on the side of the road. He put it under the front of one of the back wheels. He knew the chains were deep in the Landrover, under most of the other stuff. They set too together making a heap of the stuff and getting the chains out. While Charlie was laying the chains out, Anna packed up the Landrover, ready to leave as soon as they could. She did a double check to make sure they had not left anything. She knew that they would never make it back up again!

Charlie did not turn on the engine but inched the Landrover forward, using the slope, after he had removed the rock. Anna watched the wheels on the chains, and when they were right in the middle shouted for him to stop. Then with the vehicle in gear and the handbrake on they both started to do up the chains. When one was done Charlie put the rock in front of the wheel. Doing up the chains required lying on the cold frozen ground. Anna did not hesitate to do her share. They were both freezing cold when they had finished. Charlie removed the rock and they both got into the Landrover with blankets wrapped around them. Anna's teeth were chattering.

Charlie started the vehicle without a problem, as unlike them it still was slightly warm. In low range the Landover easily backed up and they set off down the hill. They had some frightening moments, but the chains gripped and they did not crash into the bank. Charlie was very careful to stay well away from the outer side of the road. Anna kept watch for a vehicle coming up. They did not see one. Eventually they could see the outside temperature had risen above freezing as the trees were no longer white and covered with snow. However for safety they kept the chains on and Charlie only speeded up slightly.

It was lucky they were going slowly as they did not see the road block until they were right on top of it. It had been sighted to stop vehicles going up, not coming down. Charlie brought the Landrover to a halt. The policemen manning the road block were not angry, but just concerned. There was a lot of talk and pointing at the chains. They indicated that they could take them off now. It was still cold, but it was no longer freezing. The men were amazed when Anna lay on the ground to undo the chains on her side. When they had packed the chains in their hessian bag, back in the Landrover, the men insisted on shaking them both by the hand.

As they drew away, Charlie said,

"You should be honoured, things must be changing in Turkey. It used to be a Moslem state, but I have read that it is now non-secretarian. Men do not normally go around shaking hands with lesser beings!"

"You wait until tonight, Charlie Ferguson, I will show you in bed who is a lesser being. You cheeky bugger!"

They journeyed on until they came to a small town called Iskenderun. They could just see the sea to their left. They stopped to buy some fresh food. About five miles out of town, Charlie took a sandy track off the road to their left. Soon they were in a pine grove close to the sea. They stopped and made camp. It was not really warm but after what they had been through it seemed like heaven. Making sure there was no danger of a fire spreading they made a fire pit with dry fir cones and dry pine wood. They heated up water in their metal bucket. They both laughed, as although they both did strip they bathed very quickly. They were soon back in clothes, but they only required one sweater each. The meal was very tasty with fresh lamb chops and potatoes baked in foil. Anna made a Greek salad.

When they were ready for bed, Anna stripped off like she used to in the desert, but did not waste time and was quickly into the tent and into the bed sack. Charlie was slower. As he was last he had to zip up the tent. He was on his knees when he felt, Anna's hand grab his balls. He froze.

"I think there was talk of lesser beings? A retraction is in order I think?"

"I was only saying what Moslems think."

She gave them a gentle squeeze. "I think a fuller retraction is required?"

"Anna, you and I are totally equal."

He scrabbled into bed on top of her, grabbing both her wrists and holding them above her head. He kissed her lips. He kissed her neck. He kissed and sucked her breasts.

"Bloody hell, Charlie. I must squeeze your balls more often."

She opened her legs and bent her knees. She felt him hard against her but he continued to kiss her. She raised her chest to make it easier for him to suck her nipples. Breathlessly she said,

"Please keep sucking Charlie. It is bloody amazing. I think I am going to come."

Her breathing became more ragged. She was pushing her breast into his eager mouth. He swopped to the other breast and sucked the engorged nipple. She sighed and he let go of her wrists. He felt her push him inside her. She was so moist he hardily felt her round him. He reached down and held her buttocks. They pushed for several minutes before they came together.

Eventually Anna said,

"That was really something. You sleep on top of me tonight. I love the feel of you getting smaller and then I'm briefly sad as I feel you slipping out of me." Charlie did not think she was sad that night as he was sure she was asleep before he slipped out.

Neither of them remembered what happened in the night but somehow they awoke with him on his back and her lying on top of him. She yawned and said,

"I think I like being a lesser being, if it means I can sleep on top of you and have your arms around me. Actually your hairy chest stimulates my nipples. I don't think we have had a shag for hours? How about it?"

As it was so mild they made the most of it and had a leisurely breakfast. Charlie said as they were washing up,

"I'm glad we are equal as we need to come to a joint decision on the direction which we now need to take. As I see it, we can hug the coast which will be warmer but take us two days longer, as it is much further, or we can go virtually straight to Istanbul. That way is not nearly so far, but it is across the Anatolia plateau and we will have one very cold night, as it will take us two days. Anna said,

"I think we ought to go straight over the plateau." Charlie laughed,

"I'm sure you guessed that's what I wanted to do. We are equal you know." Anna responded,

"That does not stop me loving you to bits. I know you will do your very best to keep me warm in bed."

So they set off. It was not a steep climb up on to the plateau so they could keep up a good speed without putting the Landrover engine under too much stress. It gradually got colder the higher they climbed. The road was good and there was only a little snow lying beside it. However half way through the morning it began to snow. Anna was driving. She had to slow down, as the old windscreen wipers could not really clear the screen quick enough. They ate the lunch which they had prepared at breakfast without stopping, except to change drivers. They kept pushing on, but changing regularly, as the driver really had a job seeing where the road was in the white-out. It was not a blizzard as there was no wind, but the snow just kept on falling steadily. There were very few vehicles and so it settled on the road. Obviously this was a regular occurrence in the winter, as the road was marked by high stakes either side at regular three metre intervals. It began to get dark and so they started to look for somewhere to camp. The area was barren. There did not appear to be any trees or even rocky outcrops. Then Charlie saw a dwelling of some sort about fifty yards off the road. The snow was deep now, but it was frozen and so he did not think they would get stuck. He made for the building which was a shepherds hut that was only used in the summer. He backed the Landrover up to the small door so that it would prevent the snow blowing in, if the wind got up. They both got out and went into the hut. The inside was about four metres in diameter. They lit the gas lamp as it was now dark. Anna made supper while Charlie put up the tent. He treated the ground as if it was outside putting the awning down under the tent. Anna brought him a mug of tea. He got all the bedding into the tent. The hut was a real blessing as the snow was still falling outside and everything would have got damp at best, wet at worse. They put up the table and two chairs. As they were eating supper the wind started to blow. They were even more grateful to be in the hut, as they could imagine what it was like outside. They cleared up, ducked outside for a quick pee and got into the tent. They left their shoes by the flap and crawled into bed with all their clothes on. Slowly they started taking them off, starting with their bottom halves. Anna felt Charlie, pulling her knickers down.

"So you think you are in with a chance, do you?"

"A man always has to hope and you did say at breakfast that I was to keep you warm."

The hand rubbed just where she wanted. She savoured the feeling before rolling on to him and helping him. She kissed his neck as she reached up under her shirt and sweater to undo her bra. She loved the feeling of his big hands on her bottom. She knew he was trying to hold on. She licked inside his ear as she knew that he was very ticklish. Sure enough he stopped thrusting but squirmed instead. The squirming was very erotic so she undulated her hips. She begged then, as she was so nearly there,

"Please Charlie don't stop I am so nearly there, think of the cold."As if she had summoned it the wind howled. She knew Charlie dare not move, but she needed more. She undulated her pelvis. He was in just the right spot and then they both came together.

"You wonderful man that was beautiful."

They still had their clothes on their top halves in the morning which for Anna made having a pee much quicker. It was still dark so they cuddled up to warm up before Charlie lit the light and they got dressed. The mug of tea even with the UHT was nectar. It was freezing in the hut, but the wind had dropped. They had a quick breakfast and loaded up the Landrover. Then, as the dawn was breaking they had the onerous job of putting on the wheel chains. They both prayed that the Landrover would start. Their prayers were answered and it coughed into life. The wind driven snow had obliterated their tracks, but Anna managed to hit the road at right angles. She turned right and they headed to Istanbul. They saw their first vehicle coming towards them after about half an hour. It was a real relief as it meant the road was open. The chains were a godsend in the deep snow.

Then to Anna's horror the lorry was on the wrong side of the road coming straight towards her with its lights flashing. She swerved off the road to avoid a head-on crash. As she turned back on to the road she realised her mistake. She had driven on the left hand side of the road as if she was in England! Charlie smiled,

"Your nude body is etched in my mind. You have no need to prove you are a real blond!" She was just about to apologise and then thought, 'to hell with it' and said,

"Silly me, I was just thinking what good fun we had in bed last night." Charlie replied,

"We certainly did. Let's stay in the best hotel in town to night to celebrate our survival?"

"That gets my vote. I might even get to take off all my clothes and prove to you once again that you have got the 'the real deal'!"

Charlie leant over and kissed her neck.

The deep snow continued all across the plateau. They went through several small towns which looked beautiful with their covering of snow, but they suspected might not look so good, when it melted. One town was holding a livestock market. The streets, even the main road was full of herds of cattle and flocks of fat-tailed sheep. Anna said,

"I bet this looks a right mess when the snow melts?"

"Too right, we are lucky where I work in the Northern Frontier District because it's so dry the cattle do not seem to make a mess. I actually love the smell of cattle, but my favourite smell is the ground after a downpour of rain."

Anna who was driving, was cross with herself as she suddenly started to silently cry. Unlike so many men, Charlie was very sensitive. He knew just what had made her cry. It was the thought of him being in Kenya and her being in Cambridge. He reached up and touched her neck.

"We will work something out. It is only a ten hour overnight flight!" She smiled through her tears.

"You will not have to take a day off work or rugby. You can fly back to UK on Saturday night. We can spend the whole of Sunday in bed and you can fly home for work on Monday morning!"

"Great minds think alike. Even last night in the freezing cold in a shepherd's hut was marvellous."

He leant over and licked her wet face.

"I enjoy licking you." She really laughed then.

"I enjoy being licked you sexy beast. Look out Istanbul! Can you look up in that 'Lonely Planet Guide' the best hotel in the city?" Eventually Charlie said,

"It looks like the 'Hotel Kennedy'. Let's hope there is a big bath in our bathroom. We can enjoy a really good soak."

The hotel was indeed very posh. A doorman took the keys of the Landrover so it was safely parked undercover and in a secure garage. They checked in with their two small rucksacks. The room was on the seventh floor and had a wonderful view of the city. Charlie went into the bathroom to run a bath. He came out slightly annoyed as there seemed to be no water, neither hot, nor cold. He went to the room phone and pressed 0 for reception. A voice in Turkish replied, but immediately switched to English when Charlie inquired about the water. He was told that there was a problem in the whole of Istanbul and the water everywhere was turned off until further notice. Charlie then explained that he and his wife had driven through appalling conditions across the Anatolia Plateau for two days and therefore required a bath. Would the management kindly send up some water.

Anna was laughing,

"That was very forceful for you, Charlie. Does having a wife make you more likely to get water? I suppose, 'my bit of crumpet which I picked up at an airport in Africa', does not quite have the same gravitas!" It was Charlie's time to laugh,

"I suggest they would have said, 'the bit of crumpet had better keep her clothes on until the water is brought.' I assume they will bring it in a big urn?"

He was wrong. Much to Anna's amusement, four men in the hotel uniform arrived with two crates each of small bottles of soda water together with two openers. They nodded after they put the crates down in the large bathroom and left. Anna put her arms around Charlie' neck.

"Thank goodness the room is quite warm. Sitting in a bath of cold soda water is not really my idea of a long soak, but the bubbles may be quite erotic."

Needless to say they did not spend long in the water, but did manage to get themselves clean. Anna washed her hair as she had seen there was a hair drier. She put on her little black dress which she knew Charlie liked. The very few occasions when she had to dress up travelling though Africa, it had been hot and so she had just worn the lace knickers which Charlie had bought her. She knew outside it was cold, maybe not as cold as the last few days, but it would be cold all the same. So black nylons with a suspender belt were the order of the day. Charlie looked up from his book as she was clipping on her stockings.

"Wow. I am lucky tonight. Why are suspenders so sexy?" Anna smiled at him,

"I guess the bit of bare thigh and suspenders draw the eye to where you men should not be looking."

She then added, "I think you are a little different from most men, not that I really know, but I have heard my brothers talking. You do find some clothes that I wear sexy, but basically you like me naked. You seem to like to excite me more than be excited by me. If you know what I mean?"

Charlie thought for a second, "Yes, you are right. I think other senses are very important to me. I love the feel of your skin. I love the softness of your secret place. I love the taste of you." Then he added, "I hate to see you cry. I almost cried today when I licked your face." Anna answered,

"I'm glad I don't have to wear any make up for you. I will look very unglamorous in the UK when the other girls are all dolled up." He replied,

"In my eyes you will always look the best. Come here a second" Anna walked to the bed. He slid his hand up her thigh under her skirt. "That feel is certainly extremely sexy." She smiled,

"So is the feel of your hand. Come on let's hit the town?"

They got some directions from the reception of the hotel to a good local restaurant. Luckily it was quite near, as it was now getting really cold. Anna only had a smart but not warm jacket. She teased, Charlie as he had found a sports jacket which smelt of moth balls. Although the restaurant was local they were pleased that they served alcohol. They both had G&Ts. Anna asked Charlie to tell her about Turkey.

He told about the Ottoman Empire and how in its hay day it nearly reached to Vienna. How the Ottomans sided with the Germans in the First World War, but as a result of the allied victory the empire was reduced to the size of present day Turkey. He horrified her by a story of when Ataturk came to power in the 1920's. He had got a summons sent to all the spies in Istanbul to be on the Galatia bridge one night at 2am. So the British spy, the French spy, the CIA man and the Russian spy all crept up on to the bridge. A large black limo drove up. Two men lifted Ataturk's' rival out of the limo. He's feet were in a solid concrete block. They dropped him over the bridge. Anna asked why Ataturk had done that. Charlie told her that it was, so he could show the rest of the world that he now was the power in Turkey.

They had a superb meal which ended with 'Baked Alaska' cooked for them at their table. They were both a little tipsy by the time they got back to their room at the 'Hotel Kennedy'. Once they had locked the door, Anna gave him a passionate kiss and she whispered,

"I thought that after all that drink you might not be up to it tonight but by the feel of you, I was wrong. Will you strip me? I would find that very sexy."

"Certainly, I would love to."

He quickly took his own clothes off, before very slowly unzipping her dress, letting it drop to the floor. He kept eye contact with her and reached behind her and unclipped her bra. He reached up to her shoulder straps to let her pert breasts break free. Then he slowly pushed down her knickers. Anna gave a sexy wiggle and they dropped to the floor. Still gazing at her he reached down a gently stroked her bare thighs above the tops of her stockings. Slowly his hand moved into her groin. Anna opened her legs slightly so it was easier for him to stroke her with one hand as his other hand stroked her bottom. As she became aroused she put her arms around his neck. Very slowly she became more and more aroused until she whispered,

"Take me now, Charlie."

She gave a little jump and wrapped her stocking clad legs around him. He lifted her bottom with both hands. She rubbed herself against him. It took him three thrusts to manage to enter her. She gasped,

"That feels wonderful."

He carried her to the bed and then they thrust together. Slowly at first then quicker and quicker. Anna came first with a little cry and then Charlie, who was on his knees came before burying his face in her breasts.

Charlie woke with Anna giggling,

"How is it, Charlie Ferguson, that I have still got my suspender belt and my stockings on. I remember distinctly asking you to undress me. You are almost a total failure. I suppose you did manage my dress, bra and knickers. Would you like to complete your allotted task?" Charlie murmured,

"Not really. I would rather stroke that lovely bit of your thigh above your stocking top."

"I think I might enjoy that. So feel free to carry on."

It was mid-morning when they surfaced. They were too late for breakfast, but room service managed coffee and various sweet cakes. So eventually they checked out and got the ferry across the Bosporus taking photos of the Donmabachi Palace as they left Asia and entered Europe. Their first night in Europe was in Turkey. It was freezing cold. Anna did a lot of wriggling in the sleeping sack. Charlie asked,

"What's the problem my love?"

"I was just putting my stockings on. I thought it might encourage you to try and warm me up. I am freezing. Charlie took the warming up exercise very seriously. It was still freezing in the morning so Anna made a brew of tea and helped Charlie pack up. They did not bother with any breakfast until they got to the border. There were no problems getting out of Turkey, but the Greek customs insisted on getting them to remove everything from the Landrover. Everything was then thoroughly examined in a very serious manner. It was only when Charlie was ordered to unzip the sleeping sack revealing the black stocking and suspender belt that the customs men smiled. Anna was too cold to blush.

Chapter 10

Greece, Yugoslavia and Italy February 1971

They had entered Northern Greece in the province of Thessalonica. Thanks to the delay at the border they were soon camping again. This time they got into the sleeping sack as soon as they could and made some packets of hot soup in the tent. This was followed by hot coffee laced with Greek Metaxa brandy. Anna thought Charlie had gone over the top getting seven star brandy, until he explained that anything lower that five star was virtually undrinkable. This change of the sleeping arrangements was marvellous for getting to sleep but sadly they had to get up in the middle of the night for a pee. Luckily the sack was still warm when they snuggled back in it.

The following day they had to exit Greece, which seemed to be fairly straightforward and was relatively quick. Getting into Yugoslavia was a nightmare. The main problem was currency. Every bit of foreign currency to the nearest penny had to be declared. Then they were forced to buy Yugoslav Dinars at a very poor rate. Charlie tried to change as little as possible. He said they were only going to be in the country two days and had enough food and fuel to get them to Italy, but they were forced to change £100 into dinars at this very poor rate. Anna could see Charlie was getting cross. She laughed and said,

"You will need all of the £100 to buy me sexy underwear. This place is so bloody cold you will have to shag me to death or I will die of cold!"

The customs men luckily did not understand a word, but she had made him laugh, so he stopped arguing and changed the money. They then set off on the main road north through Titograd. They stopped at a services and Charlie disappeared behind the building to change some money with a very dubious character, while Anna filled up the two petrol tanks. He returned smiling, so she knew he had got a good rate. Unwisely he bought two ham sandwiches as well as the petrol. There was a lot of rather stale bread, a little fat and no actual ham. As they were now going north and it was early February the days were very short, so they had to stop their practice of camping before dark.

Driving in the dark was scary to say the least. The main road northwards ran alongside the railway track which in turn followed a river. The road and railway often crossed and there were no crossing gates. To make matters worse the road was full of lorries carrying sugar beet from the farms to the factory. They must have been on a strict time schedule. As Charlie said, "They didn't take any prisoners."

Anna hated driving in the dark, but did not like pushing it all on to Charlie. She knew he was really tired as he fell asleep immediately they got into the sleeping sack rather than making love. She teased him so that he knew she understood, by saying, "Did he want her to put on her suspender belt and stockings on?" She also knew he was worried as the Landrover was becoming harder and harder to start in the mornings. Even she could feel that it had less power climbing the hills. Luckily they could lighten the vehicle, as they did not require nearly as much water or fuel on board.

Camping was no longer fun. It was a matter of survival. Although they had gaslights and torches, there was no light in the Landrover. Making supper in the freezing cold semi-darkness was extremely difficult. Anna hugged Charlie,

"I'm sorry the standard of cuisine has dropped. I'm bloody useless. I hate driving in the dark. I can't cook. All I can do is lie on my back with my legs apart and you are too tired to want that."

"My darling, Anna, You are an angel. I must stink that badly, you must love me a hell of a lot, just to hug me, let alone get into bed with me." With a cheeky smile he added, "If the Landrover starts tomorrow, we should hit Venice tomorrow night, I will give you a cold bath in soda water!"

Anna laughed, "I will probably strangle you with a silk stocking!"

The Landrover did not start in the morning. The night had been the coldest ever. There was thick ice inside the tent. However the sky was blue and they were in a wood so they lit a fire. Charlie tried the spare battery which he knew was charged, but he guessed was so cold that there was not sufficient current to turn over the engine. He put the battery as near as he dared to the fire. He tried the starting handle. The oil must have been very thick as he could only just turn over the engine.

Anna had made a cooked breakfast and big mugs of tea, so they sat down and ate, well rugged up in the Alpine type of weather. Their breath crystallised. After breakfast Charlie said he would walk down the track they had seen which he was sure led to a farm and see if he could get some help. Anna did the washing up and then carefully packed up the Landrover, so that she was totally ready, when he returned with a vehicle to tow them.

Charlie did return but not with a vehicle, but with a horse, all harnessed up, led by a strong, good looking, guy with his left arm in plaster. Charlie introduced him as, 'Super Yug'. Apparently it had been that cold that even the farm tractor would not start. Everything had to be conducted in sign language. Anna said,

"He's quite tasty; if it wasn't so bloody cold I would undo my shirt buttons for him!" Charlie laughed,

"I'll have to lift my game in Venice this evening."

Still the Landrover would not start. The horse could pull it, but not fast enough for the vehicle to fire. 'Super Yug' gave the horse to Anna to hold. She was rather honoured. It was a massive cart horse but stood beside her like a lamb. He indicated that Charlie should follow him. Charlie said,

"Don't go chatting up any good looking young men."

She stuck her tongue out at him and pretended to undo her shirt buttons, much to 'Super Yug's' amusement. She started to talk to the horse after they had gone. She was sure it liked her gentle tone. She looked underneath it and saw it was a gelding. She thought to herself how that zebra foal had done her such a good turn. She thought how different her life would have been. She smiled as she thought she would probably still be having temper tantrums! She felt how Charlie was so much more than a boyfriend. He was her man, for better or worse, for richer or poorer, in sickness and in health. Somehow they would have to work something out. She knew in her heart that if he asked her, she would marry him and go with him to the ends of the earth, but she also knew she would regret not becoming a vet. He was such a lovely guy. She was sure he understood. He so loved his job he would understand why she wanted to do the same.

She was stroking the horse when they returned with a second horse which Charlie said was the first horses' mother. An old man came with them. Charlie introduced him as 'Grandad'. He shook her hand and she kissed his cheek. He broke into a wide smile. They attached the second horse to the Landrover. Charlie told Anna what to do to start the Landrover as he was going to push with 'Super Yug'. 'Grandad' was going to drive the two horses sitting on the front of the vehicle.

With a great shout in Serbo-Croat they were off. Anna had the hand brake off, the engine in second gear, her foot on the clutch, the ignition on and the choke out. She had the window open. On a shout from Charlie she lifted her foot off the clutch. The engine fired, she pushed down on the accelerator and half pushed in the clutch. 'Grandad' slowed the horses from a canter to a trot and then as Anna braked to a walk. With the engine revving, the horses and the Landrover came to a halt.

Anna had to stay in the driving seat to keep up the revs. 'Super Yug' unhitched the horses. Charlie was rummaging in the back of the Landrover for a half bottle of whiskey which he gave to 'Grandad', who was delighted. Grandad then produced a bottle of local raw spirit which Charlie thought was made from potatoes. He gave it to Anna in the cab. She realised she was meant to take a swig. She will never know how she stopped herself from choking. A glow spread up her chest. She laughed as she could see Charlie was struggling not to choke,

"Wow, I nearly had to undo my shirt buttons after that!"

There was a lot of waving and shouting and Anna drove off down the track back to the road, saying to Charlie,

"I wish I could have told him in Serbo-Croat that normally I drive a chariot in the nude wearing a marvellous hat." Charlie laughed,

"I'm sure 'Grandad' would have enjoyed that story."

They drove on through Ljubljana where they saw lots of people in ski gear before they came to the Yugoslavian customs. Anna dare not let the engine stop, as it obviously, according to Charlie, was only firing on three of its four cylinders. The Yugoslavians were very helpful and the immigration man came to check her picture in her passport with her still in the cab.

The Italians in Trieste were just as helpful. Anna said,

"I'm sure you have made me stay in the cab Charlie as two of these guys are very sexy."

"I think you had better behave yourself or you will get us both in jail."

So they made it to a big garage which was on the mainland at Maestri opposite Venice. The mechanics promised to have a look at the Landrover the next day and suggested they came back the day after that. They took their small rucksacks on a boat to Venice. They had no problem finding a small hotel, as the town was virtually empty of tourists, as it was the first week in February. The hotel also seemed to be empty.

Anna was delighted. The hotel was warm and the bath water was hot. The bath was big enough for them both to have a soak together. They decided to eat in the hotel, as they felt too tired to go out. They were in the middle of their meal when there was a commotion in the reception. It was a party of French School girls in school uniform. They were wearing short skirts and gave Charlie the eye. Anna said,

"If you ogle those girls, I will go back to the Italian immigration!"

With a disarming smile Charlie replied,

"Would I ever?"

Anna was well aware that Charlie was the centre of attention for the rest of the meal. He even said,

"Bon soir" to them.

Anna just smiled sweetly and they went up to their room. Charlie was first in bed and had dropped off to sleep while Anna was still brushing her teeth. She enjoyed the room being warm. It was so lovely to go to bed in the nude. She was looking forward to a cuddle. When she saw he was asleep she remembered how she had threatened to strangle him with one of her stockings, if he had bathed her in cold soda water. She had a naughty idea. The stockings which she had worn in Istanbul were both laddered and finished with. She retrieved them from her bag. Charlie was sleeping on his back with his hands above his head. She knew he would wake when she got in bed so she very carefully put a noose round each wrist with a separate stocking and tied the two stockings to the bed head. She got in bed and lay on top of him as she often did. He woke as he went to put his arms around her.

"What the devil?"

"I think you forgot to say 'Bon soir' to me you all rogue." She kissed him tenderly and then said,

"I thought I would just remind you that you should be dreaming of me, not a bunch of French girls with short skirts!"

She straddled him which she knew he loved, but instead of putting him the whole way inside her she just rubbed his tip on her. When he thrust upwards she lifted her bottom to tease him. He was really hard now and she enjoyed the feel of him. She moved her pelvis invitingly, but always only just touching him. She went too high and he came out,

"Silly me, I think I have lost him."

Charlie was growling with frustration, as she rubbed herself against him. She was getting very excited herself and so soon she let him enter her properly and sighed as with one thrust he came deep inside her. She flopped forward on his chest and undid the stockings. Charlie asked,

"Would you like me to tie you up?"

"I trust you and I love you so much, I rather think I would love it. Now, no more 'Bon soirs', I know you are exhausted and worried about the Landrover, so we must get some sleep. Will you cuddle my back? That is lovely. Sleep well my love."

Actually they were both exhausted and slept in late in the following morning. They were amazed as there had been a heavy fall of snow which was virtually unheard of in Venice. Breakfast had long since finished at the hotel so they went out for an espresso and a croissant. It was a magical scene. There were older children having a snowball fight. There was two young children with a plastic sledge. They were using a humped back bridge across one of the canals as a slope.

Anna did not see exactly how it happened, but somehow the sledge and the two children went under the metal railings into the canal. Shouting to Charlie she was shedding clothes as she ran to the canal and dived in. The cold hit her, but perhaps not as rapidly as might have been expected, as she had been virtually permanently cold for weeks. She managed to grab one child. Charlie was right behind her but stopped at the railings to assess the situation. He then dived in to get the second child. Luckily there were some metal rungs on the side of the canal to help the gondoliers. Anna swum with what turned out to be a seven year old boy to these rungs. However she could not climb out one handed as she needed to hold the boy. Charlie was behind her with a girl who hadn't swallowed any water and so could hold his hair. Charlie pushed Anna's bottom which helped her to start climbing. He could then climb and she could use his head to support her. She managed to climb one handed.

A crowd had gathered and a strong Italian man pulled the unconscious boy to safety. Anna immediately started mouth to mouth resuscitation. She could feel his heart beating. She just concentrated on the boy and was unaware of the blankets being wrapped around them. There was a lot of Italian being voiced. Charlie had handed the girl to her mother who was too shocked to speak. A motorised boat ambulance had been summoned. Anna had got the boy breathing on his own and the paramedics took over. The mother and the two children were taken to hospital. They wanted to take Anna and Charlie, but they said they were fine. Someone had gathered their shoes and clothes, so to try and warm up they ran back to their hotel.

They had a lovely warm bath and they washed their clothes in the bath, wrapped in towels. Anna did the washing and part of the rinsing, Charlie did the rest of the rinsing in the bidet and wrung them out as best he could. They hung them over the bath. Charlie said,

"In the summer the canals of Venice are pretty polluted, but in the winter they are not so bad. It is sea water so I don't think we will catch anything. We are a good team. It was reminiscent of the Uasin Nyro!"

Anna gave him a kiss and laughing said,

"Now I am going to sit on your lap and let you comb and dry my hair. That will be reminiscent of the time at the Uasin Nyro. You were a naughty bad boy getting an innocent fourteen year old girl to sit on your lap." Charlie protested,

"I honestly thought you were eighteen!"

She kissed him again.

"I believe you. In fact you were rather sweet to me. I was naughty as well. I think if you had gone a bit further I might have let you!"

At about 6 o'clock they got on some warmer clothes although their warmest were still very wet. They went out to find 'Harry's Bar' which is famous, as it was where Ernest Hemmingway used to drink. It was a cosy little bar. Charlie ordered them a beer each. He was not very pleased, as they bought two very small beers which Anna suspected were very potent. He asked the barman if they had large beers like he was used to in Kenya. The barman replied that they only had these small beers which he assured Charlie were very good. Anna smiled as she could see Charlie was not happy. He ordered four more small beers each. She could see he was even more unhappy at the bill which was enormous. Once they were outside she said,

"I think I had better tie you up again tonight, as I thought you were going to thump him."

"I am sorry I am grumpy. I am so worried about the Landrover."

"Come on we will get back to the warm hotel. Hopefully the French girls will be back. That will cheer you up."

They got back, but Anna suspected that it was a good meal which actually made the difference. The beers had made her feel a bit randy so when they got to the room she suggested that he might like to tie her wrists to the bed head. Charlie jumped at the idea. She quickly stripped. Once he had tied her wrists he rested her thighs on his shoulders and buried his face in her groin. Soon he had her begging him to stop and then when he stopped, begging him to continue. She ended bucking her body so violently that Charlie was worried she would hurt her back. She was still gasping several minutes later when he untied her wrists. Her first coherent words were,

"Bloody hell that was good. What was in those small beers? They were rocket fuel. I'm sorry they were so expensive."

Charlie replied,

"They were worth every penny. I do love to see you in ecstasy."

The following morning when they were having breakfast, a young Italian man arrived at their hotel and was shown to their table. His English was not too good, but they learnt that he was the father of the two children they had rescued. They were so pleased that both children were now fine and had been let out of hospital. Their father asked them to come for dinner in two night's time when the children had fully recovered. He gave them his address. They said they would be delighted.

As soon as they had finished breakfast they set off to the mainland to go to the garage. The news at the garage was not good.

Apparently the Landrover needed a new valve. They had already removed the top of the engine so that Charlie could see what the problem was. They were not Landrover dealers, so they needed to get a new valve from a dealer in Milan. Charlie was given the task of procuring this valve. He was given a number to ring in Milan and was ushered into a typical garage office with calendars of nude girls on the wall. Anna kept a low profile, as she somehow found it a little disconcerting and then laughed to herself. 'What an idiot she was. She was quite happy to be in the nude herself in the casino!'

Charlie sat at a metal desk with a telephone and tried to get the number. He immediately found out why he had been given the task. There was no direct dial system, he had to go through an exchange and he kept getting cut off. Obviously Anna could see his face and hear what he said, but she could not hear what was said to him. He became more and more exasperated. Eventually she heard him say,

"This bloody *'shenzi simo'* (hopeless telephone in Swahili)." His face suddenly lit up and he starting talking away in Swahili. The conversation went on for some time. When he eventually put the phone down he was the normal happy Charlie.

"That was amazing, Anna, the operator in Milan was a prisoner of war in Kenya. He understood Swahili. He is going to find the valve and then ring me back on this number. I can't believe how lucky we are. What an amazing coincidence."

Anna now understood the man she so loved. Not only was he worried about the Landrover, but also he missed his home in Kenya. The telephone rang again and there was more Swahili. After he put the phone down he told Anna that the valve would be packed up and sent by express parcel to this garage. It would take three days. He then told the mechanic who seemed to be in charge of the job. Although the mechanic spoke only a little English, it was much easier to communicate face to face using hand signs as well as words, rather than using the telephone. They left the garage and spent the day looking around Venice. Anna was amazed at Charlie, as he knew quite a lot about the art and more importantly the history of the art in Italy. She noticed that he was more intent on explaining things about what they had seen at supper than looking at the French girls.

When they got to bed and she was cuddling his back she whispered,

"Charlie, you know I love you. I want you to know that your home is my home. I loved Kenya and I will be really happy to live there." He rolled to face her,

"Oh Anna, that is wonderful. Somehow we will make your ambition to become a vet come true."

Their love making was very tender that night and they both enjoyed it as much and maybe even more than their energetic love making on the previous two nights.

The dinner with the Italian family was great fun. The children had been allowed to stay up to greet them. They were both very shy. They stayed with their mother while Charlie and Anna sat down and their father brought them drinks. Obviously the boy did not recognise them but he must have been told that Anna had rescued him. The girl definitely remembered Charlie, but was too shy to approach him. The boy made the first move and sidled over to Anna. It was not long before he was sitting on her knee and she had her arm around him. She wished she could speak Italian and talk to him. Then the little girl became bolder and came up to Charlie and climbed on to his knee. Charlie asked her father who spoke a little English whether she had ever ridden a pony. It appeared they both had ridden donkeys on the sand the previous summer. They had also seen horses being ridden. Charlie managed to indicate that he was a horse and got her sitting on his knees with her legs apart and holding his hands, as if they were reins. She was obviously a bright child as she seemed to understand the movements of a horse. Charlie started,

"This is the way the lady rides, walky, walky." He moved his legs slowly like a walking horse. Then he said,

"This is the way the farmer rides, trot, trot, hip-pity hop, down to the shop." He bounced her up and down like a trotting horse. Then holding her hands very firmly he said,

"This is the way the huntsman rides, gallopy, gallopy." He moved her arms and made her body move as if she was on a galloping horse. She shrieked with delight. Then he said,

"Over the hedge." He bounced her up in the air still holding her hands tightly.

"Into the ditch." He opened his legs and let her bottom drop but still held her hands. Then he pulled her back on to his knees. The girl indicated that she wanted to do it all again. Then Charlie had to do it twice for the boy. After several more goes it was bed time. Both children kissed Charlie and Anna before their mother took them off to bed.

The meal was a real success. Language was a barrier, but they managed to get around that. It was quite late when they made their way back to the hotel. They walked quickly as it was so cold. It seemed all too soon that the Landrover was finished. They both had enjoyed their time in Venice. They were thankful their warmest clothes were now dry.

Chapter 11

Switzerland February 1971

Their journey now took them North West through Milan. Obviously there was a large amount of snow in the Alps but low down it had now all melted. There was no problem exiting Italy near Lake Como. However the Swiss were very thorough and checked not only their passports, but also the Landrover. They looked at the tyres and said they could not drive a vehicle in Switzerland with tyres as worn as these. Charlie offered to change them, as he had three spares, but they were also rather bald. They were in a muddle as they could not return, as they were no longer in Italy. The Swiss said there was a garage three kilometres down the road where they could buy tyres. They set off each rolling a spare tyre. It was hard work particularly for Anna, as the tyre was so heavy. After a couple of hundred metres she stopped to get her breath and then shouted to Charlie,

"We are being complete fools. What about the wheel chains?"

They left the tyres where they were on the road side, as there was no way anyone was going to steal two bald Landrover tyres, and walked back to the customs men. Initially they were perplexed and then Charlie started putting on the chains and they understood. They then escorted them to the garage picking up the spares on the way. The customs men stayed the whole time the tyres were changed. They were pleased, as Charlie bought five tyres in all, as he said he would need them in future and they still had a long way to go to get to England.

They stayed the night at a small hotel near Lake Locarno. In the morning they started the long hard climb up into the Alps. They had only gone about ten kilometres before they had to put on the wheel chains for real. The sun was shining but the temperature was below freezing and the snow was crisp. Then they came to a sign saying the Gotthard Pass was closed. Charlie said,

"Let's give it a go, it is a hell of a long way around if we don't. The Italians did a great job on this engine. Even at this altitude it is pulling well." They kept climbing up the hairpin bends. They came to a small town with a railway station. The road was totally blocked with snow which was much higher than the Landrover. However to their relief they found they could put the vehicle on a train and go under the pass in a tunnel. They drove the Landrover on to the train and it was chained down to the flat-car. They were told they should travel in the vehicle. After half an hour the train set off into the tunnel. It was very scary as they could not see anything except sparks from the rails. Anna shouted,

"This would be really frightening for children." Charlie agreed and then laughed,

"We are fools in a normal car there would be an interior light. It would not be half as frightening!"

Charlie and Anna had agreed, when they were skiing in Lebanon that they would stop for two weeks in Wengen in Switzerland on their way through Europe. Anna was delighted that Charlie knew the area so well. They parked the Landrover at Lauterbrunnen station. Anna thought it was so funny that they looked like a couple of tramps wearing the Wellington boots which they had bought in Istanbul.

Even the man at the ticket office remembered Anna. He said parking was for free, if they had bought a two week lift pass for the whole area. They only took their rucksacks. Anna was determined she would get some decent ski gear for both of them. When Charlie tried to get out of it, she had teased him saying she would measure him on the underpants she had bought him in Nairobi. That day seemed so long ago. Charlie was delighted that she always wore the knickers he had bought her when they were not camping and went out in the evening. He noticed they were washed separately from all their other clothes and were put almost religiously on a towel to dry unlike the rest of her clothes which were draped over anything. She had given him a really hard whack on his backside when he pretended to dry his face on them one morning.

They arrived at the 'Banhoff' in Wengen. They laughed together as Anna had nearly always stayed at the 'Hotel Regina' and Charlie had always stayed at the 'Palace Hotel'. These were the most expensive hotels in town except for the 'Park Hotel' which they both agreed was situated much too far away from the action, at the bottom of the lift up the Mannlican.

They decided to try the 'Hotel Eiger', as that was nearest to the station. Sadly that was full, so they walked the ten yards to the 'Hotel Silberhorn'. The middle-age owner was gobsmacked that they had driven all the way from Kenya. He said the hotel was full up, but he had a bathroom which they could rent for £35 a week. They could use their own bedding. Anna and Charlie were delighted. It was getting dark so they decided to hire their skis and boots before returning to get their kit from the Landrover. Mr. Moliter the owner of the ski shop remembered both of them. He thought it was very amusing that they were going to be camping in a bathroom. He was a marvellous salesman and soon had them kitted out in very smart, hired, ski clothes which Anna was sure were new. He also insisted on giving them a 'luge' for the two weeks, not only to help them with their kit, but also so that they could have some fun going down the new 'luge' track to Lauterbrunnen. They dumped their stuff in the Hotel and sent off.

The 'lugging' was good fun. Some way down they had a crash. Anna somehow ended up on top of Charlie. She gave him a big kiss. Even in their ski trousers she could feel him hard against her. Without him knowing she undid his zip. The first Charlie knew was a very cold ski glove in his groin, with Anna giggling, "I thought that would cool your ardour. Your poor 'Willy' has almost disappeared." Then a snow fight ensued and Anna ended up with snow inside her bra.

They got going again and managed to 'luge' right up to the Landrover. They felt like Scott of the Antarctic as they pulled the 'luge' to the train. There were only 'locals' getting on and they soon helped them lift the laden 'luge' on to the flat car at the back of the train which was being loaded with provisions to go up the mountain. No motor vehicles were allow in Wengen.

When they eventually got all their stuff up to bathroom at the hotel they were both too tired to want to go out to eat. They had brought up their tiny gas stove, which they had rarely used on the journey, as they normally relied on a fire. Anna made some soup out of a packet and they had it with some cheese and biscuits. They only had one chair so Anna sat on Charlie's lap. After Anna had made them some black coffee they had a brandy each and both got in the big bath. Charlie lay back and Anna sat in front of him and enjoyed him fondling her breasts. She was in heaven as he whispered in her ear. "I love you so much."

The bathroom was big enough for them to lay out their big mattress and their zipped together sleeping bags. They used the blanket sack which they had made for extra warmth. Anna snuggled into bed first, leaving Charlie to switch out the light which was by the door. The room was warm as there was a radiator, so Charlie opened the window to let in the very cold night air. He then quickly got in with her. Anna had warmed her hands in her armpits. She kissed him and fondled him with one hand. She whispered,

"I think I should have kept my hands cold. He has got big and hard quickly. Come on have your wicked way with me. I love to feel you deep inside me." That invitation was too much for Charlie he came after three trusts saying, "I'm sorry you are so beautiful I could not stop." Anna nipped his earlobe murmuring, "You're forgiven." Then she was asleep with him still inside her.

At about 2 o'clock Anna got up for a wee and shut the window as it was now seriously cold The heating was off. Charlie was still asleep so she lay on her back and brought his hand into her groin. He was dead to the world so she started to rub herself with his index finger. Somehow it was more arousing than her own finger. She soon sighed with pleasure and went to sleep.

Charlie was aghast when she told him in the morning. She laughed, "You have no need to worry. You just have a good shag and leave me frustrated! Come on let's get skiing you can make up for it tonight."

They had a wonderful day. They knew that they both skied at roughly the same speed which made the skiing all the more fun. They only stopped for a quick bowl of soup and some bread. It was dark when they got back to their bathroom. Anna immediately turned on the bath and stripped off. She was slightly surprised when Charlie said he would just go to the ski shop and get some wax for their skis. However the bath was lovely and even more fun when he joined her, so she thought no more about it.

The following day they took the train up to Kleine Scheidegg, then the T-Bar up the Lauberhorn. They skied down to Grindelwald.

Anna took Charlie to Bravo Peter's restaurant. She was appalled by Peter's appearance. He was very thin and his once brown skin looked yellow. His eyes were sunken and the sclera also looked yellow. When he saw Anna his face lit up. She hugged him and introduced Charlie. She indicated to Charlie to sit at a small table in the corner while she went to help Peter with the coffees. She wanted to ask him if he was ill, but was too shy. He alarmed her further by having a coughing fit. When he recovered he asked her,

"Is he the one?" She blushed and replied,

"I'm certain he is. However I have got to spend six years at veterinary college and he lives in Kenya. I don't think it is fair to make him wait that long."

"My advice, Anna, is don't wait. If he asks you, say yes and find some way to work it out. I won't embarrass you, but you have my blessing and all your children and your husband have the freedom of the mountains like your grandfather had. Good luck." She kissed him on the cheek and he held her hands for a moment before they took the coffees over to the table. Peter sat with them and asked them about their journey before he had to go back and help at the bar.

They took the train back up to Kleine Scheidegg and went up the Lauberhorn lift again. Initially they skied to the left of the lift in the direction of Grindelwald but Anna then skied off-piste, even further to the left shouting to Charlie to follow her.

They stopped above the open area of new snow below the rocky outcrop. It had taken some very careful off-piste skiing to reach this point. They were on a small flat area before the slope, dramatically fell away below them into the valley. They could see Grindelwald below and a mountain restaurant two thirds of the way down. Using her poles, Anna gave a big jump so she could turn completely around to face Charlie. She gave a small push forward so her skis could slide either side of his. They hugged and kissed passionately. As they broke apart, Anna said,

"Thank you so much Charlie for bringing me here."

"Bravo Peter was kind to welcome me. You obviously mean a lot to him. Can you tell me what he said to you?"

"I am too shy."

"You have made me shy now. Anna, will you marry me? I know it is going to be difficult wearing this at college doing anatomy practicals." He produced a jeweller's box out of his pocket. Without opening it, Anna cried out,

"Charlie the answer is yes, yes a hundred times yes. Bravo was asking me if you were the one. I said you were, but we might have to wait for six years and that you hadn't asked me yet. However when he kissed me he whispered that he could not wait and he gave you and our children the freedom of the mountains." Charlie replied,

"I don't want to make you sad, but I think he is dying of cancer."

"I guessed that, as he seemed so shrunk and yellow."

"I imagine it is his liver. I don't think he has long. He is amazing to keep working." Anna asked,

"Does alcohol affect his liver?"

"Yes,"

"That explains why he did not give us shots of spirit like he usually does." Tears were running down her face now. Then she hugged Charlie really hard and said,

"I must not be sad, Bravo and my Grandfather would not want that. We must go and celebrate our engagement. I feel like making love right now, but I know how shy you are. We will wait until we are back in our bathroom. I wondered why you rushed out last night when I got in the bath. Was it to get this ring. I have not even opened it." She opened the box.

"Charlie it is beautiful. Three diamonds like my mothers. It must have cost a fortune." They kissed again.

"Will you put it on for me?" She pulled off her ski glove. Charlie already had his gloves off and he gently placed it on her finger.

"Thank you Charlie, so much. You are a real star it fits perfectly. It's so beautiful." She hugged him again.

"Come on let's hit this slope and go to that restaurant in view and get a bottle of champagne."

Unbeknown to them Anna's family were all sitting out in the sunshine having a drink before lunch. Her Dad had noticed two skiers under the rocks. He said,

"Those two must be good skiers that is very steep. I don't think even when I was twenty, I would have tackled that." His wife added,

"I'm glad to hear it." She turned to her four sons, "Don't any of you try it. It is looks suicidal."

They all watched the skiers. Cindy one of the girl friends said,

"I'm sure one of the skiers is a girl. She is wearing powder-blue and she is smaller than the other." They continued to watch. The girl friend added,

"I'm sure they are lovers. It is so romantic." Her boy friend groaned,

"You see romance everywhere. It won't be very romantic if they end up in hospital." The girl grimaced,

"You are so down to earth and boring. Anyway they are down the steepest bit. I think they are heading this way." Sure enough Anna and Charlie were coming straight towards them up to the ski rack and were lost from view.

They kicked off their skis, threw down their poles and Charlie swept Anna off her legs and carried her round the rack laughing,

"I am going to carry over the threshold to buy the champagne."

"Put me down you great fool, you don't know where I've been!"

"Oh yes I do. You have just skied down the steepest slope in the area and you are going to be my wife. I think we will have the word obey in our marriage service."

That was the moment when Anna's mother recognised her.

"Anna, what are you doing here? We thought you were in Kenya."

Anna rarely could do anything wrong in her Father's eyes. Before his wife could say anymore, he said,

"This is wonderful. We have the whole family together. I don't know who you are young man but both of you should be congratulated on that exhibition of skiing, so I will buy the champagne."

Charlie gently lowered Anna onto her feet. He held out his hand,

"Charlie Ferguson. May I marry your daughter?" Anna's mother was about to explode, but her husband was too quick for her.

"Charlie, if she has accepted you, I won't object. However I would prefer if she completed her training. Six years will be a long engagement!"

"I know, my job is in Kenya and Anna will be in Cambridge." Anna interrupted,

"We will work something out. Thank you, Dad. This amazing that you are all out here. It is really sad we have just seen Bravo Peter.

Charlie thinks he is dying of liver cancer." Anna's father asked, "So you are doctor, Charlie?"

"No, nothing so important, I am a vet." Anna's mother was a very intelligent woman. She instantly realised there must have been some connection with Charlie for Anna to want to become a vet all those years ago. She remembered how Anna had seemed to have grown up overnight in Kenya. She asked,

"Are you a rugby player Charlie?" Anna's father interrupted.

"Well if you are as good a rugby player as you are a skier, you must be a star. Anna can you do all the introductions I will go and get the champagne. What a marvellous surprise."

To Anna's mother's surprise Charlie put his arm around her. She was still shocked and cross, but this small gesture helped her not to show too much anger. Charlie said,

"I'm so sorry Mrs. Anderton to spring this on you. I know I should have courted your daughter in the proper manner, but somehow we were so excited about travelling to the UK together that we just set off. We have been on the move ever since meeting by chance at Embakasi airport. Anna has been marvellous she has taken everything in her stride. She told me about your families' love of Wengen and so it was natural for us to aim for Lauterbrunnen on our way through Europe."

"Well it has been a shock. I was not pleased when she set off on her own for Kenya. She is only eighteen. We assumed by her letters that she was working in Kenya not gadding about in Europe!" Charlie kept quiet. He was unaware that Anna had not told her parents. He was worried. He so loved Anna, he did not want her hurt in anyway. Looking at her he could see the grave look of concern on her face. Luckily Cindy took the heat out of the moment by waxing eloquently about Anna's engagement. There was no doubt she wished Anna's brother would pop the question to her.

Anna's Father returned with a tray of glasses and a bottle of champagne. He toasted Anna and Charlie. Charlie could see the reluctance with which Anna' mother raised her glass. The rest of the family mercifully seemed to have accepted the situation. There was a general chat about the marvellous skiing conditions.

The two girl friends, Cindy and Gina who were obviously sharing a room at the 'Regina', we're delighted that they had their own bathroom. Anna just smiled and agreed how great it was to have a long soak after skiing and not have to rush, as someone else wanted the bath. Charlie said how kind the 'Beldi-Laudi' family at the 'Hotel Silberhorn' had been letting them stay at such a cheap rate as the hotel was full up. He hoped he would be able to return the favour, as their son hoped to travel to Kenya in his gap year.

In the afternoon initially they all skied together but soon it was obvious that the two girl friends were holding every one up so they split up. Charlie, Anna and her four brothers skied off leaving her Mum, Dad and the two girls to come on at a more sedate pace.

They did however decided to have one more run over 'The bumps' just below Wengen Alp and so it was almost dark when they came into Wengen village and walked up the hill to the 'Hotel Regina'. As they were dropping their skis in the ski room, Anna's Father said, "Blast I meant to ask Anna and Charlie to join us for dinner tonight." Cindy said,

"Don't worry Mr. Anderton I will walk down to their hotel. Gina you can have first bath." She walked back up the ski room steps and set off down the hill to the 'Hotel Silberhorn'. At reception the proprietor gave her directions to their room which was on the top floor. She was still in her ski boots so she took them off in the reception and climbed the stairs. She was slightly surprised that the room she had been directed to, had no number. She heard laughter inside and timidly knocked. There was no reply, but she could hear shrieks of laughter from Anna so she opened the door. Anna and Charlie were naked. Anna was doing a handstand on the mattress and Charlie had his head between her thighs and was holding her up. Cindy was about to bolt, but Anna had seen her. Anna did not seemed the least bit upset but said,

"Hello Cindy, we trying some gymnastics. We will get some clothes on." At that moment the kettle whistled. Charlie who had grabbed a towel, said, "Good timing. Would you like a cup of good bricklayer's tea? We brought it all the way from Kenya."

So Cindy was given the only chair. Anna and Charlie rapped in towels sat on the side of the bath. Cindy and Anna had mugs and Charlie had his tea in a beer mug. Soon, Cindy lost her embarrassment as they chatted away. Charlie told how they had pitched their tent inside an old Turkish shepherd's hut. Anna told her that they certainly had clothes on then as it was well below freezing. In fact she thought they were probably wearing every article of clothing they had possessed. Suddenly, Cindy remembered her errand. She said, "I must dash or I will be late for dinner. Your Dad asked you to join us." Anna answered, "We would love to. Can you placate my mother. I will look a real sight as my only suitable dress is crumpled at the bottom of my rucksack. Hell, What are you going to wear, Charlie? It is black tie at the Regina." Charlie replied,

"No problems, two nights before we left I went to Muthaiga Ball. I expect the trousers have got grass stains on the knees." He then told them a hilarious storey of wrestling on the top of the marquee and rolling down and falling eight foot on to the grass missing a big metal tent peg by inches. Eventually Cindy rushed off.

Anna had never been a girl for taking hours to get dressed so in fact she and Charlie were the first to arrive in the bar at the 'Regina Hotel'. They were both very nervous, wondering what sort of reception they would get from Anna's mother, when they were hailed by a large florid, grey-haired man.

"Bloody hell, if it isn't Ferguson. You did a marvellous job on that *'punda'* (Polo pony) of mine. She is as sound as a pound." Charlie replied,

"I am delighted. Lord Maclue. Let me introduce my fiancé, Anna Anderton. She will be a vet soon." Lord Maclue shook Anna's hand.

"Well young lady if you end up as good a vet as this young fella you will do well." Anna was shivering in her shoes, but managed to look him straight in the eye. Lord Maclue looked at her, as if she was a young filly.

"You may not be very big but I can see you have got a lot of guts." A very tall willowy women had joined them. He turned to her.

"Phillida, my dear meet this young lady vet, Anna Anderton."

"Hello, Charlie, Anna, you must not mind my husband. He thinks every girl vet should be six foot tall and built like a tank. I am sure you will manage very well. Archie can you get some drinks?"

At that moment the Andertons arrived in the bar. Charlie did all the introductions. Anna could have kissed Lady Maclue, when she turned to her mother and said,

"You must be very proud of your daughter becoming a vet and getting engaged to Charlie. We think the world of him in Kenya.

Nothing is too much trouble for him, when animals are concerned. He managed to get a lovely set of heifer twins out of my best Jersey cow."

The evening was a great success until Cindy who had a little too much wine let out that Charlie and Anna were sleeping in a bathroom. Anna's mother looked furious. They were back in the bar and the Maclues had joined them. Lady Maclue laughed,

"What a great arrangement. If you are strapped for cash, Charlie, you can hire it out for five francs a bath!"

The rest of the evening was a nightmare for Anna and Charlie. Luckily they had not had much to drink. Anna's father tried his best, but her mother would not even say good night to her daughter. Charlie and Anna walked down to their hotel very subdued, arm in arm. Anna shivered when they got into the bathroom, and yet it was not cold.

"Charlie, I will just put my ski clothes on and go out for a breath of night air." He replied,

"I will come with you. I think we have missed the last train to Kleine Scheidegg." She hugged him.

"How did you know that I wanted to go up the mountain?" He kissed the top of her head.

"I know you rather well my darling. You have done your best to hide it, but I know you have been worried all day about Bravo Peter."

So they got into their ski gear. They met the proprietor as he was locking up. They told him where they were going. He knew Peter was very ill. He said he thought such a journey was unwise, but he said they were welcome to borrow his and his wife's cross country skis. He made Charlie carry an emergency rescue pack and told them the location of the rescue huts. He was relieved that both of them knew the mountains so well and that it was a clear, but very cold night. They set off up the dedicated path for cross-country skiers and he locked up the hotel.

When they got to bed, Anna's parents had had a blazing row. Eventually to pacify her, Anna's father had got up and gone down to the 'Hotel Silberhorn'. Actually he was quite relieved to find it locked up. He could not really understand why his wife was making such a fuss. He was rather proud that Lord Maclue thought they were both good vets. He actually thought it was rather colourful that they were sleeping in a bathroom. Certainly Anna was perhaps a little young to be having sex, but he thought most young folk of her age did. He just hoped his wife would have calmed down in the morning.

Anna led. She was so grateful to Charlie, not only because he was coming with her, but also because he trusted her and was happy to follow her. She knew that he was a born leader and most men who were ten years older than an eighteen year old girl would insist on being in charge. That was not Charlie's way.

Initially they made good head way as they were young and fit, but by the time they reached the 'Water Station' at the top of the 'Bumps' the altitude began to take its toll. They had both been at altitude in Ethiopia and even in parts of Turkey but their red blood cell numbers had decreased since then. They stopped and both had a good drink of water which had not frozen as it was deep in the pack. Charlie said nothing but gently stroked her face and then they set off again. They could see 'Plum Pudding Hill' on their right. Charlie said,

"It's almost as beautiful as one of your tits!" Anna laughed,

"Do you ever stop thinking about sex?"

"Oh yes, occasionally for about half a minute!"

"At least you are honest. I have never discussed sex with either another girl or guy. However I think I am unusual as a girl. I think about sex a lot. I often wake in the night and want you. It is so lovely that I can feel you hard up against me. I think to myself, even when he is asleep Charlie wants me. Then I am happy to go to sleep again. Sometimes I do bring your hand to my groin or on to my breast. I love it as you do not wake but often nuzzle my neck or kiss my ear in your sleep." Charlie kissed her face.

"Well I am awake now and I think we ought to get going or we will get cold."

"You're right but remember I am thinking about sex as well!"

They set off and soon got to Wengen Alp. They did not stop. The going, along below the railway was less steep and they moved in the same rhythm, but covered more ground. Scheidegg was dark. They easily found the blue run down to Grindelwald. The moonlight showed some of the bumps in the snow, but even for experienced skiers like them they had to work hard and keep their speed down, particularly on the final steep icy piste near to the village. There were no lights on in the houses except for a light in a window above Peter's restaurant. They took off their skis. The door was unlocked. Everything was in order ready for the morning. Anna was relieved it seemed they had come on a fool's errand. They quietly took off their boots. The big room was not freezing cold but equally it was not warm so they kept on their ski gear except for their gloves and hats.

They froze, when they heard a terrible choking cough from upstairs. Their eyes were well adjusted to the dark so Anna had no problem climbing the stairs in her stocking feet. Charlie followed. They found Peter sitting up in bed but still clothed. He obviously had not had the energy to undress himself. The bedside light was on. The room was cold. He was in a fitful sleep. Anna reached for his hand which was icy cold. He woke at her touch and instantly was 'Compus Mentis'.

"Anna, you have caught me out. I just did not have the energy to get into my pyjamas." Then he started coughing and choking. Charlie helped her to get him sitting up better which seemed to help him. She offered him small sips of water. Although she had no experience she knew he was dying. She also knew he did not want her to summoned a doctor. She guessed that the nearest doctor was in Lauterbrunnen.

Mercifully he stopped coughing and lapsed into a deep sleep. She sat beside him on the bed and held his hand. Charlie sat in a chair. They left the bedside light on. They both dosed and soon slept. Anna woke cold and stiff as the grey dawn light came into the room. She could see Peter was not moving. She quietly got up and went to Charlie. He was awake in an instant with her touch. He went to the bedside and felt Peter's wrist. There was no pulse. He lent forward so his cheek was near to Peter's mouth. He could not feel any air movement. He didn't whisper but in a normal voice said,

"He's died, Anna. At least he won't suffer anymore. We are lucky, as vets we don't have to let our patients suffer. You did the right thing. If you had not come, he might have choked to death. At least he died peacefully. We will lie him down on his back and cover his face then it will be not so much of a shock for his old house keeper when she arrives."

He gave Anna a brief hug and they did as he suggested. It was only when they went down stairs to make a pot of tea that she wept.

Anna's father left his wife in bed and made his way down to the 'Hotel Silberhorn' before breakfast. The proprietor told him where Anna and Charlie had gone. Charlie had rung and told Mr Beldi-Laudi that Peter had died in the early hours. Charlie had said that he and Anna would have some breakfast with the housekeeper and then ski down to Wengen and probably go to bed for a few hours.

Anna's father returned to the 'Hotel Regina'. He thought Anna and Charlie were marvellous to have taken the trouble to go to the old man in the night. Anna's mother was still furious. Anna's father was fed up with this attitude. He thought they had shown a lot of courage and love for an old man. He had spoken to his wife to that affect. The family breakfast was rather tense to say the least. Eventually the whole group made their way down to the train station to go skiing. They met Anna and Charlie on their way. Before Anna's mother could speak, Anna said in a very flat voice,

"Mother, you have probably heard that Bravo died early this morning which was a relief. We were with him so we know he died peacefully. I am sorry I'm not the model daughter you want or expect. In your eyes I have been living in sin with Charlie. We are going to get married. It is up to you whether you accept it. I will always be your daughter, Mum, but I am no longer your little girl!" With that Anna and Charlie walked on to the 'Hotel Silberhorn'.

Anna's Mother burst into tears and walked on to the station with the rest of the party trailing behind her. Nothing was said until they were all sitting on the train. Anna's brother broke the silence.

"Well Mum, I don't think you should be sad. Grandmother always used to say, 'children are only lent'. I think Charlie is an honest, kind bloke. I think he will really look after Anna. He gets my vote of approval." Anna's father and his three brothers nodded their heads in agreement. Before Anna's mother could say anything he added, "I know one thing, if she had been a man, she would have been an awesome rugby player!"

Anna's mother blew her nose on the handkerchief that her husband offered her, and he changed the subject and asked where they were going to sky today.

Anna and Charlie had a Ghulvien with Mr Beldi-Laudi and went to their bath room. They were soon cuddled up together and soon were asleep. They slept through the whole day. It was dark when they woke as it was just after 6 o'clock. Charlie got up to run them a bath and make them some tea. There was a note which had been pushed under their door. Anna recognised her Mother's writing. The note was simple, 'Dearest Anna and Charlie, please join us for dinner tonight. The table is booked for eight but hopefully we will have time for a drink in the bar first, Love Mum'

Charlie could see how pleased Anna was with the note. He said,

"While you are having a bath, I will go out and buy you a dress for the occasion, if you tell me the size. I think you look great in black." Anna laughed,

"What a marvellous man you are. Up here in the mountains, dresses are going to be horrendously expensive. Also I don't know what size in Switzerland would fit me, but if you find a shop with an assistant my size, she will tell you!" With a grin Charlie replied,

"You might have time for quite a long bath." He did not wait for tea and was soon walking up the main street. However he had a bit of luck as he bumped into Gina. He knew she was about Anna's size so he asked her if she would help him. Gina thought he was being very brave and was happy to volunteer. Charlie made Gina laugh as he took her into the first dress shop they found and in very poor German explained with the help of a lot of hand signs what he wanted. Then, once the assistant understood and had a dress which would fit Gina, Charlie sent her off saying, "Gina thanks, I want it to be a surprise so I don't want you to see it first."

Anna was delighted with the dress. It fitted her well. It was long and came high up to her neck. It was low at the back but not too risqué.

"Charlie it is lovely. Well done. I thought you would either get a very short one or a dress with a very plunging neckline. Either of which would not have pleased Mum. However this is great. I won't wear a bra but Mum won't know that. I will wear my favourite Nairobi knickers. You are the most lovely, lovely man."

So they were in high spirits when they walked the short distance up to the 'Regina'. The Andertons were all in the bar. Anna immediately went and hugged her mother and then did the same to her father. He whispered,

"Well done. Your Mother expected you to be dressed totally inappropriately." Aloud he said, "What a beautiful dress. You look marvellous." Anna replied,

"Thanks Dad. Charlie went out and bought it for me an hour ago all on his own." Anna's Mother was now determined to say the right thing but somehow she just had to have the last word.

"What it needs is a piece of jewellery." Anna's Father scowled at her, as he knew this would be taken as criticism by Anna. However graciously she reached behind her neck and took off her diamond pendent and said,

"Why not wear this? Dear. It belonged to your father's grandmother." Anna received it with very good grace,

"It is lovely Mum. Can you put it on for me."

So the evening got off to a very good start. Gina said,

"Charlie, you are a real star. Can I borrow the dress sometime? Anna, it is lovely. I know it would fit me."

Anna replied,

"Of course, Charlie told me you had modelled for me. I would have loved to be a fly on the wall and watched Charlie trying to make the shop assistant know what he wanted." Charlie laughed,

"The young lady was rather Rubenesque. I would have really struggled without you Gina!"

Anna's Mother added,

"Well Charlie you have certainly put the 'cat amongst the pigeons'. I will expect great things next Christmas from the male Andertons."

No one saw Anna squeeze Charlie's hand.

The rest of the Anderton's stay was a very happy time. Anna and Charlie kissed and hugged them all goodbye at Wengen station. Then as soon as the train had drawn out they rushed around the back to their luge and raced down at breakneck speed to Lauterbrunnen. There was a lot of laughter when they saw them off for a second time.

Two days later it was not such a happy time. It was Bravo Peters funeral. Word must have got around, as Charlie was asked to be one of the pallbearers and Peter's housekeeper asked Anna to walk with her behind the coffin. Anna and Charlie felt very honoured. They both knew that they would always be welcome back to these mountains.

Chapter 12

The final part of the journey

Charlie and Anna left Wengen two days after the funeral. They both were down-hearted, but tried to put on a brave faces. Charlie suggested as it was so cold and wet, that they planned to stop any idea of camping and stay in small hotels. This made packing up the Landrover much easier as they just needed access to their small rucksacks or so they thought.

They were both keen to get back to the UK so they drove out of Switzerland at Basle and followed the Rhine. Although the Landover seemed to be going well Charlie did not want to risk problems with the new valve so they kept at a sensible speed. The second night they found a cheap truckers halt near Rotterdam at 9.00 pm. The landlord was rather hesitant about them having a room, but he said they could have it, provided they gave his wife time to prepare it. Charlie said that was no problem, as they would sit in the bar and have a drink. They actually had a couple of drinks before they got the Landlord to show them to the room.

It was pretty dirty and Anna took one look at the sheets and declared they had been used before. Charlie suggested they turned the sheets over. As they started to turn the sheets over they both started to laugh. Obviously that is what the landlord's wife had already done! The other sides of the sheets were ten times worse. So they made two journeys back to the Landrover and brought their mattress, sleeping sack and pillows up to the room. They were much happier on the floor! Surprisingly the breakfast was really good in the morning. They got to the Hook of Holland by mid-morning only to find they could not get on a sailing to Harwich until the evening.

They drove into Rotterdam and parked up the Landrover. They had an enjoyable day walking around the city, sightseeing and window shopping. The dark came early and so they drove back and waited in the car queue to get on to the evening ferry. They were glad they had booked as there were plenty of cars containing rather glum skiers on the way back from skiing holidays.

They had booked a cabin, as the crossing took eight hours if the sea was calm and longer if it was rough. There was a heavy swell. Anna teased Charlie asking him if he wanted her to go and get to their cabin early, so that she was naked when he arrived, like she was when they were in Alexandria. Charlie thought that was a great idea, so when they started loading the vehicles. Anna went on ahead. She had the booking reference for the cabin. Charlie memorised the cabin number, telling her he expected her to jump into his arms when he arrived.

It was a drive on, drive off, ferry. Somehow two truck-drivers thought they had been waved on at the same time. There was a collision. It was at a slow speed, but there was a real delay, as they both had to back up. They did this very slowly to lessen the damage. Eventually all the vehicles were loaded. However the sailing was behind schedule so the Captain ordered the engine room to go ahead with the departure before the rear ferry doors were lifted. The helmsman turned the helm quickly to lessen the delay. A big freak wave hit the ferry door, damaging the hydraulics. The ferry had left the jetty. The ramp dropped and scooped up a very large volume of water. The ferry continued to turn. More water was scooped up. The ferry was destabilised and rolled allowing the sea to pour in through the open rear doors. The ferry sunk, but as it was still in the relative shallow water of the harbour it did not sink totally but rolled on to its side.

Anna had found their cabin. She had brought her small rucksack. The cabin was warm so she decided to surprise Charlie. She locked the door. She took off her thick clothes and was rummaging in her rucksack to find her sexy knickers which Charlie had bought in Nairobi. She was standing on one leg putting them on and so was not prepared when the floor of the cabin lurched violently. She fell backwards hitting the back of her head on the side of the bottom bunk. Her world went black as she lost consciousness. She came round rapidly as she was lying in very cold water which was pouring in around the door which was slightly buckled, as the ship had rolled. The door was directly above her. The main cabin light had gone out but there was a glow from the small emergency light. She was lying on the wall of the cabin between the bunks. There was about six inches of water, but the level was rising. Anna had never been frightened of water but she was afraid now, as she realised she was trapped in the cabin. She had the sense not to try and open the door. It would have crashed inwards with the weight of water above it. She knew she had to wait for the cabin to fill up with water before she could attempt it. The whole ship moved as it settled on to the bottom. The water kept coming in.

Charlie was on the stairs when the ship rolled. He hung on to the banisters. Water poured into the stairwell and the lights went out. He could see a green emergency exit light and then the emergency lights started dimly glowing. He immediately thought of Anna. He guessed she was in their cabin D6. She would be trapped. He had to get her out. He started pulling himself to the green light so that he could get his bearings. He got to a passage which was at right angles to the stairwell. The rush of water had carried other passengers away so he seemed to be on his own. He started hauling himself along. He now had about a foot of air above him, above which was cabin D23. He soon came to D21. He was going in the right direction but he realised to his horror that Anna, unless she had got out was in cabin D6 which was directly in the row of cabins directly below him. He renewed his efforts. At last he got to cabin D7. He took a big breath and went down under water. He felt the number on the door below the water. It was cabin D8. He came up for air and hauled himself further along the passage until he had cabin D5 above him. He ducked down again after a big breath. He felt the number D6. He dreaded what he would find. He came up and hyperventilated.

Anna had heard the scratching outside of the door. She now had about two foot of air left to breath in. She moved to the side of the door just in time as Charlie released it. It crashed inwards with a massive amount of water. Charlie was catapulted in. She grabbed at him and hung on to the belt on his waist as the water swirled them viciously around the cabin. Charlie was kicking out and as the water pressure eased he, having felt hands in his thick leather belt, kicked upwards and using his hand on the door-jam he propelled them into the passage and up to the air on the other side.

Anna let go of his belt, kicked with her legs and flung her arms around his neck. They both gasped for air. She shouted in his ear, "I did as I was told. I was waiting naked for you!" She felt his hands squeeze her bottom. He shouted, "We need to get out of here pretty quick. Follow me and stay close." Hand over hand they hauled themselves along the passage. All the while the water level was rising, but at least they could still breath. When they came to the end of the passage, Charlie's instinct was to try to go upwards but he used his intelligence and led Anna sideways. She followed without a thought. He was her leader. She did as she had been instructed.

As the ship had settled on its side, they needed to traverse to another stair well and try to get out of the ship. The water was cold, but as they were moving and working hard they did not feel it. The dim emergency lights were their salvation without them they would have been totally lost. Eventually they came to a bulk-head. There was only one way forward. They had to swim under-water and hope they came to another air pocket. Charlie shouted to Anna, that he would do a recce. He told her it was best if he went alone and then if he was running out of air he could turn round and swim back. If she was behind him then he thought they would both get in a muddle and drown. Anna shouted, "I'll wait, good luck, I love you."

Charlie took three very deep breaths and he was off. Initially he was terrified but he kept swimming breast-stroke, counting his strokes. In eight strokes he broke the surface as the light became brighter. He quickly turned as he knew Anna would be worried. He took three very deep breaths. He was not so worried on the return journey. Being more relaxed he swam more efficiently and only took six strokes. As he broke the surface on his return journey he felt a strong little body wrap itself around him. He told her the good news. Anna was soon off and this time Charlie followed behind her. They both knew they had to keep going as all the while the amount of air above them was diminishing. Then to their horror they came across a drowned couple. They were in their ski gear which obviously was difficult to swim in.

Each time they came to a new obstruction which meant they had to swim under water, they carried out the same procedure but each time it became harder as the pocket of air was thinner. Anna was beginning to panic. It was particularly bad when she could not see Charlie. Charlie was a good leader, he realised how she felt and at the next obstruction he made her go ahead. She nearly flunked it, but her tough nature did not let her down and she felt better after she had achieved it. Suddenly to their relief they got to a stairwell. There was much more air above them. They could breathe easier but they still could not decide how to get out of the hull. Then they both realised what they needed to do. They had to dive deep down into the water to get to the door which would let them out on to the deck. They would then have a long swim upwards to break the surface.

Charlie shouted,

"Let's both try together, my darling, I'm afraid there will be no going back." Anna shouted,

"You go first, Charlie, I'll swim close behind you. Good luck."

Three big breaths and Charlie set off with Anna right behind him. The light got poorer as they descended. At last Charlie reached the bottom and hauled himself under the obstruction. He got a glimpse of Anna behind him. There was no going back now. He had about ten feet to swim horizontally before he dared to try to come up. At last he made it. His lungs were crying out for air. Self preservation was in his subconscious, but he willed himself to stop and turn to see if Anna was behind him. He could not see her. His love overcame his fear. He started to swim back.

Anna had tried to come up too early and now was panicking as there was no way above her. She was kicking out with her legs. Holding on to a banister he grabbed one of her ankles and yanked her downwards. Anna immediately stopped panicking and doubled over and swam downwards past him. Charlie followed. They both were desperately short of oxygen now. They swam with short less effective strokes. Anna made it to the upwards turning place first. To her credit she waited a couple of seconds to make sure he had made it before pushing off upwards with all her strength.

Up and up they went. They both thought they wouldn't make it, but even in the darkness they could see the bright lights of the rescue boats on the surface above them. This helped to spur them on. They both broke the surface together. Thankfully they both had exhaled some stale air during their ascent so there was no danger of rupturing the blood vessels in their lungs. They gulped in air being careful as there was a chop on the sea. As soon as Anna had recovered her arms went around Charlie, "Thank you my darling, twice you came back for me. I don't deserve a wonderful man like you. I will follow you forever."

"Rubbish," shouted back Charlie, "We will walk together holding hands, but first we must get out of this bloody freezing cold water."

They were soon picked up by a Dutch rescue boat. It was only then that Anna realised she was naked. "Oh Charlie, I have lost my favourite knickers."

The Dutch seaman laughed with the other seaman, as he wrapped her in a blanket. "A typical girl. She is nearly drowned and she is worried about her knickers!"

Anna was not having that,

"You cheeky bugger. I give you a real eyeful and you laugh at me because I am worried about my knickers. They were very special. They were the first present my fiancé gave me." She cuddled up to Charlie under his blanket and kissed his neck.

"I still have my engagement ring. It is my extra special belonging. In fact it is my only belonging!" Charlie cuddled her under the blanket and fondled her breasts whispering, "Great tits."

She reached down to him whispering back, "I'll soon harden him up."

They were soon taken up to the harbour wall still in their blankets. After they had given their names to an official, they were whisked into a taxi and taken to a hotel. Sadly they realised the ambulances were being used to take the drowned bodies to the morgue. The car was lovely and warm but Anna still hugged Charlie, as if someone would try and steal him away from her. When they reached the hotel, Anna gave Charlie a cheeky grin, "Shall I give the driver a flash, as I seemed to have mislaid my money for a tip." Charlie whispered a reply,

"I think that is a little excessive." Anna laughed and retorted,

"So you think just the top half is sufficient?"

They had to register at the hotel. Luckily Charlie had still got their passports which were sodden but the receptionist who was a young chap was not worried. In fact he could not take his eyes off Anna as he had guessed she had little, if anything on under her blanket. He told Charlie that there was a telephone in their room. Charlie knew that Anna's family did not know that they had been travelling on that ferry, but he thought it was only fair to let them know that they were both safe and well. Charlie guessed that the casualty rate for the disaster was going to be high. Soon they got to a warm bedroom with an en suite bathroom. While Anna laid out all his clothes and the contents of his wallet to dry on the radiators, Charlie managed to get through to Anna's mother who was delighted he had rung. She said they had worried a little, but did not think the Landrover would have got them to the channel ports that quickly. Anna had a quick word with her Mum as Charlie ran a bath. They were soon in it. Anna just sank into the water sitting in Charlie's lap, bringing his hands on to her breasts saying,

"This is heaven." She giggled as she felt his rough chin on her skin as he kissed her neck.

"I don't even mind that rough old chin." Actually they did not stay in the bath that long. They thought they both had been in water too long already that night.

They dried rapidly and jumped into bed. Charlie had just managed to get her underneath him when there was a knock on the door. Anna laughed, "Whoever is at the door will guess exactly what we were up to. You only have a towel to wrap around you which won't hide anything." Charlie thought what the hell and went to the door. There were two Dutch chambermaids who both giggled when they saw him. They had brought two bathrobes, two pairs of towelling slippers and a tray of coffee and light snacks. Charlie went bright red but managed to open the door without his towel dropping off. He indicated to put the tray down on the table and mumbled, 'Merci'. Anna just laughed half sitting up in bed, but covered by a sheet, and said, "Thank you very much. I'm sure you both speak English. My fiancé has a thing about French maids. He has forgotten we are in Holland!"

When they had left, Charlie locked the door saying rather wistfully, "I imagine you would like some coffee and food rather than carry on where we left off?" Anna jumped out of bed, saying, "I think we can manage both. I'll sit on your knee." Their late supper was most enjoyable.

They were both very subdued in the morning. The extent of the disaster was still not fully known as they were still bringing drowned passengers off the boat and out of the sea. The staff at the hotel found them some clothes. Anna of course had none of her own and

Charlie's were still damp. Anna kept hugging Charlie. He knew how grateful she was, that twice he had come back for her and twice had saved her life. She kissed him,

"Poor you, sadly I think you have lost your faithful old Landy forever." He kissed her back,

"But I haven't lost you. That would have been the end of my world." Anna burst in tears.

There was no reason for them to stay in Holland so when they were offered air tickets from Amsterdam to Heathrow they readily accepted them and went on the bus to the airport. At Heathrow they took the airport bus to Victoria coach station. Charlie asked Anna if she would like to go shopping for some clothes but she said she would rather get home, where she knew she had plenty of clothes. So they got on a train to East Grinstead after they had rung Anna's home to tell them which train they were on. Anna's youngest brother was at the station to meet them. Normally he would have been casual, but today he gave Anna a big hug. Charlie could see tears in her eyes. When they got home the whole family gave them a terrific greeting. Then Anna could not stop crying. She had to tell them all about Charlie, rescuing her twice. Even Anna's mother was in tears as she hugged Charlie. "Oh thank you, Charlie for bring her back to us."

Supper that night was a really happy occasion with all the family. Anna was amazed that her mother took it as read that Charlie would sleep in Anna's room even though there was just one tiny bed. As they were cuddling up naked together, Anna whispered,

"I think Mum imagines that we can't get up to any hanky-panky in this tiny bed or one of us would fall out." Charlie reached a gentle hand between her legs and replied quietly,

"Let's prove her wrong?" Anna gasped and kissed him passionately. Then she murmured,

"Oh that's lovely. Oh don't stop." After a few minutes she gave a gentle sigh. Then she reached and picked a towel up off the floor. She tucked it under her bottom and whispered, "Now have your wicked way with me. You won't make a mess of the sheets."

As he entered her, she wrapped her legs around him and thrust upwards. Then she giggled, "I think I'm so wide open and ready for you, that you will have to work hard. Wow that feels good." She buried her mouth in his neck so that she wouldn't cry out.

Chapter 13

Time for Charlie to return to Kenya March 1971

Anna's mother was not delighted, but she accepted that Anna would return with Charlie to Kenya as his long leave was finished. Anna still had several months of her gap year left before she had to go up to Cambridge and, not only start her veterinary course, but also start coaching the St Catherine's rugby squad. Before actually flying back to Kenya, Charlie had to go the Ministry of Overseas Development Administration (ODA) in Stags Place in Victoria. This was normally just a routine, but unbeknown to Anna, Charlie did enquire whether he could make a sideways move into a more laboratory based job and hence get a posting back to the UK, but still be employed by the ODA.

Charlie's flight was paid for by ODA but he insisted on paying for Anna's flight. Although he had not received any money, he had been notified that he would be compensated for the full value of his Landrover and all his equipment. Anna also would receive full compensation on a new for old basis for all her clothes and rucksack. She had not really bought any clothes, but she had bought a new rucksack. Charlie had done the same.

They flew out together on an East African Airways VC 10. They were lucky it was barely a third full so after supper Charlie put up the arm-rests of three seats and lay back so Anna could lie on top of him. However the stewardess was not happy with this arrangement and said they had to move. Actually it had not been very comfortable for either of them, so they each separately slept on three seats. In the morning they discussed, as they were eating their breakfast what was going to happen on their arrival. Charlie told her there would be a car at the airport from the vet labs to take them to Kabete. He would then report to the Director of Veterinary Services (DVS) who would tell him where was going to work. This was called his posting. Anna was amazed that Charlie had no warning of where he was going to be sent. His previous job had been in the vast Rift Valley Province which stretched from the Sudan in the North to Tanzania in the South. When she had first met Charlie, he had been based in Nairobi but had been seconded to the Livestock Marketing Division (LMD) so that he worked moving cattle country-wide. She teased him by reminding him of how when they had first met, he had got her sitting in his lap when he wasn't wearing any underpants. She teased him further as the memory still made him blush. Charlie told her he was so delighted that she loved the life in the bush. He said many of the veterinary wives hated it and so any posting might be a real drama.

As the plane was so empty and they had little luggage, they were soon through immigration and customs. Anna could see how pleased Charlie was to be back in Kenya. In fact she was also pleased to be back, but she was also a little sad, as she knew she only had five months before she had to leave him. Charlie was a sensitive man and he guessed the reason for her sadness. He squeezed her hand. She kissed his neck. There was a tear in her eye as she simply said, "Thanks, I'm being a silly little girl." He replied,

"Well I love that little girl with all my heart."

They both failed to notice Moses, the Kabete driver standing beside them. He cleared his throat. Charlie then immediately greeted him and introduced Anna as the girl who was going to be his wife. Moses who was quite an old man smiled and remarked that she must have cost a large number of cows. Anna shook him by the hand and said, "Oh yes, together with several camels!"

Anna was fascinated by the drive in from the airport as five months before her head had been in a complete whirl and she really hadn't seen anything. Moses noted how different Anna was from most of the other wives. Charlie sat in the back of the car, expecting Anna to sit beside him. Instead she sat in the front and chatted to Moses. She asked him about the things they were seeing and also asked him to teach her some Swahili.

When they reached the veterinary HQ at Kabete. Charlie went inside, but Anna said she would stay in the sun with Moses. The DVS seemed pleased to see Charlie and asked him about his trip. He was appalled by Charlie's account of the ship wreck. He was standing by the window looking out and asked, "Who is that girl talking to the three drivers?" Charlie guessed it was Anna but he moved to the window to make sure.

"It is my fiancé, Anna Atherton, Sir. She will be staying with me until September when she returns to Cambridge Veterinary School." The DVS grunted,

"Well she will be pleased, as I have promoted you to Provincial Veterinary Officer (PVO), Coast Province. She will have the most sort after house in the Department. You both deserve it. You did very well on your last tour with the LMD and she seems to have an easy manner with subordinate staff. Many European wives are too stuck up and snooty with us Kenyans. Come on it is time for coffee. Let's go across to canteen and I can meet your fiancé." At that moment, Anna must have said something funny as the three drivers were splitting their sides laughing.

When the DVS and Charlie emerged from the building. They were seen by the drivers who stood to attention. Anna ran to Charlie and hugged him. "I haven't been wasting my time I have learnt a lot of Swahili." Charlie replied,

"Anna I would like you to meet the DVS." The DVS added, as he shook her hand,

"I'm glad you have been learning Swahili, as where you are going you will need it."

Anna might have got a place at Cambridge on account of her rugby coaching ability, but she also had secured her place by her academic achievement. She was very bright and she knew that best Swahili in Kenya was spoken at the coast, so she answered the DVS, "Thank you Sir, I guess that means you have posted Charlie to the coast. I will give him as much support as I can to get the Coastal stock routes working as efficiently as possible."

The DVS was impressed and smiled, "I can see you don't miss a trick. What you don't know is your fiancé has been promoted and so you will have a very smart house to live in." Anna replied,

"Then I have a double thank you. I do hope you will come down and visit us."

The DVS beamed with pleasure at the invitation. They went for coffee and the DVS enjoyed introducing Anna to some of the senior staff at the Veterinary Laboratories. Charlie was not idle he used the time to find out how he could perhaps move from the field service to the laboratory service.

After coffee, Moses drove them back into Nairobi. They had some lunch at the New Stanley. In the afternoon they went to Benbros Motors and Charlie bought a Long Wheel Base (LWB) safari type Landrover. He did not actually take delivery of it because it would be cheaper, if he bought it directly went it arrived by sea in Mombasa.

While they had been at Kabete, the DVS's secretary had booked them first class tickets on that evening's train to Mombasa. So they had a cup of tea at the garage and the garage owner who had played rugby with Charlie gave them a lift to the station.

Anna was enchanted by the train. They had a compartment all to themselves. They were brought tea and biscuits before they had set off. When the whistle blew, Charlie encouraged her to look out the window and see the steam train slowly pulling the old train out of the station. Almost immediately they were travelling through acacia scrubland which was Nairobi Game Park. There was game everywhere. Charlie reeled off the species to Anna; Masai Giraffe, Common Zebra, Defassa's Waterbuck, Hartebeest, Impala, Thompson Gazelle, Grant Gazelle, Warthog, Baboons, Buffalo and Elephant. Although Anna had been on safari before, she thought this was fantastic to be seeing them all from the comfort of a train, while they were drinking a cup of tea! Even when they left Nairobi Game Park they could still see a lot of game on the Athi Plains. Sadly it swiftly got dark.

They went along to the dining car. They had a little table for just the two of them facing each other with a small light like a romantic candle on the table. They each had a 'Tusker' before they were brought a bowl of tomato soup and a hot roll, with a pat of butter. Charlie lent across and squeezed Anna's hand, "Welcome back to Kenya."

"Oh Charlie, this is so lovely. I wish it could go on forever. I dread leaving you in September." Charlie replied,

"I've an idea. How about inviting your parents, and any of your brothers, with their girl friends, for Christmas out here. You could come out as soon as term finishes at Cambridge and they could come out whenever. In that way we can have as long together as possible. I know your Mum will want you at home in UK for the holiday otherwise."

"That's a marvellous idea. That's the first thing I'm going to put in an air-letter. They go quicker than postcards. Charlie you are a star. You always know how to cheer me up. I was about to cry."

Diner was sensational from then on, with roast Guinea fowl, followed by chocolate mousse and coffee. They also had a glass of 'African Cream Liquor'. When they got back to their carriage, their beds were all made up. After they had locked the door, Anna wrapped herself around Charlie, saying, "Tonight is going to be awesome. I remember how good our love-making was on the train in Egypt. Can I go on top so you don't hit your head? We will get on the top bunk as there is more head room."

Charlie could not believe how quickly she got out of her clothes and started to climb the ladder. He buried his face between her legs and held her thighs.

"Charlie Ferguson, you are a very naughty boy! Don't stop that is lovely." So it was a fun night, making love to the rhythm of the train. They awoke at dawn and lay together on the top bunk looking at the game in Tsavo National Park and then they could not resist making love again before going for a massive breakfast.

Ted Sykes, the outgoing PVO, met them at the station. He was an affable bloke and apologised that they could not move directly into his house. He said he thought Charlie was a bachelor. He had not realised he had a fiancé. As always, Anna soon charmed him. She said they were really happy to go into the Manor Hotel which had been booked for Charlie. With a cheeky grin she said they would enjoy the single room which had been booked! Also she said that they actually didn't have any kit as all Charlie's stuff was still at Kabete waiting to come down in a lorry. She then told Ted about their ordeal crossing the channel. She implied that having no clothes was not a problem. Ted coloured, when he imagined her naked being rescued. He took them to the Hotel and said there was no need for them do anything. He would pick them up so they could come and have lunch with him and his wife. Charlie said he had no need to pick them up as Charlie was sure he knew, where Ted's house was and they would make their own way there, to save him diverting into town. Ted insisted the Hotel gave them a double room before he went off to the office. He expected them to rest. They had other ideas.

Charlie knew there was a water ski club down in Tudor Creek. They put their swimming things into two good thick polythene bags and went down in a taxi, to see if they could join. There were two pretty girls down at the club who had small children with them. They weren't skiing but we're just enjoying the sun with their families. They said that they would propose and second Charlie and Anna so they could immediately start skiing. There was a boat-boy called Sea Lion who said he would be happy to drive the boat for them. Anna knew Charlie had water-skied before, so she made him ski first. She put her bikini on and sat in the boat. She saw that Charlie was rather good. He used a mono-ski. His turns were so tight he slowed the boat down. She enjoyed looking at his hard stomach muscles which she loved to feel in bed. Then as they passed the club house, Charlie threw away the rope and gently skied into the beach, hardly getting his feet wet.

To her horror she realised it was her turn. She was doubly nervous, as she could imagine the two girls were very good like Charlie. She thought they had been pretending to be talking but they actually had been watching Charlie. She not only did not want to let Charlie down, but also she did not want to let herself down.

Sea Lion brought the boat in after he had coiled up the rope, so that she could jump off into shallow water. She turned to thank him. He gave her a wide smile, "Don't worry, I will drive carefully for you. I'm sure the Bwana will help you. He is a very good skier and he looks a kind man. Look he is coming with extra clothes for you." Sure enough Charlie was coming into the water with a life-jacket and a pair of his shorts. Anna said,

"Thanks Charlie. I'm really nervous." He replied,

"Don't worry I will help you. I suggest you wear this pair of shorts, so you don't get a salt water enema. This life jacket will stop your bikini top flying up." As Anna did a sexy wiggle to get into his shorts, he gave her a kiss on the cheek and said,

"Have I ever told you that you have the most sexy bottom in the world." Anna smiled at him as she realised he was trying to calm her nerves. It must have worked as she felt a trill, as he helped her in to the life jacket and therefore got a good view of her tits. She asked,

"Do my tits meet with approval?"

"They are the best! Now I am going to help you. You have only got two things to remember; keep your arms straight and your legs bent. The rope will pull you out of the water. Only when you feel stable may you straighten your legs. You must never bend your arms. If you feel you are falling backwards just bend your legs. You are a great snow skier. You will do fine."

Charlie collected the two skis which Sea lion had pushed out of the boat across the water to him. He adjusted them for Anna's small feet. Then Sea lion threw Charlie the wooden bar attached to the ski rope. Charlie caught it and gave it to Anna. He positioned the rope between her skis. Then he came behind her and held her thighs so that she was stable in the water. She whispered, "This is cosy."

Slowly Sea Lion took the boat out into the creek. When the rope tightened, Charlie shouted, "Hit it."

Anna was off, she followed Charlie's instructions. The rope lifted her out of the water. She felt her bottom bouncing on the surface. She was glad of the shorts. Slowly she straightened her legs. She was up and skiing. Sea Lion took her in a wide circle and headed up the creek. Anna followed in the wake. When they both were going straight Anna started to shift her weight and so she came out of the wake. She shifted her weight the other way and she crossed the wake. She was now really enjoying it. She crossed the wake twice more and then she saw Sea Lion indicate he was going to turn and that she should stay in the wake. She turned with him, but could not resist accelerating over the wake out of the turn. This was great fun. She was getting tired, as they came back to the club house. She threw the rope in the air and skied into the shallow water aiming at Charlie who had his arms open wide. She didn't quite make it but sank gracefully into the water ten yards in front of him and shouted, "That was magic."

While Sea Lion was sorting out the boat, Charlie and Anna walked up the beach holding hands. The two girls called to them to come and have a drink. However Charlie insisted he bought them a drink. They congratulated Anna when she told them it was her first attempt. One of the girls obviously fancied Charlie as she said,

"I can see you have done it before. You will be a great asset to the club."

Anna was slightly surprised as Charlie did not get her a drink or one for himself. He knew her so well she only had to raise her eyebrows and he said,

"I'm not getting us a drink as we have a bit of a swim to do before lunch. Luckily the tide is going out. We can swim to Ted's house it is just round the corner. I remember the PVO before Ted, saying the garden runs down to the creek."

So they said goodbye to the girls, put their clothes into the two polythene bags and tied them tightly to keep them dry. Charlie wore his wet old shorts over the top of his swimming trunks and tucked their flip-flops into the big pockets of his shorts. They swum out from the beach. They could feel the tide helping them. They kept fairly near in shore. They did not want to be swept past the house. Anna thought how typical this was of Charlie, to arrive by sea in his swimming things. She loved him for his adventurous behaviour. She knew she was out of the same mould. Soon Charlie said,

"There's the house. Luckily the tide has not gone out too much, we have not got much of a climb. We will put our flip-flops on as the coral is quite sharp. You go first. I will give your bottom a push up. Anna only had to climb about five feet. It was easy as Charlie was treading water and he could almost post her up to the top. She lay on the top and reached to help him up. They walked up to the house..

The PVO's house was a big old two storied house with a very large upstairs veranda. There was a long coffee table on the veranda with a long settee and easy chairs. Ted was sitting with his wife, Mary, having a glass of cold lemonade with added fresh lime juice. He looked up,

"Good God, my replacement PVO has swum here!" He called down, "Come up and have a lime and lemonade. You must deserve a drink after your swim."

When Anna and Charlie got up to the veranda, he introduced them to Mary. Anna apologised for arriving in a bikini. Mary replied that she should not worry, as she was sure Ted would love it. Anna enthused about the house. She said she thought it was lovely. When Mary said she was worried that it would be too big for them, Anna explained that she would have to go back to the UK at the end of September. However she then said how she wanted to invite her whole family out for Christmas and so the house would be marvellous. Mary kindly offered to leave the curtains as she said, when they came back from their long leave they were unlikely to be posted to a place where the PVO had such an enormous house.

Mary showed them to one of the five guest bedrooms which were all 'en suit', so that they could put on their clothes which were still dry. After lunch Ted and Charlie went back to the office to start the hand over. Anna stayed and had a happy afternoon with Mary, who gave her ideas on how to run the house. Anna told Mary that Charlie had a cook called Timmo who would come down in the lorry with Charlie's things. Mary advised Anna to let Charlie give all the orders to Timmo. Mary said that often cooks who had worked for bachelors did not like a woman in the house. As it happened Anna got on really well with Timmo. He was old enough to be her grandfather and within in a few days it was obvious he was devoted to her.

The ten day handover was soon over. Ted and Mary drove up to Nairobi, the lorry with Timmo and Charlie' stuff had arrived the evening before. Several of the veterinary staff were co-opted to help, unload and load up the lorry. Anna enjoyed working with Timmo to sort everything out in the house. Charlie left them to it and went to collect his new Landrover.

Ted had not been very keen on leaving Mary for a night so he had tended to do day safaris. This was fine for the Districts of Kwale, Kilifi and Taita which were relatively near to Mombasa. Ted had used a long range radio call to organise the more remote parts of Coast Province. The very remote North Eastern Province had largely been left to Kabete and the LMD. The DVS knew that Charlie was a keen flier and so he had instructed Charlie to visit Tana River District and Lamu District, the northern two districts of Coast Province together with Garissa District, Wajir District and Mandera District, the three districts of North Eastern Province. What the DVS did not know was that Anna loved going on safari and so she was delighted to go with Charlie and leave Timmo in charge of their home. Anna loved the massive greeting which Charlie received when they arrived in these remote areas. They all remembered him from his days with the LMD.

Obviously Charlie had to spend quite a large amount of time doing boring office work. He anticipated that Anna would get bored sunbathing, waterskiing or having coffee at the Mombasa Sports

Club, which Charlie had joined, so he could play rugby when the season started. The sports club also had a squash court. Anna was delighted that often she could get the first three games off Charlie before she got hot and tired. There was no viewing gallery so Charlie was delighted when Anna played in the nude. He was sure she won more games as she looked so sexy just in her socks and trainers.

So it was that after a few days, Charlie suggested to Anna that she should learn to fly, as to learn in Mombasa was very inexpensive. Anna jumped at the chance. Charlie said he was going to pay as he had never given her a Christmas Present. Anna was not happy, as she knew it was a lot of money, and so she insisted she paid for half as she had the money she had never spent which her Dad had given her for her gap year, and also she would get the insurance money for her clothes which were lost on the ferry. She added with a cheeky grin that she certainly did not need any squash gear as she would always play in the nude. Charlie laughed and said she would have to be careful at Cambridge, or she would be sent down for indecent exposure!

Anna was a natural flier as Charlie had guessed, when he first flew her down from Samburu to Nairobi. She joined the Mombasa Flying Club and had most of her lessons in the early in morning when there was no wind and there was no other air traffic. It suited her instructor, as it meant he could get his hours teaching her and still get to work on time. So Charlie and Anna had a pattern, Timmo would wake them with a cup of tea in bed, then Anna would get up and have a quick shower while Charlie got on the Veterinary Radio Network. Then they would both have breakfast together. Anna would go off for her flying lesson. Charlie would have a shower and then go off to the office. As The Veterinary Office was off Mombasa Island on the causeway it was on the way to the airport. Often Anna would drop in for a cup of coffee with Charlie on her way back. Charlie loved it that the staff all seemed so pleased to see her. He did not realise, how well he was respected by the staff. They thought it was hilarious that he took the use of Government Vehicles so seriously. If he was off on a day safari he would get a driver to pick him up, on the other hand if he was going to be working at the office he would use a bicycle.

Anna always came if he was going to be away for the night or longer on safari. She and Timmo would be in charge of packing up the new Landrover. Anna loved going on safari, but now she was learning to fly she particularly loved going on an airborne safari. Sometimes they would stay at Government Rest houses or sometimes they would camp. As she was still learning and Charlie was not an instructor, she had to sit in the right hand seat. Charlie was the pilot in charge and sat in the left hand seat. He was said to be P1 and she could still log the hours, but she was said to be P2.

They were flying back from Wajir one day after a visit to find out why camels seem to be dying. It was a long boring flight. Charlie was flying but not really paying attention when he felt Anna wriggling out of her shorts and knickers. He had not noticed that she had already taken off her shirt and bra. He just said, "Wow, this is a treat."

Anna laughed and replied, "I imagine you have forgotten that you tried to get me as an innocent fourteen year old to join the 'Mile High Club'. I think I declined saying it was 'Out of My League'. Well we are at six thousand feet. How about it?" Charlie gulped and replied,

"I was all talk and no trousers. I have never joined. I don't even know how we go about it." Anna grinned, "One thing I know about you is that you will make a hell of a mess! Let's get this towel under you and get your shorts off?" Once she was happy, Anna lent forward and swung her left leg over the top of him. That was too much for Charlie, he buried his face between the cheeks of her bottom and started kissing her. That brought a response of, "Bloody hell that's good. Don't stop." Soon Anna was panting and she came. As her breathing came back to normal she said,

"I'm going to love this. Now it's your turn." She came down on him. Charlie groaned. She knew him so well. She took right him to the brink. Then she stopped and he moaned, but she just swung her leg over him so she was facing him with her bottom in his lap and pushed him inside her. She pulled his face into her breasts. Charlie gave one thrust gripping her bottom with both hands and he came as the plane lurched. Anna giggled, "I don't think you were meant to let go of the stick,"

Charlie said, "That was so bloody lovely. I don't care if we are upside down!" Anna whispered, "If I hadn't put a towel under you, I would have made you turn the plane over to stop the mess on the seat. You are still hard. Can you feel me gripping you?"

"Yes, Yes, I can feel you."

"I want to come again." With that Anna started rubbing her tummy. Charlie kept thrusting and they both came together. Then Charlie tenderly kissed her erect nipples.

"Oh Charlie, you are so gentle. My nipples are so sensitive. I'm going to come again." She sighed.

"You know even when I was fourteen, I felt really turned on when you put you hairy arm between my thighs to adjust the seat. We would have got into no end of trouble if we had done anything more. It brings me out in a cold sweat thinking about. It would not have been your fault. I kept up the pretence that I was in my gap year. I had every opportunity to tell you I was only fourteen. There must have been a bucketful of oestrogen in my blood stream. You gently sucking my nipples now is causing a massive hormone surge. Thank God, I'm on the pill. I would get pregnant for sure. Please keep sucking. I love to feel you getting smaller." She sighed as she felt him slip out of her. Charlie looked at the altimeter. Somehow they had lost three thousand feet!

With all the extra flying with Charlie and her regular flying lesions, Anna soon went solo. She has no problems with Navigation and so she soon accomplished her two cross countries, one with her instructor and the other solo. She took the written exam and the radio-telephony in her stride. She was a little nervous on the morning of her flying test. Her examiner was a jovial chap in his forties. He made her complete her own flight plan at the tower. As she was walking out to the plane with the examiner, she had a very naughty thought. She was dying to tell him she had joined 'The Mile High Club. Somehow this made her relax and so she passed with flying colours. She had done all her lessons in a Piper Colt which was an extremely simple aeroplane. However most of the time Charlie and her flew in Cherokees. The smallest was a 140 which only actually took four people if they were light. Then there was a 180 which took four people and some luggage. There was a much faster version of this called a Cherokee Arrow. This had a variable pitch propeller and a retractable under-carriage. When her examiner had told her she had passed. He did what was normally done. He suggested she just did a couple of circuits to celebrate being a pilot. Anna said,

"Can I be really cheeky. I fly a lot with Charlie my fiancé. Would you mind checking me out to fly a Cherokee Arrow as I understand the club rule is that only pilots who have been checked out by you are allowed to hire the Arrows. Obviously the examiner had taken a liking to Anna so he readily granted her request. He only made her do two landings, making her raise and lower the under-carriage twice before he said, "Well done, that is fine. I think you are the most accomplished pilot I have ever examined. When we walked to file the flight plan, you seemed to be very nervous and then suddenly you relaxed. How did you manage that?" Anna blushed,

"I was very naughty. I had a great desire to tell you that I had joined The Mile High Club. The examiner chuckled,

"You must be very athletic. Was it fun?"

"Rather!" Replied Anna with a grin.

Charlie and Anna had the most marvellous time. The rugby season started at Easter with the long rains. Anna was delighted as she became their coach. The midweek games were all against Royal Navy Sides. There was normally at least one Royal Navy Frigate in Mombasa for refit and R&R, as they were patrolling off Beira to prevent oil reaching Rhodesia which had declared unilateral independence (UDI). They had the occasional visits from sides from Nairobi, Arusha and Dar Es Salaam and equally they sent Mombasa sides to play away in return. Charlie and Anna were in demand, as between them they could fly seven players. The end of September came much too soon. Anna had to report in Cambridge for fresher's week at the beginning of October. Luckily Charlie had to attend a PVOs meeting in Kabete so they flew up early that morning. Anna booked a flight to the UK that evening. Charlie hired a car to take her to her flight in the evening. Anna was in tears in the car, but they kissed in the car park and then she ran in with her rucksack. It was an overnight flight and her Dad met her at Heathrow. Charlie had a miserable flight back to Mombasa the following day. However they both consoled themselves that in fact it was only ten weeks before Anna flew out again to Nairobi for the Christmas vacation. Her Mother and Father together with two of her brothers and their girl friends were due to fly out a week before Christmas. She had a week to get ready for their arrival.

Although Anna missed Charlie, she did not have time to be sad. Fresher week was very busy. She was meeting masses of new young people, not only in St Catherine's College, but also in the vet school. The veterinary students were mainly boys, and girls were in demand. However except when they were doing practicals, Anna always wore her engagement ring and soon word got around that she was not available. That did not mean she was not good fun and she was invited out by many groups, particularly the rugby boys. She also joined the University Aero Club so she did get a little flying. She converted her licence into a UK licence and checked out on a Cessna 150 which was the cheapest plane she could hire.

The anatomy, physiology and biochemistry came easily to her. However what she really loved was the animal management and husbandry. Thanks to Charlie she was much more knowledgeable than the other students. Also she was much more mature than most of the other students who were straight from school. Her veterinary tutor who was also attached to St Catherine's obviously found her interesting. He had two sons who thought she was marvellous as she coached rugby. Much to their delight she took them up one at a time in the Cessna.

Her own parents knew she flew a lot in Kenya but somehow she had not mentioned that she had actually got her Private Pilots License (PPL). She thought it would worry her mother. She knew she would have to tell her when they came out Kenya, but then she would be sort of on her home territory, and so in a strange way that would give her more confidence, particularly as she was with Charlie.

So her first term at Cambridge went by quickly. She regularly wrote air-letters to Charlie and he wrote to her. She loved all his news. However she was not prepared for the Charlie who met her at the airport. He was stooped and lame like an old man. As she ran to him she cried in anguish,

"My darling what has happened. Have you been hurt playing rugby?"

"No, I ought go back to vet college and redo my animal husbandry. I was hit by a bull yesterday up at Burgoni, the holding ground in land from Mkowe, where we take the boat to Lamu island. At my age I ought to have known better!"

"I will kiss every bit of you better. I can be very gentle you know when I try. How are we getting home?" Charlie replied,

"I love it when you call here, home. I flew up in an Arrow. I could not face the road journey. Can you fly home. I'm not up to the mile high club today, that's for sure!"

"I will love to fly us back, you know that. I will be so gentle in bed tonight." She gently kissed him on lips. They took a taxi from Embakasi to Wilson. Anna did all the checks and filed the flight plan. Charlie just watched her as he lent on the wing. As she was flying she would be in the left hand seat and had to get in first. She had a short skirt on. She had taken her tights off in the VC 10 before she landed. Charlie reached up under her skirt and touched her. She turned,

"I hoped you would do that. I have really missed your cheeky ways."

By the way he got into the plane, Anna could see he was in a lot of pain. She was thankful. It could have been worse. The arrow was swift and they were back home for lunch. Timmo was delighted to see Anna. He had made a special fish pie which he knew she loved. Pudding was mango with vanilla ice cream which was another one of her favourites. Anna drove Charlie to the office. He protested, but she persuaded him that it would be less painful for him and that she was keen to see all the staff, who were delighted to see her. Charlie worked in his office doing boring office work. He could hear loud laughter outside which he guessed was Anna hearing their news and learning some Swahili. All the staff seemed worried about Charlie and so Anna had no difficulty getting him to leave promptly at 4pm which was the official knocking off time.

They had an early supper and Charlie had a hot shower which was unusual for him, but he said he thought the hot water would lessen his aches and pains. Anna, as she had promised was very gentle in bed but the sex was no worse or less passionate for that. They both slept very well and we're still asleep when Timmo brought in their tea in the morning. At breakfast Timmo introduced his nephew, Peter, who Charlie had arranged to work under Timmo for a month as Charlie knew there would be a lot of extra work with

Anna's family arriving. Anna had insisted she drive him as she did not want him going on his bicycle. However she did notice that Charlie was quite a bit better. She was delighted that Charlie had got an extra fridge from the office brought to the house which would make catering easier. She laughed to herself as all the bedrooms had big double beds and big mosquito nets. Her brothers and their girl friends would be pleased. There was no way she was going to make the girls share!

To make the most of Charlie's local leave they had agreed she would fly up and meet her family at Embakasi. They had a friend who was a rancher with a plane at Nanyuki who always kept a big Landrover at Wilson, so it was available for him when he flew down. He had said Anna was very welcome to borrow it. She was there in good time to meet them and take them to the Norfolk Hotel where they could have a relaxing day by the pool. Actually they had a very cramped flight as the plane was full, mainly bringing young folk out to be with their parents for Christmas. These flights were nicknamed, 'Lollipop Specials'. Her parents were therefore particularly pleased not to have a long drive down to the coast. However they all wanted to have a game drive in Nairobi National Park in the evening. They were lucky and Anna found them a pride of lions. Anna's mother just could not believe how Anna took charge and did all the driving.

Supper was good fun, but they all were glad to have an early night. Anna missed Charlie, but knew she would see him early in the morning. She was going to drive them to Wilson and then meet Charlie when he arrived at coffee time. They reached the aero club before him. It was only after Anna had sat them all down and got them coffee and went to check over the plane, that Anna's mother realised that Anna was going to fly them down to Mombasa. However in all credit it to her, she didn't say anything. Charlie soon arrived. Anna was grateful, as he took charge of them and said he thought it was best to have two men and two girls in each plane and therefore if Anna's Mum would like to come with him and her Dad went with Anna the others could sort themselves out. Anna and Charlie had purposely not brought any luggage so weight was not a problem. Anna's Mother watched Charlie and Anna walking hand in hand to file their flight planes. She saw suddenly Anna grab Charlie and kiss him passionately. When they were all in the two planes,

Anna's mother and Gina were in the back so that the weight was evenly distributed, Anna's Mother could not resist asking why Anna had kissed him. Charlie laughed,

"It was because I had to tell her what my Christmas present was to you all. We are going to have a night at Kilaguni on our way home. It is a great lodge. I hope you will enjoy it. Now we are off on an airborne safari, Have any of you been in a light aircraft before?"

They all said they hadn't, so Charlie said, "I'll talk you all through what I'm doing. Anna will be doing exactly the same in the other plane. I imagine Mrs. Atherton that you are very proud of her?"

Anna's Mum hardily managed more than a whisper,

"Actually Charlie I'm terrified, but after Wengen, I now know what she is really like and I am just trying to live with it. I know you are the right man for her, but that does not make it easy."

Charlie made an instant decision. He asked Anna's brother, Gavin, if he would mind swapping over so Anna's Mum could sit in the front. Charlie knew that the extra weight in the back would not be critical. He had been a little pedantic making the two ladies sit in the back. When they had swapped over, he got Anna's Mother to hold the stick and he moved her seat forward so her feet were on the foot pedals. Gavin was grateful as it gave him much more leg room in the back. He put his arm around Gina and gave her a hug.

Anna had been watching and had guessed what Charlie had done. She therefore got clearance from the tower and set off taxiing ahead of Charlie. Charlie heard on the radio, but Anna's Mum was in such a flap she missed the exchange. All the while Charlie was talking to her to try and get her to relax. Getting her doing something certainly helped. It also helped as Charlie pointed out Anna's plane ahead of them. He got Anna's Mum to listen to the radio. She did relax more then, as she could hear how cheerful, but always correct Anna was. Mrs Anderton actually smiled when she heard Anna say, "November Quebec taking off on 14. Right-hand circuit. Will report visual marker."

When Charlie reported the visual marker and set the course for Kilaguni, he turned to her and pointed out Anna ahead. Then he said, "I think you are actually enjoying this? You look so like Anna in profile." She smiled and replied, "If you can't beat them you have to join them."

"Well done." Replied Charlie, "Now we will get you using the controls and looking at the instruments." Anna's Mother in fact was very good, but got Charlie to take over after half an hour. She turned round to say something to Gavin and Gina only to see they had gone to sleep with Gavin holding Gina against him. She pointed them out to Charlie and said, "Can we talk? I don't think we will wake them." Charlie nodded. She asked,

"What happened in Samburu when we were all on safari. How did you meet Anna?" Charlie gave her a very simple, but abridged version. She then said, "I always wondered what happened. Anna was a different girl after that holiday in fact the night you had saved her from the crocodile. Will you accept an apology for my behaviour in Wengen?"

Charlie reached over and squeezed her hand, saying,

"It's me who should apologise." This elicited her more characteristic reply,

"What rubbish. If you hadn't fished her out of the water, I wouldn't have a daughter at all. Is that her?"

It was Anna calling that she had Kilaguni in sight on the standard frequency for unmanned airfields of 118.1. Charlie called her saying he had her in sight and his P2 would land behind her. There was a dirty laugh on the radio. Anna's mother did not miss a trick and asked,

"Why is she laughing?" Charlie replied,

"I just said you would be landing the plane."

"That I won't, but I will buy the first round of drinks. I certainly deserve a double gin after all this." Charlie knew he could relax, as he realised his future mother-in-law had accepted him. Kilaguni was magical, they all went swimming after an excellent lunch. Among a lot of other things they saw a cheetah on the evening game run. Supper was a riot and as they were having their coffee, elephants with their calves came to the floodlit water-hole and played in the water. They then quite wisely all went and had an early night. Charlie arranged with the Rangers that they would wake him if anything real interesting arrived at the water-hole. Gina and Gavin together with Rufus and Rachael we're delighted that the embargo of them not being allow to share bedrooms had been lifted.

When Charlie came out of the bathroom in their room, naked, Anna was lying on the bed in a new, very sexy, short, black nighty which she had purposely allowed to ride up her thighs so her bush was visible. She chuckled,

"Shall I go and tell the Rangers that you have seen something interesting in your room? Your Willy certain seems to think so!" Charlie replied,

"You know my battered body suddenly feels a lot better. In fact that nighty has revealed something which needs kissing. He buried his face in her groin." He reached up under her nighty and gently squeezed her breasts and nipples while he kissed her. She brought her knees up and stretched her thighs apart to make it easier for him. She had her hands on the back of his head to direct him to all her sensitive places. She very earnestly requested him,

"If I tell you to stop can you totally disobey me. You lovely man I want you so much and being gentle because of your injuries has been very frustrating." She continued to encourage him with endearments until she could no longer bare to be licked. "Oh Charlie I've come. I've come, you must stop!" However Charlie was under orders and anyhow he did not want to stop. Her smell was driving him wild. He brought his hands under her buttocks and drew her as hard as he could on to his tongue. She bucked and struggled but still he would not stop until she viciously pulled his hair, dragging him up her body, crying,

"I'm so bloody ready for you that you won't know you have entered me!" However he could feel her clenching her muscles around him as he gripped her bottom and thrust in time with her. He only just managed to stop himself from biting her neck as he came. They lay locked together until Anna broke the spell,

"I am certain I can tell the Ranger that two interesting things came in the night!"

In the morning, Charlie had arranged that they all were woken in their rooms with tea. Then they went on a game drive. After a couple of hours they were met by a Landrover from the lodge with their breakfast. It was a bizarre experience sitting in the bush on a long table in sight of elephant, buffalo and all manner of other species of game. When they got to the lodge they had a quick swim after they had packed and then they got a lift to the airstrip. Anna's Mother insisted on coming in the plane which Anna was flying. Anna really felt she had 'Come of age'.

Anna's family were very impressed with the large house. Laughing, Anna showed them to their rooms, saying,

"Now we have some house rules for visitors. Timmo is in charge in the kitchen, by all means ask him for something e.g. tea but leave him entirely alone or he will get confused. Actually he understands a lot of English. He and his nephew, Peter, will do all your washing, except I think it is more polite if us girls wash our own knickers. Lastly please don't leave any money anywhere unattended in the house. Charlie will lock anything in the gun safe. The reason is Charlie and I know that Timmo is 100 percent honest, but it is so easy for visitors to spend money and forget they have spent it. Timmo would be mortified if anyone thought he was a thief."

Anna's Dad whispered to Anna's Mum,

"She is even more bossy than you dear." Anna chipped in,

"I heard that Dad. I have made up another house rule. You buy the first round of drinks when we go out for supper. You are let off tonight as we are eating in. Timmo will be making a massive fish pie which will follow the soup."

Anna absolutely love entertaining her family. She was little sad that her two oldest brothers who were both married were celebrating Christmas with their in-laws but that could not be helped. The main thing she was with Charlie and the second thing was she had been accepted by her parents as an adult and that she was mistress of the house. It was a far cry from the bathroom in the ' Eiger Hotel' last Christmas.

The next few days were a very happy time for all of them. Charlie had to work, but he got home as soon as he could. Anna had the use of the Big Landrover and took the visitors south of Mombasa across the Likoni ferry to the small game park of Shimba Hills. They were lucky and saw both Roan and Sable Antelope. It was one of the few places in Kenya where you could see these species. They stopped at Diani which has a spectacular beach, so they all had a refreshing swim before having drinks in the shade. Charlie managed to join them for lunch as he had arranged a morning meeting at the Kwale Veterinary Office and he had also blood-tested some cattle for a Trypanosomiasis survey he was doing throughout the Coast

Province. Straight after lunch Charlie had to get back to the Veterinary Office, but the others stayed on a Diani sitting in the shade of the very high coconut palms before going for a walk along the beach, when it got a little cooler towards evening. They had another swim before heading back for the ferry. There they were lucky as the majority of the traffic was coming off Mombasa Island at the end of the working day. Not many vehicles were heading their way. They got home soon after Charlie and they all had tea on the upstairs veranda with its wonderful view of Tudor Creek.

That evening they had a drink on the same veranda before walking down to the Mombasa Club, which was very nearby, for a very formal dinner. Men had to wear jackets and ties. Charlie in fact was not a member, but he was allowed in, as he was a member of Nanuyki Sports Club which had reciprocating rights. Anna teased her father, as she said although he should be buying the first drinks he was not allowed to, as only Charlie could, by signing a chit. Then it was everyone's chance to laugh at Anna. She was wearing a very fashionable black trouser suit, a fashion which Charlie thought had not reached Nairobi and certainly not Mombasa. The doorman knew Anna and Charlie and very quietly whispered in her ear.

"Madam, I am so terribly sorry. Ladies are not allow in the club for dinner wearing trousers." Anna laughed,

"That's not a problem, Josiah."

Much to everyone's amusement she promptly took off her trousers and gave them to the smiling Josiah. The top of her suit just covered her bottom. "Before you ask, Charlie. Yes, I am wearing knickers, but I can assure you I won't be bending down in a hurry. I don't want any old buffers having heart attacks."

A year ago her Mother would have been appalled. Now she said,

"Well done, dear, I do hate girls who make a fuss about petty regulations." She turned to Josiah and added, "Thank you for being so helpful, Josiah. I know you have to uphold standards." He beamed with the recognition of his problem. The club secretary came out of his office. He took one look at Anna's legs' went very red in the face and bolted back into his office.

The meal was amazing. It was a set menu and had nine courses. First consommé, then thick potato and leek soup, then a tiny prawn cocktail followed by fried fish. A small curried chicken dish preceded roast beef. Fresh mango and pineapple was followed by cheese and biscuits. A lemon sorbet finished the meal before they retired to easy chairs for coffee. Anna's Dad said,

"Thank you both. That was the most magnificent meal I have ever had." The others echoed with, "Here, here." They staggered home to Charlie and Anna's beautiful house.

Charlie set off on the office bike in the morning for the last day of work before Christmas. Anna took her mother, Gina and Rachael off on a shopping expedition. Leaving her father and the boys to go on a short walk and visit the old Portuguese castle called 'Fort Jesus'. The plan was for them all to meet back at the house and take a picnic down to the water ski club. Charlie met them down there. Gavin managed to get up on his second attempt at skiing but Rufus really struggled, but at last did manage to get up. Anna's Mother said she was very happy not skiing, but she was amused that her husband was obviously dying to have a go. Anna whispered to him that she thought it would be better if he waited until Charlie arrived as he was such a good teacher. Then Anna had a ski. Her family were amazed at how good she was. As soon as she saw Charlie coming down the steps she indicated to Sea lion that she wanted to stop, so that she could run to him when he reached the sand. Much to his amusement she wrapped her arms round him and got him wet. Then she got in the boat with Sea lion, Charlie quickly changed and got in the water to help Anna's Dad. Much to her Dad's delight he managed to get up first time. Gina and Rachael then both wanted to have a go. Anna got them to wear shorts and shirts over their bikinis. Then laughing she said,

"Really you ought to wear long trousers as I don't trust Charlie's hands on your thighs!" Gina replied,

"Don't worry, Anna. I know what a rascal he is. Remember he got me modelling for him in Wengen!"

As it was Charlie managed to get them both up first time. They were really pleased, as Anna said they had done better than their men.

The next day was Christmas Eve. After the early morning radio call up, Charlie was free so they had a leisurely breakfast and then packed up only some of their things, sufficient for two nights on a flying safari. They were off to the magical island of Lamu. Anna's

Mum, Gina and Rachael were apprehensive, as Charlie had them in fits of laughter about the hotel, called 'Petley's Inn', which was hot and noisy in the middle of town. He said it had an upstairs long-drop. One night he went to the loo in the middle of the night and managed to drop his torch down the long-drop. It landed with the light pointing upwards. He said several people visited the hotel in the morning to see the only illuminated upstairs long-drop in the world!

The visitors enjoyed the flight as Charlie and Anna could point out to their respective passengers all the landmarks on the way up. In a few minutes they could see Mtwapa bridge, soon followed by Kilifi Creek which was crossed near its mouth by the Kilifi ferry. They saw the large acreage of sisal before they came to Mida Creek. In a couple of minutes they saw Malindi Airport which lay just south of Malinda resort on Malindi bay. As always because of the erosion of the soil in the hinterland the bay was red from the mouth of the Sabaki River. Then they left the land to cross the large bay south of the Tana river which had a more sandy colour from its erosion. Then, soon, they were making their approach to the airfield on Manda Island which was where they were going to land for the short boat trip across to Lamu Island. Charlie had organised the Veterinary Boat from the mainland at Mkowe to meet them at the jetty on Manda.

They parked up the two planes and tied them down to the concrete blocks provided, as they knew that planes had been damaged by freak winds on Manda in the past. As they were unloading the luggage, there was a shout from the path up from the jetty, "Bwana Charles, Habari." It was Kassim coming surprising fast for an old man. Habari *'Bmabu' (Chest)?* To Anna's surprise he started to unbutton Charlie's shirt. Once he had looked at Charlie's chest, he hugged Anna. The whole story then came out which Anna had to translate for her family. According to Kassim, Charlie had saved his life. A great big angry bull had charged Kassim who was too old to get out of the way. Charlie had jumped in its path and that's how he had got hurt the day before Anna had arrived from UK. Anna was so proud of Charlie. Her parents were amazed how revered both Charlie and Anna were by Kassim and the other veterinary staff who had now arrived to carry their bags. The staff except for the two boatmen all stayed at jetty so there was enough room in the boat for the visitors.

They crossed the short distance to Lamu Town on Lamu Island. The District Commissioner came to welcome them with the Livestock Officer. They all went into 'Petley's Hotel for a beer. Anna's Mother said nothing, but it was worse than she had expected. She was not looking forward to spending two nights here. Anna's Father on the other hand had guessed that there was a joke as, their luggage had been left on the boat and no effort had been made to show them to their rooms. When they had finished their beers they got back on the boat and headed north but keeping close inshore. Twenty minutes later when the town was a couple of miles behind them, they came around the headland and there were four beautiful white thatched (*makuti*) beach bungalows with a central, bigger, building which was the reception/dining room. There on the beach was a tall Somali Man wearing a white Kansu and a white embroidered fez. He called, "Welcome."

Anna had taken off her shirt and shorts to reveal her bikini. She did not wait for the boat men to lower the long gang-plank but jumped into the surf which came up to her waist. She ran up the beach and hugged the man, "Elijah, it is great to see you. How are your family in Wajir?"

"They are very well, but my father would not be pleased to see me talking to you, virtually naked in a public place!" Anna laughed,

"Well I'm not going to tell him! You must send them my Salaams and now you must meet some of my family which is nearly as big as yours."

Charlie had also taken off his shirt and shorts and had jumped into the water in his swimming trunks. He helped Anna's Father and Mother down the gang-plank by standing in the water close to it and holding their hands. Anna's Mother shook Elijah's hand, saying,

"Do you think your father would be able to control my wayward daughter?" Elijah gave a deep throated laugh. "I don't think so, Madam. He is already under her spell, but she does wear more clothes when she sees him!"

Anna's family were enchanted by the 'Peponi Hotel'. After they had been given their rooms they met for a drink and then had crayfish and mayonnaise followed by the legendary Lamu mangos.

They spent the afternoon sunbathing and relaxing before they were brought tea. Then in the cool of the evening then went for a walk on the totally deserted beach, out towards the sea.

Supper was consommé soup followed by tuna steaks with sweet potato and corn on the cob. Desert was a fruit salad of pineapple, mango, banana and oranges. They even had milk with their excellent Kenyan coffee. It was a magical evening in an amazing idyllic setting. When they went to bed, Anna warned them not to delay too long as Elijah would soon turn off the generator. Anna and Charlie were in the furthest room out to sea with her parents next to them. The others were the other side of reception. There were twin beds in the rooms. Anna whispered to Charlie,

"No hi jinx, Mum and Dad will hear everything. I bet my lucky brothers will have a whale of a time. It is so romantic." Charlie whispered back,

"How about a walk in the surf?" Anna was definitely up for that, so as soon as the generator cut out they crept out of their room. They walked out naked on to the beach and away from the hotel. The moon had not yet risen and so it was fairly dark. The night sky with no ambient light was magical. After they had gone about a hundred yards. Charlie wrapped his arms around her and they kissed passionately. Then she knelt in front of him and took him in her mouth. She kept sucking and rubbing him until she tasted him, as he gave a relaxed sigh. He drew her to her feet and they kissed again. It was so erotic with them both tasting him. Then Charlie knelt and Anna opened her thighs wide. Normally he would have licked her but tonight he parted her delicate lips and ,

"This elicited,"

"I want more more and more." Then to Charlie's amazement he felt her moisture on his chin as he continued to blow. It became a trickle and she cried out and gripped his hair. She tried to move away from him but he gripped her bottom with both hands and pulled her hard to him and then he licked deep inside her. She screamed, "Stop Charlie. I'm too sensitive." She pulled him up. She stood on tiptoe and was just tall enough so she could push him into her. Her arms went around his neck. He pulled her bottom on to him and lifted her thighs so she could curl her legs behind him. He was strong enough to take her weight but as he had already ejaculated he needed more stimulation. She realised and undulated her hips. They were both panting now. Then Anna cried out and they both came. They kissed again, but stayed locked together until Anna felt him slide gently out of her. As her legs dropped she felt the juice running down her thighs.

Charlie kissed her neck and said,
"I love you so much. That was wonderful."
"Oh Charlie, I so love you."

After they had swum a little they walked back to their room. They dipped their feet in the washing up bowl of water to get off the sand. Then as quietly as they could they each had showers. They crept into separate beds under the mosquito nets as they knew they would be too hot together.

Anna' parents were awakened not long after dawn by Anna's shrieks. Her Dad said,

I haven't heard such a racket on Christmas morning since she was about seven and she woke to find her stocking."

Then they heard sounds of a pillow fight and Anna saying,

"How could you keep it a secret. Why didn't you tell me before. You are a real rogue!"

Then Anna wrapped in a kikoi, burst into their room. She thrust a letter at her mother. Jumped on top of her father saying,

"Poor old you, Dad. Can you afford a wedding in September? Charlie has got a job in Cambridge in the autumn so we can get married and not wait for me to finish my training!"